EZRA SNUKAL

Barnaby Stump and the Soul Thief

Copyright © 2024 by Ezra Snukal

All rights reserved. No part of this publication may be reproduced, stored or transmitted in any form or by any means, electronic, mechanical, photocopying, recording, scanning, or otherwise without written permission from the publisher. It is illegal to copy this book, post it to a website, or distribute it by any other means without permission.

This novel is entirely a work of fiction. The names, characters and incidents portrayed in it are the work of the author's imagination. Any resemblance to actual persons, living or dead, events or localities is entirely coincidental.

Ezra Snukal asserts the moral right to be identified as the author of this work.

Designations used by companies to distinguish their products are often claimed as trademarks. All brand names and product names used in this book and on its cover are trade names, service marks, trademarks and registered trademarks of their respective owners. The publishers and the book are not associated with any product or vendor mentioned in this book. None of the companies referenced within the book have endorsed the book.

First edition

ISBN: 978-965-597-052-4

Cover art by ebooklaunch.com

This book was professionally typeset on Reedsy. Find out more at reedsy.com

Barnaby Stump and the Soul Thief

Ezra Snukal

*To Bubbie Fran (Z"L) and Sabba Josh,
who introduced me to the magic of books
and sparked my imagination all those years ago.*

CHAPTER 1

"*Yo ho, yo ho, a pirate's life for me.*"

Centuries ago, these words echoed across the Seven Seas. They weren't just a shanty sung by hardworking sailors—they were a calling. An invitation to escape the mundane and enter a life brimming with adventure, treasure, and freedom.

Today, those words still echo in certain places, especially the ones I've been to. People still sing them with pride, as if the life of a pirate is something to celebrate, a choice they dreamed of making for themselves.

A choice I never had.

No one ever asked if I wanted to be a pirate. No one gave me the chance to hold onto my ordinary life, my ordinary school, my ordinary grandmother. If I'd had the choice, I would've picked ordinary every single time. Because, while a pirate's life sounds adventurous, it's as dangerous as it is thrilling. It's as terrifying as it is exhilarating. And it almost always ends in death.

You'll see. Everyone in this story has at least one run-in with death.

For me, those words are nothing more than a punch to the gut—a painful reminder of the path I was forced to walk.

My name is Barnaby Stump, I'm fourteen years old, and this is my story. Let it serve as a warning that the life of a pirate isn't always the dream they make it out to be. By the end, you can decide if it's the right choice for you. I envy your ability to make this decision.

Consider this your final warning.

Sometimes, I wonder if everything that happened to me was just karma's sadistic idea of payback for being late to fencing that Sunday morning.

I know what you're probably thinking:

Dude. It's just ten minutes. What's there to freak out about?

Um, for me...*a lot.* I'm not talking about just any run-of-the-mill fencing class. I've missed my share of those. No, I'm talking about the Junior Regional Tournament. The biggest fencing competition I've ever been a part of.

Let me rewind a bit.

My love for fencing goes back several years when I came across a flashy flier for fencing lessons on my school's notice board. I took it home, made my grandmother sign me up—and it was love at first sword. While everyone else was playing basketball and football, I was showing up to practice the precise movements and swift footwork of fencing. I mean, come on; the fact that there's still a sport where you can go around swinging a sword at people? Count me in!

Yes, I'm aware my opinion is an unpopular one. I can testify firsthand that fencing hasn't exactly drawn in the ladies.

Yet.

One thing it had drawn in, on the other hand, were tournaments. I've competed in just about every local fencing

CHAPTER 1

tournament my county of Florida offers. I actually did so well in the last bunch, my fencing coach felt it was time to try at something bigger, so he signed me up for Divisionals.

To his surprise, I breezed through the competition and finished third, which was good enough to earn me a ticket to Regionals. That meant I was now only a handful of wins from Nationals. As in, the United States National-freaking-Fencing Tournament. The largest and most elite fencing competition in the country.

So, of course, it was only natural that I slept through both my alarms that morning.

Grandma was already waiting for me in the kitchen by the time I made it downstairs.

"You're lucky I already started on breakfast. It'll be ready in a second, sleepyhead," she said with a wink. "How are you feeling this morning? Did you sleep well?"

"Mmm...fine," I replied like a total idiot.

Grandma smiled. She knew all too well how excited I was.

"Just remember to text me the results right away, okay, darling?"

Unfortunately, Grandma couldn't come watch me. Some last-minute registration paperwork had slipped through the cracks, and today was the *absolute* final day to get it filled out. If she didn't handle it today, I wouldn't be able to start school on time next week.

Ninth grade—already causing me problems.

Not wanting her to feel guilty, I downplayed my disappointment by giving her a soft kiss on the cheek.

"Of course, Grandma. I promise."

A sudden "ding" from the toaster interrupted this affectionate moment. Not wasting a second, I pounced around the island to snatch the breakfast pastry out of the toaster's rack.

"Good luck! Be careful!" Grandma called after me as I grabbed my bike helmet and ran outside.

"I will!" I hollered back with a grin.

Grandma. Overprotective as always.

That grin had all but vanished by the time I arrived at the local recreational center, the location of the tournament. Not only was I ten minutes late to my first match, but I was also potentially *eliminated* from the competition before I even got to swing my sword. To make matters worse, I was in such a hurry, I flew right past the tournament's sign-in table, wasting another thirty seconds before remembering that I needed to sign in.

Face flushed with embarrassment, I shifted both my mental and physical gears into reverse and headed back over.

"Good morning!" I shone my brightest, most polite smile for the petite, brown-haired lady sitting behind the desk. She smiled right back.

"And a good morning to you as well! Competing today? May I just have your name please?"

I nodded. "Of course. It's Barnaby Stump."

The lady's eyebrows rose an inch upon hearing my name.

"Barnaby Stump," she repeated, searching her papers for my name. "Now that's not a name you hear every day."

Lady, tell me something I don't know, I grumbled in my thoughts. I've long grown used to people's reactions when they hear my name for the first time—a must if you plan on going through roll call with a new homeroom teacher every year. I'd be lying if I said that I've never considered changing it—not that I ever actually would. Grandma would be devastated. It was one of the three things I had from her son: my name, my

CHAPTER 1

blue eyes, and my messy mane of undeniably unusual light blond, borderline *vanilla* hair.

He left me with Grandma when I was one. I haven't seen him or my mother since.

"Ah, there it is," the lady remarked as she found my name in her papers and crossed it off. She looked back up with another smile on her face. "Well, you're all done over here. Head on in, and good luck!"

"Thanks."

I checked my watch as I darted through the Center. It read 8:27. Only three minutes until my first match!

Thankfully, the changing rooms weren't far off. Reaching them, I hurled myself into the one labeled Men's and headed straight to the lockers. Hastily undoing the lock on mine, I began tossing on my gear—jacket, pants, and glove for my sword hand. I didn't need to put on my mask yet, so I just tucked it under my arm for the meantime.

After performing some final stretches to check everything was on properly, I reached back in for my final, and most important, piece of equipment: my sword.

Without a doubt, it was my most prized possession. The hilt alone was a work of art, the grip's protective shell constructed out of individual strips of sleek silver that came together in an elegantly curved helix. The sword was a gift from Grandma, given to me just before my first match in the Divisionals.

"A new sword to reach new levels of success," she had told me beamingly. "I'm so proud of you, Barnaby."

Tightly clutching the sword's grip, I closed my now-empty locker. Butterflies began fluttering within my stomach as I made my way over to the second exit of the locker room, the one that led directly into the gymnasium.

With a deep breath, I pushed the door open, and stepped into the room that would forever change my life.

It just wouldn't be in the way I expected.

I didn't make it more than two steps inside before Coach spotted me.

"STUMP! Get over here ASAP!"

I winced as his deafening voice hit me, my eardrums aching in complaint. I sure was eager to compete, but it was still way too early for something that loud. Even worse, several of the gymnasium's other occupants also heard Coach's bellowing and were now eyeing me questionably.

Great. Just what my nerves need.

"Come on, Stump! PRONTO!"

Mustering a deep breath, I did my best to ignore the oglers as I sprinted across the gymnasium to Coach. On my way, I caught my first look at the tournament's setup: two-and-a-half dozen pistes laid out across the hardwood floor. These long thin mats are what we dueled on, and their long, yet thin, boundaries allowed for the two permitted directions of movement: forward and backward. Or, as I've always seen them, *attack and retreat.*

Apart from the mats, a small refreshment area had been erected beside the gymnasium's bleachers, which had already begun filling up. Despite knowing I wouldn't find Grandma there, I couldn't help but glance bitter-sweetly at the handful of sitting parents. How I wished that, just once, one of those cheering mothers and fathers was here for me. Sure, Grandma was my everything, what with her basically raising me from birth and all, but can you really blame an orphan for wanting

CHAPTER 1

his birth parents for a change?

Not too far from the bleachers was Coach, and I tried speeding up as I reached him. Hopefully he'd notice the extra effort and would go easier on me.

"What took you so long?" he asked me, his bushy mustache curling downward in a frown. "Were you not there when I addressed everyone at the end of our last session?"

Of course I'd been there. Coach had asked everyone to arrive early for a little pre-tournament practice. But I knew better than to argue. Coach definitely hated tardiness, but if there was something he detested even more, it was excuses.

So, instead of defending my case, I simply hung my head and apologized.

"I'm sorry, Coach. It won't happen again."

For a lingering moment, Coach said nothing, simply continuing to glare at me. Then, after a moment, his expression started to soften. His stern scowl even shifted into a smile.

"Well, you're in luck. You missed your initial match, but some other fella was also late, and I was able to get you matched up against him. You're over at Piste Six."

I was lost for words, which Coach noticed.

"You can thank me with a win, Barnaby. Now, let's go!"

Wrapping his beefy arm around me, Coach led me over to one of the nearby pistes, where the match's official was already waiting. I turned to step onto the mat, but not before Coach stopped me.

"Relax, Barnaby, you still have time for a quick pep talk from your ol' coach." He winked at me. "Just remember what we discussed, all right? Stay calm, have confidence in your stance, and bring the fight to him. Oh, and please, for the love of God—don't do anything stupid."

"Fencers, please approach the center of the mat," the referee called out.

"You've got this!" Coach cheered me on, delivering one final pat onto my back as I stepped onto the piste. I half expected him to depart and assist my other fellow classmates but no, Coach remained where he was and watched on with a face filled with pride.

Boy, I can't tell you how much of a boost of confidence this gave me. I seriously looked up to Coach, and with Grandma being absent today, his support meant the world to me. It almost filled the void I felt when I passed the parent-filled bleachers.

Almost.

I walked across the piste toward the referee, where my opponent joined me a moment later. He was dressed in gear completely identical to mine, although in a different color. While mine was stark white, his was jet black.

The referee began to speak to us.

"Gentlemen, welcome to the Summer Regional Fencing Tournament!"

His bright green eyes darted in both of our directions, checking that we were listening. At first glance, I thought he looked rather young to be officiating. Tall, and in his late teens, he had a tight blond ponytail and a face infested with pimples.

Probably just making some last-second cash before school, I figured.

"Now, we'll be doing things a little differently today," the referee continued. "Due to the large number of matches today, each round will consist of only three bouts, instead of the five that you are probably used to. One round, best of three. Got

CHAPTER 1

it?"

My opponent and I nodded, although I couldn't help but feel a small tug of pressure at this last-second update, as it most certainly raised the intensity level that each bout carried. With only three chances to score, the margin of error had shrunk. To win, I would need to be flawless. I would need to be *perfect*.

The referee went on.

"Target area remains the same: waist up, with the arms included. Also, if either of you steps off the mat at any time throughout the match, that's a point for your opponent. Finally, we ask, for safety reasons, to please not remove your masks until the entire match has been completed. Now, are you both clear on everything I've just said?"

Once again, we nodded.

"All right then." The referee stepped off the mat and motioned for us to take our positions at the two ends, which we did. "On the count of three."

I slipped on my mask and got into my stance.

"One."

I raised my saber, inhaling deeply. Here I was, only two seconds away from another step closer to my dream.

"Two."

I closed my eyes in anticipation, waiting for that final number to be called out.

"THREE!"

CHAPTER 2

"*Bring the fight to him.*"

Coach's words echoed through my head as I thundered across the piste at my opponent. I refused to waste even a millisecond. I wanted this first point *bad*.

My opponent barely had enough time to raise his saber in defense as I ferociously swung at his chest. As for the one feeble attack he managed in reply, I smacked it aside with total ease. All that remained was a swift lunge to retrieve my first point.

It was almost too easy.

"Point, white!" the referee declared.

My heart did a back flip.

"Well done, Barnaby!" Coach applauded from the sideline. "Well done!"

Turning around, I gave him my brightest grin—only realizing afterward that he couldn't see it as I still had my mask on. Fortunately, that meant that he couldn't see me blush in embarrassment either.

"Fencers, please return to your starting positions."

I rushed back to my end of the piste, absolutely energized by the first bout.

You've got this in the bag, I told myself, heart pounding with adrenaline and joy. *Nationals, here I come.*

Once both of us had returned to our respective corners, the referee continued with the next countdown.

"One. Two. Three!"

This time, I decided to let my opponent make the first move. Even though Coach had advised otherwise, something in my gut was telling me to mix it up. After all, my opponent could very well be expecting me to charge again at full throttle.

So, altering my strategy, I held my ground and braced for his first attack to come.

The thing is, it never did. He didn't charge at me like I presumed he would. Instead, my opponent began walking toward me. Vigilant with each step, he treaded slowly—almost casually—toward me.

How odd, I thought. This maneuver was unlike any I'd ever seen before.

And then it got even weirder. Still a distance away, I watched as my opponent released his grasp on his saber, letting the blade drop to the floor. Now reaching for a zipper at the side of his fencing jacket, and slowly sliding it open, I watched on, bewildered, as he began to withdraw a *second sword*.

Don't ask me how he managed to fit it into his jacket, but I'm sure it wasn't comfortable. The new sword was nothing like his other one. While it shared the long, narrow profile of the fencing saber, that's where the similarities ended. This new blade was both thicker and sharper, with an unnervingly jagged tip that gave it a menacing edge.

In other words—definitely *not* a fencing sword.

Suddenly, my opponent's pace quickened. Panic flooded through me as it morphed into an all-out sprint, and before I knew it, he was on top of me. Roles now reversed, I barely had enough time to lift my saber to block his menacing blade from carving through my side.

Except I missed.

A blast of excruciating pain rippled through my chest, as if I'd been doused by a pot of scalding water. Eventually my eyes made their way down to the inflamed area, and it took everything within me to not scream. A blotch of dark crimson began seeping through my jacket's side, which now had a massive gash through it.

"What the heck?" I gasped. Seeing my own blood was starting to make me lightheaded, and I found myself stumbling off the piste in dizziness.

"Hey, uh, ref?" My eyes darted for the fencing official. "That sword's got to be totally illegal, right?"

For some reason, the guy didn't answer. Motionless in his spot, he didn't even look at me—his eyes just stared ahead aimlessly.

"Coach?"

Again, no luck. Like the referee, he too was still as a statue. *What the heck was going on!*

My answer arrived in a gale of dark laughter.

"Oh, they can't help you," my opponent jeered from beneath his mask. "Nobody can."

The callous joy in his high-pitched voice was unmistakable. The psycho was enjoying this.

Sickened, I grimaced and gripped my saber even tighter. The lukewarm blood was now trickling down the side of my inner thigh, which felt eerily reminiscent of peeing my pants.

"Who—who are you? Why are you doing this to me?"

My masked assailant continued to laugh.

"Who am I, Barnaby Stump?"

CHAPTER 2

Hearing him say my name completely threw me off, which seemed to be exactly what he wanted. Using my moment of hesitation to charge again, I once more found myself fending for my life, parrying a vicious swipe that nearly took my head off.

Would my mask protect me from such a blow? I wondered.

I didn't really want to find out.

After evading another deadly blow, I watched as my opponent bobbed his concealed head in approval.

"Not bad, not bad at all," he taunted me. "He told me you would be good. But let's see if you can handle *this*."

He pounced again at me, slashing diagonally this time, as if trying to engrave a grisly X into my torso. I evaded the first swipe by hopping aside and swung my blade up to meet the second. Miraculously, the slender steel of my saber survived yet another tough collision. However, as our swords met, my foe shot a swift kick straight to my ribs. The hit—delivered right below my already-flaring wound—doubled me over and forced me back yet again.

"This isn't fencing," I heard him hiss at me. "Get that in your head."

Reeling, my tear-filled eyes were scrunched up so tightly they might as well have been closed shut. The pain in my side was bordering on unbearable, and it was a miracle I was still standing. That said, I doubted I would be able to take another shot like that.

But what else was I supposed to do? I was wounded, and a butter knife could do more damage than my fencing blade. I could see no way to fight back, let alone harm my opponent.

But what if I didn't need to harm him?

I thought back to a particular lesson with Coach last year.

Half the class was gone that day—they'd all been old enough to compete in some tournament—so Coach decided he would teach us younglings something special. It had just been for fun, nothing he claimed any of us would ever use in an actual fencing match.

But this isn't fencing anymore, Barnaby, I reminded myself. *Time to accept that.*

It was nearly a year since I tried the move, and I wasn't even sure if I had performed it correctly that day. Could it really be my chance at surviving this madness?

Only one way to find out.

First things first, I needed him to attack again. The joints in my legs begged for mercy as I forced them into my fencing stance, something my opponent was quick to take notice of.

"Well, then," he leered. "Someone wants a little more, eh?"

I waited until the last moment, right when he threw his blade forward in a lunge. Then, summoning up all the remaining strength I had left, I launched myself to the side and slammed my saber down on his sword, twisting and interlocking the two blades together. An alarming, cracking sound began emitting from mine, and I prayed to God that my thin blade would hold.

It did.

I twisted my sword-arm even farther, which forced my opponent's arm to do the same. He grunted in discomfort from his wrist's newfound angle.

C'mon, almost there...just a little more...

And then—

SNAP!

"ARGH!"

My eyes widened as, like a wounded animal, my opponent

yelped from beneath his mask. The pain must have been unbearable. I watched as he released himself from the bind through his only available option: by dropping his sword.

I swooped down and scooped it up in a heartbeat. Along the way, I managed to glance at my own sword to see the damage done, and instantly let out a dismal groan. While the hilt appeared unscathed, the steel blade had completely shattered and was barely clinging to a sliver of metal protruding from the hilt. It would have to be completely replaced.

As I straightened up again, armed now by both swords—well, his and whatever remained of mine—I caught my opponent reaching yet again into his jacket. His hand began to pull out something else—something shiny and made of metal.

Alarms sounded off in my head. Only one thing came to mind.

GUN!

My heart raced. My brain turned to its primal instincts, and I did the only thing that made any sense: I lunged forward.

"Argh!" my opponent cried, clutching at his side. He let go of whatever he'd been gripping and collapsed to the floor.

I pulled the sword back and looked down. The blade's tip shone a dark, glistening red.

NO.

Throwing off my mask, I rushed toward my foe, who was now sprawled out across the hardwood floor. Kneeling beside him, I watched as his hands slowly moved toward his mask, which he struggled to pull off. For the first time, I was able to see my attacker's face: late teens with youthful golden locks that fell over his blue eyes.

But more importantly, I saw the fury in his eyes. I saw the pain which'd been dealt to him. The pain *I* had dealt to him.

NO NO NO NO NO.

I watched as he snapped his fingers.

Suddenly, the referee—who, last I checked, had been frozen solid—came rushing over to his aid. The bloodied sword fell from my hands with an echoing *clang*.

"What happened?" he demanded.

"He stabbed me in the gut!" my attempted murderer croaked.

No. This can't be happening.

"Barnaby," my coach's voice came from nearby. "Is this true?"

Finding myself unable to speak, I scanned the room, desperately searching for a single soul of support. I looked first to my coach, then to my fellow classmates, all of whom had halted their matches to check out the commotion. All their eyes, as well as those of the parents in the bleachers, were on me now. Each one of their expressions was grimmer than the last.

THIS CAN'T BE HAPPENING.

Suddenly, the boy's body began to shake. His mouth opened, like he was trying to get something out but to no avail. A gagging sound began emitting from his throat, and we all watched in sheer horror as blood began to shoot out of his mouth.

Then he fell back and was still.

CHAPTER 3

Everyone held their breath as the referee checked the boy for his pulse and breath.

"He's not breathing!" he shouted, his voice rich with dread. "Someone get medical in here QUICK!"

What have I done?

"Out of the way! Please, let me—EVERYBODY MOVE!"

I watched helplessly as a pair of paramedics pushed their way through the stunned crowd, continuing to shout until people finally stepped aside. Despite being in agony myself, I didn't dare say a word to them about my cut. It was clear who needed medical attention first.

So much blood...

The "authorities" arrived shortly after, in the form of a yawning, puffy-eyed police officer. Yet despite the evidence of a good nap, Officer Gallman—per his name-tag—was swift and diligent when it came to his work. Right away, he began questioning the people nearest to the scene, jotting down what they said in a notebook.

I watched, the lump in my chest growing with every testimony, as each person he questioned—Coach included—all answered in the same, earth-shattering way:

"All I saw was that boy stabbing him in the chest."

The last person on Gallman's list was the referee. I held my breath, praying that he'd say something in my favor.

He was right beside us the whole time. He had to have seen what happened. He HAD TO.

"I really don't know, to be honest," I overheard him say. "The last thing I remember is seeing *that boy* standing over this poor one here with a bloody sword in his hands. I don't think I'll ever forget the sight of it, to be honest."

My heart sank a thousand leagues when he pointed in my direction after the officer asked him who he was referring to as "that boy."

"And that's all you remember?" Gallman asked him.

"Afraid so, Officer. Everything else is, well…fuzzy."

"I've lost his pulse!" one of the medics suddenly yelled. "Beginning compressions at a hundred-per-minute rate."

Officer Gallman finished with the referee and thanked him for his time. I bet you can guess who he went to interview next.

When the officer's eyes spotted my fencing jacket, he stiffened.

"How'd you get all that blood on you?" he asked me.

I opened my mouth to respond but couldn't even muster a sound.

"Did you stab that boy over there?"

Again, silence—but this time I was able to give him a frail, jolted nod.

I watched as he jotted something down in his notebook. It was by far the longest I'd seen it take to write something down. Definitely didn't feel like a good sign.

"He had a gun!" I forced myself to blurt out.

Gallman halted his writing and looked up. His eyebrows

CHAPTER 3

narrowed.

"A gun," he repeated skeptically, "in a fencing match?"

I nodded.

"This is nothing to kid about, son. Are you sure?"

"Yes! I was attacked!"

The officer appeared to ponder this. He turned and called the referee back over.

"You were the first to reach the boy. Did you find any sort of gun when you treated him?" he asked him.

The referee gave a curious look upon the question, but still shook his head. "Gun? Um, no, sir, nothing."

"But I saw it! I saw him pull it out," I insisted. "It was silver!"

"He was wearing a silver necklace," he said to me grimly. "But no gun."

"No, that can't be true. No—I know what I saw!"

My plea went unanswered. Thanking the referee for the second time, Gallman returned to his notes and continued writing. I bit my nails as I waited.

When finished, he looked back at me, a stern look now on his face.

"Son, I don't want you to overreact, but it looks like I'm going to have to take you down to the station for some questions. Are your parents here?"

I shook my head, quick and nervous, unable to meet his eyes.

"That's okay," he said, his voice softening. We'll call them on the way. Come with me."

Throat closing in, I had no choice but to follow. We didn't get that far, however, before one of the medics called at us to stop.

"Were you really going to take him without letting us treat

him first?" he asked the officer, a hint of skepticism in his voice. "What, do you *not* see the blood on his uniform?"

Gallman's face turned red as a tomato.

I bit my lip, wincing as the medic probed and poked around the wound on my side.

"Well, it's not deep, so that's good," he said. "The bleeding's stopped too. You'll need to get it properly cleaned and checked, but for now, just keep it covered with one of these." He placed a bandage over the cut and handed me a small bundle of extras. "They have disinfectant on them."

"Thanks," I managed.

The medic nodded at me and then once more at Gallman, signaling that he was finished.

"That cut, it happened during the match?" the security guard asked me.

"Yes. Like I said, *he* attacked *me*. I only fought back to defend myself."

"I see," Gallman said with a nod. "All right, we'll discuss it more at the station. This way, please."

He picked up where he left off and ushered me toward the exit.

Cue the Walk of Shame music. That walk out of the gymnasium was *brutal*. All along the way, I felt the crowd's eyes pierce through me, as if I was under a microscope. Man, I wished I still had my helmet to hide behind.

We walked right past my solemn faced coach, whom I pleadingly tried to make eye contact with. But the way my would-be mentor just ignored me—the only pair of eyes in the room that wouldn't look my way—it felt like I was being disowned.

Right then and there, it took everything from me to not

CHAPTER 3

burst into tears.

Finally, we got out of the gymnasium. Officer Gallman and I passed through the very lobby where I had signed in less than twenty minutes ago. The Floridian heat greeted us outside as Gallman led me to his ride—a county police cruiser.

"Hop in the back, all right?" He continued to speak to me with a gentle tone. "There's no need to be worried, son. We're just going to get to the bottom of this."

Clearly, he realized how this all must look to someone my age—to get in the back of a freaking police cruiser. I appreciated him trying not to scare me.

But, um...too late.

I buckled up and glanced out the window as Gallman started up the engine. My bike still lay idle in the rack beside the Center's entrance. I glanced wistfully at it as we pulled out of the parking lot and turned onto the main road, in the direction of the nearest police station. We were also headed in the opposite direction of my home—and of Grandma.

Oh crap. Grandma.

I'd totally forgotten about my grandmother. *What will she think?*

I've always hated disappointing my grandmother. Whether it be from pride or personal morals—or both—she's always held me at such a high standard, and I've never wanted to let her down. I could barely stomach bringing home a C+ to Grandma. Just the thought of her poor face receiving a call from the police station—it was making me downright sick.

Stomach throbbing, I tried opening the window, but it was locked. *Dang.* It looked like I would have to try and hold it together until we arrived at the precinct.

But then, all of a sudden, the cruiser came to a sharp halt.

"What the heck…?" I heard Gallman murmur from the driver's seat.

Glancing out the window, I saw that we were now parked in the middle of a main road, cars still zooming past us. Strange.

Why would Gallman stop here?

Trying to get a better look of what he was seeing, I craned my neck to the space between the two front seats, which ended up being a waste of time. The cruiser had a metal separator between the rows of seats, protecting the officers from whoever sat behind.

Whether I liked it or not, for the moment I was blind.

I heard the "click" of the driver's door being unlocked, which could only mean one thing.

Gallman was getting out.

"Stay seated," he called out to me before stepping outside. For a moment, there was just silence. Then—

"Sir, please stop where you are. Return to your vehicle and remove it from the middle of the road. You are blocking the way."

For a moment, nothing. I didn't hear any response.

Then suddenly, Gallman shouted: "Sir? Sir, I'll say it one last time. Return to your vehicle and—SIR! You are under arrest, do you hear me? You are under arrest! SIR! PUT DOWN THE—"

Gallman stopped mid-sentence. Or so it seemed…

But by who?

Panicking, I reached for the door handle and attempted to pry it open. Like the window, it too was locked.

You idiot, I thought to myself. *Do you really think they'd make it that easy for criminals to get out?*

Heart racing, I unbuckled my seat and braced for whatever

was coming. Sure, I may have been swordless (both my attacker's sword and the remains of mine were currently sitting in the trunk), but that didn't mean I wouldn't go down without a fight.

Hearing the door click open, I clenched my hand into a fist, ready to swing at whoever was out there, when a familiar voice cried out—

"Wait, don't! I'm on your side!"

Sunlight poured in as the car door swung open, blurring my vision, and it took me an extra second to make out the figure standing before me. But once my eyes adjusted, and the boy took off his motorcycle mask, I was able to see who it was.

It was the referee from the fencing match.

CHAPTER 4

"You?" I stammered, baffled. "What the heck are you doing here?"

"Um, saving your butt? What does it look like?" the referee replied coolly.

No longer in his striped officiating uniform, he was now sporting a crisp, leather biker's jacket atop a plain white tee. Combine that with his baby blue jeans and he really pulled off the whole "boy band" look rather well. Well, he would've, if it weren't for the pair of blades in his hands.

Ever the sword enthusiast—*thank you, fencing*—I recognized them instantly. They were cutlasses, short, curved swords used historically by sailors and pirates. I'd only seen a handful of them before, and they were all in museums or movies starring Johnny Depp.

So what was he doing with a pair?

"Well? Are you just going to sit there, or can we get out of here?" He grinned valiantly, like he saw himself as my knight in shining armor or something.

It was all so random, so *ridiculous*—I almost laughed.

"Um…why should I go anywhere with you?"

The referee's grin evaporated. Definitely not the reaction he'd been expecting.

CHAPTER 4

I folded my arms and frowned. "How could you say that I attacked him? You were right beside us; you had to see him attack me."

"Hey, I never said anything like that," he argued in defense. "All I said to that officer was what I saw, which was *you* standing over him with a bloody sword. That's it. I told the truth—I really don't remember any of the match happening."

"No way." I shook my head. "That's impossible."

"I wish I could explain it." The referee shrugged. "Now, I definitely remember giving a second countdown. But after that, for some odd reason, my mind goes completely blank. But really—are we just going to keep arguing until we *both* get arrested, or can we get out of here?"

"Um, and go where, exactly?"

"Some place safe. Some place far away from here, where you don't need to worry about the police finding you."

I stared at him distrustfully.

"Again—why should I believe you? Do you even know how utterly insane you sound? I don't even know your *freaking name*, and you're asking me to run away with you!"

The referee took a second to contemplate my logic.

"First off, my name is Reed," he began. "Reed Sable. And I get what you're saying. I probably look like a total stranger to you. But I am one stranger who can promise you one thing, and that's that I'm your best shot at not ending up behind bars. I mean, that's what you want, right?"

Now it was my turn to pause. Despite his testimony in the gymnasium, he did sound like he genuinely wanted to help me. As for why, exactly, I had no idea. But I didn't see anyone else standing in the middle of the road, taking out police officers to try to rescue me. It seemed absolutely insane to consider, but perhaps my best option *was* to go with Reed—if that was even his real name.

My day's been nothing but insane, I thought, *and I've already hit rock bottom. What more do I honestly have to lose?*

With a deep breath, and much hesitation, I nodded.

"Great! Now follow me!"

I stepped out of the cruiser, and immediately noticed the motionless figure lying on the concrete.

Gallman.

"He'll be fine," Reed assured me. "C'mon! We really got to go!"

We raced down the street toward Reed's parked ride, which as Grandma would put, was a "dandy:" a sleek, all-black Harley Davidson. Two seconds later, a helmet was shoved into my arms.

"Riding is pretty simple," Reed explained, his helmet already on. "Just wrap your arms around my waist and, no matter what, don't let go. That is, unless you intend on flying into the car behind us."

I had no such intentions, so I leaped on behind Reed and latched on tightly around his waist. I released a hand—my sword hand—to lower my helmet's visor, and that's when the realization came.

"HEY!" I shouted over the revving engine, but Reed didn't appear to hear me. Hoping that the referee wouldn't decide this very second to speed off, I quickly released my hold and rapped lightly on the top of his helmet.

Reed shifted. He turned his head around and lifted his visor.

"What is it?" he yelled over the rumbling. "We gotta go!"

"My sword, it's still in the car!" I answered him. "I can't leave without it!"

CHAPTER 4

Reed hesitated for a moment—but nodded.

"All right but make it fast! We're going to be late!"

Huh? Going to be late for what?

Contemplating this as I leaped off the bike, I hurried back over to the empty cruiser. Running my hands along the trunk door, I prayed for it to be unlocked.

Click!

Thank God.

I swung the truck open and reached into the bulky evidence bag. A wave of comfort washed over me as my hand reunited with the ever-familiar leather-bound grip of my sword. As I pulled its remains out of the bag, another sparkle of metal caught my eye. The warm, homely feeling within me evaporated when I realized what it was.

By now, the blood covering the blade had crusted over. It resembled dry paint, like some grotesque piece of crimson-colored art titled *Barnaby's Worst Day*. Even worse was the fact that it was impossible to tell which of the blood was mine, and which had come from the other boy.

Truth be told, I didn't want to know.

Stomach in knots, I closed the trunk with a heavy breath. I turned around, leaving both the cruiser and the wretched sword in the past.

"Don't do this, son," a faint voice suddenly called out from nearby. I immediately knew who it belonged to.

Gallman.

"Please don't make this mistake," he pleaded from where he lay on the ground. A dazed look filled his eyes, and a dark purple bruise bloomed on his forehead, ominous against his skin.

The work of Reed, no doubt.

I continued on my way to the motorcycle, attempting to ignore him. Hopefully, Gallman would just give up on trying to convince me.

"You leave with him now and you're officially a fugitive. Is that really what you want?"

Well, I mean, *that* would get anyone to freeze.

Reed hadn't mentioned anything about being deemed a criminal. Was that really what would happen?

It was at that very moment that I noticed, for the first time, the lengthy line of halted cars on the opposite side of the road. Miraculously, none had come our way since the cruiser had stopped, but on the other side of the road, roughly half a dozen cars going in the other direction had come to a complete stop.

Within their windows, I made out the faces of the drivers and passengers. Every single one shared the same look of fear in their eyes as they watched me face the injured officer. Their pale, slack-jawed expressions matched the ones I had received from my fellow teammates—and the one from Coach.

Is this...is this how people see me?

Clearly, Gallman must've noticed my hesitation because he tried speaking to me again.

"We can fix this," he urged me. "Help me up, son, and we'll fix this together. If it's just like you said—self-defense—I promise you, it'll be okay. I mean, what would your parents want you to do?"

My parents...

Was I really going to abandon Grandma, just like that? Just like I had all those years ago?

Maybe I should help him, I began considering. *They could hook me up to one of those lie detector machines and see I was telling the truth about it being self-defense. Yes! I could try again in the next qualifiers and still earn my spot in the Nationals. I could still live a perfectly normal life.*

And on top of all of that, I couldn't just leave Grandma like this. Not after she'd taken me in, all those years ago. I owed her that much.

I owed her everything.

Decision officially changed; I started moving toward Gallman, who immediately noticed this.

"You're making the right choice here, Barnaby," he reassured me. "We'll get this all sorted at the precinct. Just help me up and over to the car's radio…need to call this in."

"Okay."

I bent down and extended a hand toward Gallman—when a blazing pain suddenly rang across the back of my head.

Eyes spinning, I managed to turn around as I collapsed onto the street—and there, standing above me, was Reed. The two swords were back in his hands.

"I told you to trust me, Barnaby," he said. "I'm sorry it had to come to this. But don't you worry. Everything will make sense once we get to the island."

And then everything went black.

CHAPTER 5

After who knows how long, I finally regained consciousness. When I did, I prayed to the heavens that I would find myself back in my bedroom.

Please Lord, just let this all be some twisted, terrifyingly lifelike dream. Please let me open my eyes and see that I'm still in my bed. Please, PLEASE let this all just be a dream.

Taking a deep breath, I slowly opened my eyes—and instantly groaned.

Dang. Not a dream.

Not that my new surroundings were unpleasant. The room I was in was tidy and quaint and reminded me of the reception area at a fancy restaurant. I was lying on an extremely comfortable couch—one-half of a pair that furnished the room. Both couches, as well as the coffee table and just about everything else in the room, were all white. The only offering of color was a hand-painted pattern of golden seashells that adorned the walls. The tinge of gold within all the white gave the room a real elegant vibe.

My whereabouts weren't the only thing that was new. Someone had also changed my clothes. Gone was my torn, blood-splattered fencing uniform; a fresh-smelling navy shirt and a pair of cotton khakis in its stead.

CHAPTER 5

There was one last thing to check. Holding my breath, I reached for the hem of my new shirt and slowly lifted it to examine the wound underneath. Someone had covered the cut with one of the bandages the medic had given me, and I felt the cold and soothing antibiotic underneath.

"Looking good, eh, sleepy head?"

I craned my head upward and met the green eyes of Reed, who hovered over me with a smile on his face.

I didn't offer one in return. Instead, I leaped off the couch and scurried over to the other side of the room, determined to get as far away from Reed as possible.

"Where—where are we?" I demanded. "How long was I out?"

Reed looked at me, unrattled. Clearly, after our last encounter, he'd been expecting something like this.

"Several hours. You didn't even flinch when we tended to your wound."

"We?" I asked, eyebrows hunched. "Who's 'we'?"

Reed took a step toward me, hands now raised in a gentle, reassuring manner.

"If you'll just sit back down, Barnaby...I promise, I'll explain every—"

"No way," I cut him off. "I'm not sitting anywhere with you!" Taking another step back, my back was up against the wall now. "You stay away from me!"

Now Reed frowned. His calm demeanor beginning to waver, he quickly motioned for me to keep my voice down.

"Okay, okay. I'll stay right where I am. Just...try being a tad quieter, all right? There are other people aboard. We don't need a whole commotion right now."

"A *commotion?*" Spit flew from my mouth as I repeated

Reed's words, eyes widened with disbelief. "YOU KIDNAPPED ME!"

Reed winced at the word.

"Well, that's a strong way to put it."

"You knocked me down and took me against my will!"

"Okay, yes, I may have done that." Reed's hands remained raised as he stepped closer to me. "But if you'll just let me explain, I promise you, I can—"

"No! Stay away from me!" I yelled as he reached for me.

I need to get out of here.

Frantically glancing at the doorway by the other side of the room, I tried to measure the distance in my head. It would take roughly four steps to make it to the door, and another one to get outside. But to do so, I would need to get past Reed, who was completely blocking the way.

Thinking on my feet, I tried my best to play to Reed's blatant urge to help me. Slumping my shoulders, I let out a long pitiful sigh and showed him my finest attempt at a troubled expression.

Trying to be the hero, Reed took the bait. Stepping forward, he reached out yet again, offering his support.

"Barnaby, I promise you, everything—"

NOW.

Without hesitation, I shot my fist at Reed's face. There was a blunt *crack* as the jab impacted his nose, blood spurting from his nostrils. As a result, both of Reed's hands flew to his face, which was *exactly* what I wanted. With him distracted—and no free hand to stop me—I flew past the former referee, hopped over the loveseat, and ran straight out that door.

Along the way, I caught a glimpse of the teenage boy's bloody reaction to my escapade. It was not one of anger, but of shock.

CHAPTER 5

"Barnaby?"

Once outside the room, I found myself in a narrow corridor, the same seashell decor visible across all the walls. Numerous other doors lined the walls as well, all of them closed. I looked to the left and there, at the end, was a thin wooden staircase leading up .

Electing to head for the stairwell, I heard Reed's muffled voice call out to me from back inside the room.

"Barnaby, der's no way—"

I ignored him and pressed on.

Increasing my pace to avoid Reed catching me, I flew up the first two steps before a violent jerk suddenly sent me crashing into the wall. Wincing, it took all my strength to hang on to the handrail as my universe kept lurching violently to either side.

Where in the world was I?

Eventually, I managed to recover my footing and reached the top. Feeling the stairs swaying again, I grasped for the door's handle, twisted it, and stumbled through as fast as my body allowed.

And my jaw dropped.

I was on a ship—and an old fashioned one at that. Long, tall masts stuck out from the deck like tree trunks; white, linen sails hanging from the tops of them.

Well, that explains the shaking.

On each side of the deck, I counted a dozen cast-iron cannons, their intimidating mouths poking through holes in the wooden railing. I also noticed that, like downstairs, everything—cannons included—were painted white. But it wasn't that unusual albeit elegant feature that had caused me to gasp so dramatically.

No, that had to be attributed to what was going on *around* the ship.

I stared speechlessly at the miraculous scene before me, stumbling back a couple of feet as a school of bright, blue-and-yellow angelfish swam by my face, completely minding their own business. Atop the starboard side of the deck, a bed of eels fluttered around without a care in the world. Something suddenly zoomed over my head, and my heart fluttered in awe as I watched two manta rays soar over the ship like a pair of fighter jets.

My mind couldn't come to grips with what I was seeing.

Somehow, this ship was underwater.

Somehow, *I* was underwater.

"How—how is this possible?"

I found myself blurting out this question despite being the only person on the deck. I also assumed that my words would just be drowned out in a burst of bubbles. It was only natural then—what with also being completely dry aboard a freaking underwater ship—that I heard them echo across the deck instead.

"Incredible, isn't it?"

The familiar voice came from the stairwell, where Reed appeared a moment later. A wet-looking wad of reddened tissue clogged up both sides of his nose.

"Go away," I muttered, still too furious to speak to him.

Reed ignored my demand and continued with his approach.

"I tried telling you back there," he said, "that there's not exactly a way off right now. But there will be one soon."

"Oh yeah? And then what? And where is this ship even going?" I asked all this while still refusing to look at Reed.

Only when I received no response from him did I finally

glance up. There was a conflicting look on the former referee's face.

"I don't believe it," I shook my head. "You ask for a chance to explain yourself, and when you get it, you've got nothing to say?"

Reed looked crushed.

"It's not that I don't have the answers, Barnaby. I'm just…I'm not the person you should hear this all from. If you'll just trust me and wait, I can assure you—"

"That's the thing," I interjected. "I *don't* trust you, Reed. I trusted Gallman! He gave me his word that he would help me figure a way out of this mess. But you—you just went ahead and made everything worse! I'm a fugitive now because of you!"

"I only did all that to save you!" Reed cried. A look of bewilderment was cast across his face, and I knew exactly what he was thinking: *How could he not see what I did for him?*

"I don't care why you did it. All that matters is that right now, I'm stuck on some weird, underwater boat that I never asked to be on, going to God knows where. So, unless you plan on telling me where this ship is going, we're done here." I walked away before Reed could get out a reply.

This time, he didn't appear intent on following me. At least he got *that* right.

Once I felt like I put enough space between the two of us, I released what must've been my millionth sigh of the day.

How could Reed not see what he'd done to me? I never asked to be here. I never asked for any of this!

Frustrated, I shook my head. The more the guy spoke, the more he made his original offer of help seem less genuine. My stomach churned at the thought of that; that if *this* was the vibe of where we were heading—lying, no-good scoundrels—I sure wasn't going to like it there one bit.

But it wasn't just that. All this uncertainty was making me sick. I hated not knowing what was next. I liked sticking to my routine and doing things in order. Who knew what chaos lay ahead?

A pair of barracudas swam by at a furious pace, pursuing what appeared to be a school of much smaller, clearly helpless fish. Desperate for a distraction, I turned my attention to their hunt. It did the job for a good while, but when the barracudas disappeared, the negative thoughts started creeping back in.

I need to figure out a way home, FAST. There's probably still time for me to go to the police station and clear my—

"Barnaby!" Reed suddenly called out to me. "Grab hold of something!"

I had half a mind to ignore him, but I did as I was told—and thank goodness for that. No sooner had I snagged onto a length of the ship's rigging did the entire ship begin to shake. It began lurching upward too, and I tightened my grip onto the rope as I felt myself sliding back.

We were rising.

CHAPTER 6

Elevating through the various levels of the sea, I watched on as the cluster of sea animals occupying the deck began to dwindle, the water encompassing us becoming brighter and brighter. Like an airplane, we continued to rise higher and higher, until—

SPLOOSH!

Clutching on for dear life, I braced as the ship plowed through the surface like a battering ram, engulfing the deck in an eruption of frothy foam. Upon opening my eyes, astonishment washed over me as I realized that both Reed and I remained totally dry.

Meanwhile, the splash had conjured a thick curtain of mist that enveloped the ship, obscuring our view of the surroundings. Peering through the haze, I struggled to make out much, although I did manage to spot a cluster of palm trees on a nearby shore. As the mist evaporated, the rest of the island's features were revealed, far beyond anything I had initially imagined.

We floated in a large lagoon, its waters a sparkling sapphire blue. We must have entered through an underwater cavern that opened into the sea. A tropical shore encircled the crystal-clear waters, the sandy beaches adorned with palm trees that stretched into a dense forest in the distance. The vibrant greenery buzzed with life—I could hear wildlife rustling within the thick foliage. In the background, gray mountain peaks loomed majestically, completing the breathtaking scene.

The sound of multiple sets of feet hitting the deck disrupted my study of this stunning paradise. I turned around to see, for the first time, the other passengers of our vessel. While a handful looked around Reed's age, the majority appeared to be younger than me, around eleven or twelve. The sight of them stirred an unsettling thought within me.

Were all these kids dragged here, stolen from their lives, just like me?

But as I watched them, they sprinted to the bow with excitement, faces beaming, eager for a better look at this tropical paradise.

"Oh. My. GAWD." I heard one girl cry out in delight.

Hmm...maybe they actually chose to come here, I thought, shooting Reed another bitter glance before turning back to the approaching coast.

The shoreline we sailed toward held a harbor filled with an extraordinary collection of vessels. Ships of all shapes, sizes, and time periods—from medieval warships to a full-armed military destroyer—were anchored there. Despite their differences, they all flew the same flag: a black flag with a sword and spyglass crisscrossed under a grinning white skull.

The Jolly Roger.

I recognized the flag right away. With my love for fencing, I often imagined myself on ships donning flags like these, engaged in grand sword fights. But pirates were supposed to be a thing of the past. Why were these ships still flying their flag?

CHAPTER 6

Lost in thought, a massive shadow fell over the deck. Like everyone else, I looked up to see what cast it.

"Oh, my GAWD," I gasped.

The boat before us was unquestionably the largest on the lake, dwarfing the others like a colossal titan. Numerous wooden masts soared skyward like urban skyscrapers, each sail sprawling out to the size of a small house. Its stern boasted an oversized triple-decker cabin, its many windows suggesting a multitude of rooms within.

But whose rooms are they? I wondered. *Who did this all belong to?*

Our ship sailed into the harbor, anchoring with a splash. A gangplank clattered onto the docks, inviting us to disembark.

Once everyone was off the ship, the older teens took charge, leading the group toward the colossal warship. Unsure where else to go, I followed along.

Once aboard the new ship, the group turned left, descending stairs that disappeared into the ship's depths. As I moved to follow, a hand grabbed at my shirt and pulled me back.

It was Reed.

"Wait a second," he said. "We're not going with them."

I grimaced, sick of his antics.

"You want answers, right? Then trust me, Barnaby. Just this once."

I studied Reed's face. There was a genuine vulnerability in his expression, his eyes earnest and open. He didn't appear to be hiding anything.

"Fine," I nodded, my lips still pursed. "Lead the way."

Reed's way was somewhere within the towering cabin that

made up the ship's rear. Once inside, the former referee led me down a long, lantern-lit hallway that seemed to have no end. We passed numerous doors along the elegantly carpeted path, but Reed didn't stop until we arrived at the final doorway of the floor. I was quick to notice that it was significantly larger than all the others we'd passed to get here.

I glanced at Reed for our next move.

With a sharp and deep breath, I watched as his hands slowly moved toward the large door standing before us, and softly rapped twice.

For a second, no response came. Then—

"Enter," a rough, gravelly voice emitted from inside.

Reed took *another* breath and twisted the doorknob open. He stepped inside and motioned for me to follow.

A wave of warmth greeted me as I entered the room. I seemed to be standing in the living quarters of someone—and an exceptionally furnished set at that.

Bookshelves and cabinets covered every wall, bursting with tomes and trinkets, all except for the rear wall, which offered a breathtaking view of the tropical island below through a huge expanse of glass. A cozy-looking bed stood in the corner to my left, draped from head-to-toe in crimson silk. And finally, dominating the center of the room was a grand mahogany desk, the likes of which you would find in the offices of mega-million-dollar executives. A throne-like chair appropriately accompanied the impressive desk.

And within it sat the room's sole occupant.

His skin was dark as oak, and he was a behemoth of a man. With a rugged, scarred face, he stared us down with piercing brown eyes that radiated authority. His jagged, disfigured nose wrinkled disdainfully. But what truly captured my attention was his beard—a magnificent mass of black, swirling curls that seemed to stretch endlessly, disappearing behind the desk.

After two minutes of lingering silence—all of which I spent taking in the bearded man's daunting appearance—the man cleared his throat and spoke.

"Yes? May I help you?"

Reed tugged at his collar. "Aye, sir, and we're really sorry to interrupt you. You, um…you may not remember me, but my name is—"

"Reed Sable," the man interrupted. "I remember you. It's been quite some time, eh?"

It took quite a while for Reed to muster a reply.

"Aye, sir…it has been a while. But I'm back now, and with a candidate as well. Barnaby here—"

"Great." The man cut him off again with the wave of his hand. "Initiation should begin any minute now. Take the boy to the mess and—"

"Actually, sir," Reed interjected, returning the favor. It appeared to take him a lot to speak up, as I noticed beads of sweat had begun forming across his forehead. "We were actually hoping to hear everything from you. Barnaby here has been through quite a lot today, you see."

"Hmpf," the bearded man huffed, clearly displeased with being cut off. Everything about him gave me the impression that this was a man who was more accustomed to *doing* the cutting off. Someone who, when he said something, it was final—with no buts afterward.

And Reed's request quite defied that.

"Well, that would be rather unorthodox, wouldn't you agree?" While the man's tone was coarse and gruff, I noticed that it remained surprisingly polite, like his engagement with us was done entirely as a favor. "Unfortunately, I'm a little preoccupied at the moment with some matters relating to tomorrow's tryouts."

His expression shifted from calm to hostile as he leaned over the desk and narrowed his brown eyes at Reed. "Take the boy to the mess where he can hear it all from Roberts. *Please.*"

From both his tone and expression, it was clear that he meant this as an order, not a request.

"Yes, sir."

Visibly defeated, Reed shuffled from his spot to the door and opened it. Only then did he look at me, his face flushed with a pitiful look that read plainly: *I tried, man. C'mon, let's get the hell out of here.*

But I remained where I stood.

"Barnaby?"

I ignored Reed's pestering and continued to stare fixedly at the man sitting behind the desk. All the anger and frustration that had been festering inside of me had finally reached its tipping point.

"No."

Reed gasped. Beardy raised an eyebrow.

Eyes trained onto the bearded man, I stepped over to the big desk and slammed my hands onto its polished-wood surface.

"Look, mister, I don't know who you are, or how you normally do things around here," I snapped, "but my day was *anything but* normal. I've been stabbed at and accused of murder. I was also arrested, broken out of custody, and kidnapped onto some sixteenth-century submarine. Reed promised me answers—and I'm going to get them *now!*"

CHAPTER 7

Eyes widened like saucers, Reed looked like he was about to faint. His lips quivered, forming an "O" of disbelief as he stared at me, flabbergasted.

In stark contrast, the bearded man behind the desk remained as steady as a lighthouse in a storm. He studied me with a calm gaze, seemingly unfazed by my rant.

"Is that so?" he asked me most casually.

I nodded rapidly, heart still racing with adrenaline.

"Yeah, it is! So you better get started, Mister…?"

My voice trailed off when I realized that I still didn't know the bearded man's name.

"It's Teach," he chimed in without a drop of hesitation. "Edward Teach."

"Okay, well then, Mr. Teach, I would—"

Once again, I stopped mid-sentence. That name definitely rang a bell in my head. *Where do I know it from?*

Searching for answers, I studied the scene before me. Reed's face was etched with fear, like I was about to burst into flames for talking back. The bearded man almost looked bored behind his desk, continuing to observe me like he was waiting for me to figure this all out.

Reed seems downright spooked by this guy—but why?

And then, in that moment, it hit me like a ton of bricks. A wave of clarity came crashing over me.

Reed's pair of cutlasses—pirate swords.

The ensemble of strange old ships, all flying the Jolly Roger—the flag of pirates.

This man's bushy and magnificent black beard.

How could I have been so stupid?

"Yes?" came the bearded man's voice. "Everything all right?"

Jaw slack, I began coughing nervously—taking a substantial step back in the process. As I did, I noticed that the bearded man's expression had changed as well. Bushy eyebrows raised, he now stared at me like I'd suddenly become interesting.

He knows that I know.

"You…you're," I swallowed. "You're Blackbeard."

The dark, bearded man nodded.

"Aye, boy. I am who you say I am."

"I didn't know that Blackbeard was…" I started to say before hesitating, unsure how to phrase it properly.

"*Black*beard?" The man offered a hint of amusement in his voice.

"Uh, yes. Sorry. I just didn't expect…I didn't know…" I stumbled over my words, feeling the weight of the misunderstanding.

"Many don't. I'm afraid reality doesn't always match the stories people tell."

Fear flooding through me, I shook my head incredulously, as I'm sure anybody would upon hearing such a ridiculous claim.

"But it's impossible. Blackbeard lived centuries ago!"

"There are ways to cheat death," the bearded man replied, his voice firm and definite, suggesting that any more questions

CHAPTER 7

on the matter wouldn't end well for me.

I couldn't help myself. "Okay, but still. His head was cut off in battle!"

The man's gaze hardened. "Does my head look decapitated to you, boy?"

I swallowed hard.

"Um…no, it doesn't," I stammered. "But the history books, they say that the British—"

"The British never came after me, boy."

"What do you mean?"

The man claiming to be Blackbeard sighed in exasperation. Rolling his eyes, he gave me a look like he was asking if I was seriously going to make him have this conversation.

"I mean, everything you've read in the 'history books' about what happened to me and the rest of the pirates is a complete and utter *lie*."

My eyes shot back and forth between Reed and this man with certainty that one of them was going to crack a smile and admit this was all some exaggerated prank. After all, pirates like Blackbeard were supposed to have been wiped out centuries ago.

Surely this was a joke.

To my dismay, neither of them smiled. Rather, the bearded man saw my silence as his cue to continue.

"Back during the Golden Age of Piracy—as today's 'historians' like to call it—my kind ruled the sea. We proudly warred against the cruel monarchies of the time and stamped our mark of independence and democracy in the world, a mark that many in power feared would fester into further, more concerning revolutions. Like the one that led to the establishment of the United States, for example.

"The *civilized* world couldn't bear it for much longer," he continued, "and they desperately craved a solution. They needed to be rid of us, and that was when The Offer was brought to the table."

"The Offer?"

Blackbeard nodded. "Aye. To give us pirates a world of our own. Someplace to run as we pleased, in exchange for leaving *their* world alone."

"You—you mean like your own country," I deduced, mouth agape at what I was hearing.

"Aye. Escaping the self-centered plutocracies of the time was always our endgame. We'd made several attempts to settle—first in Madagascar, and again in the Bahamas—but neither endured. We could never seem to find ourselves a permanent home, until The Offer was brought before us, that is."

"So…what was given to you?"

Leaning back into his seat, I swear I saw the beginnings of a smile curve into Blackbeard's lips. "You would know it as the Bermuda Triangle."

"Ever wondered why all those planes and ships went missing?" Reed sprung in excitingly, his earlier panic gone. "It was us!"

"Indeed," murmured Blackbeard, shooting the former referee a look.

Reed shrunk back without another word.

"However, these self-righteous, high and mighty monarchs were still faced with one final dilemma. They needed a way to tell their menial subjects that they had solved the pirate problem *without* confessing that they had conspired with us to do so."

"But why though?" I asked. "Why couldn't they just tell

everyone the truth?"

Blackbeard's smile widened, revealing a set of filthy, yellowish teeth.

Jeez, somebody's gotta get this guy a toothbrush.

"Because," he said, "we're pirates."

Fair enough.

Blackbeard went on.

"It was obvious from the initial discussions that they were ashamed of our potential collaboration. They required a method to inform their subjects of the resolved situation without revealing *how* they came to it. And so, after sitting on it over cups of *slave-harvested tea*, the solution appeared. Why not *stage* the deaths of all the greatest pirate captains?"

My mind was spinning as I tried to take this all in. History as I knew it was being rewritten right before my eyes.

"How could they get away with such a deal? How could the deaths of all those pirates be faked?"

Unexpectedly, it was Reed who answered this time. Opening his mouth to speak, he paused beforehand and glanced reluctantly at Blackbeard, who nodded and motioned for him to proceed.

"Barnaby," he said, "you must understand, the world then was vastly different to the one you live in today. There was no social media back then. Newspapers were just getting going, and most people either relied on those higher in society for news or asked those who'd returned from being at sea. Sure, some cash had to be passed around to hush some people, but if you really think about it, it probably wasn't such a tricky thing to fabricate."

"Also," added Blackbeard, "there *was* proof. Judging by some of your earlier remarks, it seems like you have some familiarity with the gruesome end of pirates like myself. Many of these events *did* indeed happen, but the prisoners facing the hangman's noose weren't the pirates the public thought them to be—just simple landlubbers also facing death sentences. No one ever knew the difference. No one *wanted* to know the difference."

"Um, landlubbers?"

"Men who never tasted life at sea," Blackbeard explained to me. "Those too cowardly to live the life of a sailor."

"Ah. Right. Those guys."

Smiling, Blackbeard nodded like I was finally getting the picture.

"Anyways, from that moment on there was peace. We stuck to our waters—for the most part—and they stuck to theirs. Shipwreck Cove became the capital to our nation. And on another island, we built a school where we could train future generations in our beliefs and ways."

"A school. For pirates," I repeated slowly, struggling to comprehend the reality of what I was being told.

"Aye. And that's where ye come in."

"Come in. Me. *Me?*"

Blackbeard must've thought me a dolt based on how long it was taking the realization to kick in.

"Wait. *This* is the school?"

Blackbeard nodded. "Aye."

"Uh uh." I shook my head. "No way."

I now spun around toward Reed.

"This is insane!" I snapped at him. "You realize that, right? Do you really expect me to believe that this is where you dragged me to? Something as crazy and convoluted as this?"

The acne-faced, ponytailed teen remained silent.

CHAPTER 7

"I mean, why *me*," I continued, practically ranting again. "Why am I here? I'm no pirate. My family's been in America for generations. I don't belong here!"

"Barnaby," Reed spoke with great care, "if the school only took in pirates and their descendants, it would have shut down *centuries* ago. The number of families still passing on their pirate heritage is exceptionally small. Most have moved on."

"So, who goes here then?"

"Those who the world has turned its back to," explained Blackbeard. "We take in those who, because of some mistakes in their lives—ones they might not even be at fault of—their potential-filled lives have been deemed over by society. We, unlike the rest of this unforgiving world, give people a second chance."

"By training them to be pirates," I said.

"By training them in the ways of pirates, " growled Blackbeard, clearly losing his patience with me. "Teaching them to be fast on their feet. To face anything this harsh world may throw at them. I'd argue our curriculum's goals aren't that different from those of mainland schools—if not better."

I scoffed. "Mister, I don't know if you heard me properly when I first walked in, but Reed needed to *kidnap* me to bring me here. I wouldn't exactly consider that better."

"Don't worry, boy," Blackbeard reassured me. "Over time, ye will learn to appreciate the actions of Mr. Sable here."

Over time?

I wasn't liking the sound of that.

"Um, my apologies for not being clear, Mr. Blackbeard," I began, choosing my next words very carefully. "But I'm afraid I don't intend on staying around. It all sounds really neat, what you've got going on here, but if you could get me a ticket for the next departure of that super-cool white ship you've got, I'd really appreciate it."

While trying my best to sound respectful and mannerly when I spoke, I also wanted to make my intentions perfectly clear:

There was no way I planned on staying.

So I found it very unsettling when Blackbeard began to laugh.

"Oh, ye've got pluck, boy," he chuckled, dark facial hair flapping with every chuckle. "That's good—it'll definitely come in handy when dealing with some of our more...*difficult* students. But I'm afraid I cannot heed your request—it's quite an inconceivable one. If Reed brought you here, it means you've got no place else to go."

Baffled, I opened my mouth to object, but Blackbeard went on, completely disregarding whatever I was going to say.

"Now," he said, "I bet you're mighty hungry, eh? Yes, some food could do well to that complaining mouth of yours. Mr. Sable, why don't you take our *new student* to the mess for supper? It was a pleasure meeting you...Barnaby."

CHAPTER 8

I didn't say another word until we were back outside.

Fists clenched, I marched down the cabin's hallway with Reed, biting my lip to stop myself from blurting anything out. The moment we were back on the deck—as Reed turned to close the cabin door behind us—I swung around and, for the second time today, took a shot at the boy's face.

"YOU RUINED MY LIFE!"

This time, Reed managed to evade my punch. Perhaps he'd even seen it coming. But what surprised me most was the fact that after he dodged it, he once again tried consoling me. The guy was a human broken record.

"Barnaby, just please, listen to me—"

"NO, YOU LISTEN TO ME." I stomped on the deck in full-blown fury. "You've taken everything from me! My home, my friends, my fencing—my grandma! And if that wasn't enough, I'm now trapped here, on this ridiculous pirate island, because of you!"

"Oh yeah? Well, what about *me*?" Reed shot back. "Huh? Have you even considered for a moment how much I've put on the line for you? I was the one who took out that police officer, not you. I *broke the law* for you!"

"I never asked for you to do any of that," I reminded him,

my aggressive tone faltering. This conversation was taking a completely unexpected turn. "I didn't need your help. Gallman, he promised me—"

"To help you get out of this mess," Reed finished for me, rolling his eyes. "Yes, you've said that already. But you'd be a fool if you actually believed him. Do I really need to remind you that everyone saw you stabbing that boy with a sword?"

"IT WAS SELF-DEFENSE!" I roared. My voice echoed across the twilight lake and through the jungle beyond. A long, downhearted sigh left my mouth afterward as I gloomily glanced down at the wooden planks of the ship's deck.

Reed took the moment as his chance to approach, gently laying his hand on my shoulder in an act of support. All it did was make me feel even worse.

"I can't just leave her, Reed," I sniffled, tears beginning to roll down my cheeks. "I'm all the family she's got left."

Reed said nothing, keeping his hand resting on me as I continued to weep.

"Listen," he said after some time, when my tears seemed to slow, "take all the time you need. I'm heading down to the mess to arrange some warm food for us. When you're ready, come down and find me there. It's the big, bright room straight ahead after you reach the bottom of the stairs—you can't miss it."

I nodded. "Thanks."

After Reed left, I wandered to the side of the ship, letting its gentle sway guide my steps. Leaning on the railing, I absorbed the view of the torchlit harbor below. Amber shadows from the ships danced on the waves, creating a scene of unexpected beauty. The jungle had quieted too, the sounds of wildlife fading, wrapping the island in a serene silence that brought an unfamiliar peace—a stark contrast to the turmoil inside me.

Peace. I almost snorted at the thought of the word. How could I even think of peace after everything I'd just endured?

If only I had seen Reed coming at me on the freeway, I lamented. But despite my guilt, Reed's words weighed on my mind. What if he was right? What if there wasn't anything Gallman could do—what would happen to me then? Juvie? Prison? Neither of these situations would have brought me any closer to Grandma.

Well, except on visiting day, perhaps.

Oh, how I missed her. I thought about her warm, comforting presence, the way she ran her hands through my hair to tidy it and told me everything was going to be okay. I missed her welcoming smile, the kind that could chase away any storm brewing inside me. These memories sent a wave of homesickness into me, accompanied by more tears. There was no use in holding them back, so I let them flow freely down my cheeks and onto my shirt.

"I'll come back to you," I promised, my voice shaky but determined. "I don't know how long it'll take, but I'll find my way back. I swear it on Gramps's grave. I will make it home."

After my oath, I took a deep breath, trying to let go of the lingering sadness. Wiping my eyes clear of tears, I was startled by a gentle rumbling in my stomach.

Dinner time.

Taking the hint, I mentally repeated Reed's instructions as I crossed the deck. *Down the stairs and straight ahead.* Sure enough, as I descended to the lower level, the sounds of clattering utensils and people grew louder. And that was when the smells hit me. Mouth-watering aromas of spiced meat, warm bread, grilled veggies, and other unknown delicacies wafted through a massive doorway at the end of the torchlit hall.

Oh, man. Those Pop Tarts felt like a lifetime ago. And in some ways, they really were.

The doors to the mess were wide open, but a group of older teenagers were blocking the way. They all wore identical black T-shirts, each one bearing the same Jolly Roger I'd seen earlier—the one with the sword and spyglass.

"Boy, is it good to see you again, Sable!"

Sure enough, as I edged closer, I saw that it was indeed Reed being spoken to.

The one talking stood in the center of the pack. With his close-cropped black hair and bronze skin rippled with muscles, he looked like he stepped straight out of military boot camp. But what really caught my eye was the menacing hammerhead shark tattoo etched across his neck. It glared with a bloodthirsty ferocity, its message clear: *I mean trouble.*

I watched as Shark Tattoo stepped toward Reed and embraced him in a bear hug, one looking so tight I thought Reed's spine might crack.

Perhaps that was the point.

"So, Sable, how ya been?" Shark Tattoo asked him. He didn't appear to spot me yet, his focus solely on the former referee. "Boy, last time we saw you must've been when we were given our assignments. That was what, two years ago?"

"Yeah, Roger, two years," Reed's voice wavered, his gaze shifting between the different boys standing before him. "But—"

"And what was it you said back then?" The boy named Roger shined a polished grin. "You declared in the mess, for the whole school to hear. Care to help me out, Devin?"

The boy to Reed's immediate left answered gleefully, "I think it went something like, 'I'll find someone before all you roaches!'"

Roger chuckled, and his lackeys followed suit. Reed just stood there rigidly, mouth struggling to stammer up a reply.

"Ye-yes, I know. But you see—"

"See what, Sable? Who did you finally manage to bring? Where is he, by the way? Surely he should be here, right by your side!"

"Probably made a run for it the first chance he got," one of the guys suggested. "Reed probably had to tie him up to get him here."

Roger and his gang cackled with laughter.

"No, boys, you know what I think?" Roger was so consumed by his laughter, he had to wipe tears from his eyes. "I bet he *lied* and didn't even bring anyone. Probably chickened out and just wanted an excuse to bail. I mean, why else would he skip orientation?" He smirked devilishly. "Boy, Sable, you really are the worst crow —"

"HEY!" I yelled, cutting the guy off. I'd heard enough from him. My feelings for Reed aside, no one should be treated like this.

Roger shoved past Reed and stared me down.

"Yeah?" he sneered, his brown eyes narrowed. "What do *you* want?"

"I'll tell you exactly what I want," I declared, taking a confident step forward until I was practically nose-to-nose with Roger. "I want you to scram, get lost, and lay off Reed."

Roger's gaze flicked back to his pals, and they all burst into laughter. To them, I probably sounded absurd.

Which is exactly what I wanted.

In that split second, I lunged toward Reed and snatched one of the swords hanging from his belt. Before Roger could even blink, I had the blade's tip mere millimeters from his throat.

A stunned gasp broke out from Roger's friends. The tattooed teen looked stupefied himself.

"Now, you listen here...punk," he demanded. "You better put that sword down right now and show your *elders* some respect or it won't end well for you."

The fury in his voice was unmistakable, but I thought I detected something else as well.

Fear?

"I think I can tell who deserves respect, and who doesn't," I shot back, not breaking eye contact with Roger for a second. Nor did I lower the sword.

Roger's face was redder than lava.

"You don't want me as an enemy, boy," he snarled.

Finally lowering the sword, I responded to his warning with a shrug. "Too late for that, I guess. Come on, Reed, let's get something to eat."

And with that, I led the older boy past the flabbergasted teenagers and into the bright dining hall.

Rustic chandeliers hung from the high rafters, their warm lantern light creating a cozy ambience. The air was rich with the enticing aroma of spiced dishes and freshly baked bread. Throughout the expansive wooden hall, roughly four dozen circular tables were arranged, each filled to the brim with teenagers. They sat in silence, their curious eyes tracking our every move as we entered.

It didn't take a genius to understand they had overheard my little "chat" with Roger. But I didn't care. Today had been challenging enough, and I didn't have the energy to tell someone else off. I just wanted to be left alone—and to eat.

"Show's over," I announced to everyone. "Back to dinner."

CHAPTER 9

For a moment, the silence in the mess hall dragged on. Everyone's eyes remained locked onto Reed and me.

But then, slowly, heads began swiveling away, as if a collective realization swept through the room that the conflict had ended. One by one, diners shifted their attention back to their meals and conversation, the sound of cheerful chatter once more filling the room.

Out of the corner of my eye, I spotted Roger sulking back to his table. The same group of buddies from before were right on his tail and seemed to be encouraging him to brush off what just happened, but I highly doubted that would be the case. Roger didn't seem like the kind to let people like me get the better of him. Besides, his warning had been quite clear.

"You don't want me as an enemy, boy."

As I ventured deeper into the mess, Reed popped up by my side, looking stunned.

"Dude," he gaped at me. "What did you just do?"

"What's the big deal?" I shrugged. "I hate bullies, all right?"

"Okay sure, but still. You just pulled a sword on Roger Riaz in front of the entire mess.

"So?"

"*So*, he's a pretty big deal around here," Reed warned me.

CHAPTER 9

"People don't just go around messing with Roger Riaz."

Once more, I offered nothing but a shrug, brushing a vanilla-blond strand of hair out of my eyes in the process. Seeing that I still wasn't shaken, Reed's initial panic eventually gave way to a smile.

"Well, foolish or not, that move was pretty sick," he admitted. "Frankly, I was more amazed by the fact that you chose to help me."

"Me too," I replied, wiping the grin off Reed's face. "I don't know. I'm still furious at you. I just really, *really* hate bullies."

Saying this, my mind was flooded with memories of all the other tormentors I'd been forced to deal with in the past. I've always been an easy target for bullies—the combo of being an orphan with a strange name and a love for fencing made quite the credentials for a misery-filled school life.

And truth be told, I've never been good at confronting my bullies either. But for some reason, this time around, something felt different. Maybe it was due to the circumstances, but when I faced off against Riaz, I'd felt a sense of resolve wash over me, urging me to hold my ground. Like I had no reason *not* to stand up for myself. Things couldn't get any worse than they already were, right?

I guess that's what being a wanted fugitive does to you.

"Well, even so, I'm still extremely grateful you did," Reed said. "If there's anything I can do in return, let me know."

I almost rolled my eyes at Reed's offer.

Like I hadn't heard enough of that from you already.

"I'm serious this time," he added, clearly sensing my skepticism. "Go ahead. Ask away."

"Okay, well, why don't you start explaining what a crow is? What did Roger mean when he called you that?"

Judging by how Riaz used the term, I'd assumed it was some sort of pirate insult, but Reed's eyes lit up positively at the question.

"Um, it's my job, basically," he said, somewhat pridefully. "It's short for *crow's nest*, named after the part of the mast where sailors sit and scout out approaching ships and land. A crow is what we call the people the school sends to scout out new students. More often than not, they're former students themselves."

I folded my arms. "So, what, you just go around and wait for kids to do bad things, then break them out of police custody?"

Reed winced. "I mean, it's a bit more sophisticated than that. We use things like police reports, social media, and the local news to try and make it *before* anyone actually commits a crime. If that's not an option…well, then at least before the authorities get their hands on him. But this is serious, Barnaby. Lots of kids really need our help, and we need to get to them, no matter what it takes."

Even if it's against their own will?

"Okay," I continued, steering clear of that conversation rabbit hole. Reed and I would just go on and on in circles. "So, did Roger tell the truth? Am I really your first 'spot' after two whole years?"

Reed flushed but nodded.

"Yes. And it's not something I'm proud of. You see, each crow gets a special compass that's supposed to lead us to potential recruits—but mine never seemed to work. Maybe it was broken, or maybe I just had no luck getting to them in time."

"Okay, but I bet that happens to a lot of crows," I suggested.

Reed's expression hardened. "Not really. We're not given

that many supplies as crows. Expectations are to find someone in a week or two. Not *two whole years*. It was tough, but I pressed on, following my compass across the mainland, until finally—*finally*—it led me to you. It was like the compass knew you were in danger. So I made it to Florida, to the tournament, and the rest is history. Like…you know what I mean."

"Yes, I do," I said with a solemn nod. *Yes, I do*.

Reed's face turned even redder.

"Listen," he began, "if there's anything I can do to make your time here even a little bit pleasant, please let me know. I know it's hard for you to see it now, but this is actually a really great place that offers a lot, and people here tend to turn out quite well. Riaz is a bad example for that, but my point is…I'm here to help."

"You'll be the first to know," I told him with a curt nod. That seemed to do the job, because I could've sworn I saw Reed's eyes twinkle a bit.

I was about to ask what drew him specifically to my fencing tournament when a voice from a nearby table called out to us.

"Yo, Reed!"

Spinning around, I expected to be faced with another teenager with a grudge. Instead, I found myself looking at a table full of people, all of whom appeared to be waving at us.

"When were you going to let us know you were back?"

"Get over here! We've got spice brew!" someone called out.

Reed's face lit up with a smile.

"Friends of yours?" I asked, gesturing toward the group.

Reed nodded. "You wouldn't mind if I…?" he started, trailing off as I shook my head.

"Go for it," I replied.

Reed beamed. "I'll see you later then," he said, giving me

one last pat on the shoulder. "And remember, if you need anything—"

"You'll be the first to know," I reassured him. Reed's smile widened, and he waved as he jogged over to his friends.

Funny, I thought, watching him head over. *Dude kidnaps me and makes it back in time for dinner with his friends. Boy, do I love how the universe is working today.*

Punctual as always, my tummy chose then to rumble.

I know, I know, I told my stomach. *You're next. Now, where can I find a plate around here—*

"HEY! HEY, YOU!" an ear-splitting voice suddenly erupted from the opposite end of the room. "OVER HERE!"

Given the chaos of the night so far, it seemed only natural that the voice was addressing me. Sure enough, when I shifted my gaze, I came across a boy who looked roughly my age, standing on a chair by a table in the far-left corner of the room, and waving frantically at me.

"WELL? DO I HAVE TO SPELL IT OUT FOR YA?" he continued shouting in my direction. "GET OVER HERE!"

Aware that I was starting to receive some looks from nearby tables, I took a deep breath and quickly made my way over to the boy's table. I'd already caused enough commotion for one night.

As I reluctantly approached, I noticed that the strange boy—still standing on his chair, by the way—wasn't alone. Beside him sat a smaller boy with dark skin and thin, round spectacles that perched delicately on his nose. He smiled at me too, though not nearly as enthusiastically as his friend. It wasn't that he didn't seem happy for me to join them, it's just that I'd never seen anyone look as giddy as his pal.

"Sit! Sit!" the taller boy urged, motioning to one of the

vacant seats at the table—the only table in the mess that seemed to have any. Only when I finally took a seat did he plop his tall, weedy frame into his own chair, a bundle of curly blond hair tumbling over his blue eyes

"Um...thanks, I guess," I offered awkwardly.

"You're absolutely welcome! Anyone who stands up to a wartface like Roger is welcome at my table!" The boy's excitement was infectious, his bright blue eyes sparkling with energy as he grinned at me. "I'm Miles, by the way. Miles Whittaker."

"Barnaby Stump," I introduced myself.

"Huh, talk about a name," the dark-skinned boy said, examining me with interest. "Where do you hail from, Barnaby?"

"Florida."

"All right!" Miles clapped me on the back. "Another kid from the coast!"

I raised an eyebrow. "You're also from Florida?"

Miles shook his head, his grin widening. "Nope. Shipwreck Cove."

The name clicked in my mind, and I felt a jolt of recognition. "Wait a minute. You mean...the pirate island?"

"Aye. The one and only," Miles said with a grin.

"Woah. So that means your family...they're—?"

"Pirates?" Miles chuckled, his eyes twinkling with amusement. "Not exactly. My parents never went plundering or anything like that. They both studied here, got married, moved to Shipwreck Cove, and now they run the local inn on the island. My older brother also studied here. He just became a crow."

"Wow." I found myself fascinated by all of this.

"Yup, surprise—this place isn't exactly a criminal training

ground," the other boy remarked, extending his hand to me. "Jefferson Monroe."

"Are you also from Shipwreck Cove?" I asked him.

"Nope, but a place just as legendary," he said to me with a grin. "Cleveland."

"Jefferson is the 'brains' of our operation," Miles explained for me. "He's especially useful for last-second homework copying."

"And that's going to end this year, Miles," Jefferson interjected, pushing his glasses up his nose. As his voice got serious, it took on a higher pitch, like he was trying to emphasize his point with the extra squeakiness. "You've got to do your own work if you want to pass from now on."

"Ah, come on, man. Just one more year, I swear."

Jefferson turned to me. "Miles here can't do squat unless it involves either a sword or a boat."

"Hey, don't exaggerate!" Miles objected. "Although," he said with a grin, "I am top five in the class for sword fighting and sailing."

"And bottom of the class in history and biology," Jefferson reminded him.

"Yeah, yeah, whatever." Miles appeared to have enough of disputing his academic capabilities. He turned back toward me. "You hungry, Barnaby?"

On cue, my tummy started rumbling again.

"Famished."

Miles's radiant smile lit up his face once again.

"Perfect. HEY, BONES!"

"Yesss? Can I get something for you, Master Whittaker?"

Eyes squeezed shut from the deafening volume of Miles's voice, I opened my eyes, turned toward the direction the raspy drawl came from, and literally toppled out of my seat at what I saw.

Standing above me was an actual human skeleton.

"Um, watwazat?" I stammered from the floor, unable to release any actual words. Meanwhile, Miles and Jefferson had both burst out laughing. As for the skeleton, its mouth emitted some sort of strange scratchy noise, like it was trying to *groan*.

"Every wretched time," it complained. "Why do the new ones always frighten when they see me?"

"Because, Bones," replied Jefferson, still struggling to refrain from giggling, "seeing a *walking, talking* skeleton for the first time really tends to freak people out."

Appearing to ignore the snide comment, Bones turned its skull toward Miles.

"Well, what will it be, sir?"

"Oh, I didn't call you for me; I already ate." Miles pointed in my direction. "He's the hungry one."

The skeleton swung around to me now.

"Well, boy? What would you like to have?"

Still reeling from the surreal experience of being spoken to by a freaking walking, talking skeleton, it shouldn't be surprising that my next words came out a tad redundant.

"You mean…like food?"

Okay, maybe they were completely redundant.

"No, I mean like an extra *femur*," Bones snapped (pun intended). Man, this skeleton had an attitude. Wasn't it supposed to have a funny bone?

"Okay, well, what can I have?" I asked, returning to my seat.

"Anything."

"Anything?"

"Anything."

"Wait, so like literally anything—"

"YES!" shrieked the skeleton. I shrunk back into my chair. *"Literally anything."*

"Um, okay, I guess I'll have a cheeseburger then."

"Excellent choice, sir," replied Bones, tone completely shifted. Full of sass before, it was now downright obedient.

"Don't mind Bones," excused Miles as the skeleton ran off—if such a thing was even possible. "He's just, well…"

"Got a bone to pick with me?" I suggested. Miles laughed approvingly.

"Not bad! I'm liking you even more already. Oh look—your food's here!"

The blond-haired boy pointed to my part of the table, which had been empty just seconds ago. I almost cried from the beauty of it. Sitting there, on a plate, was the juiciest-looking burger I'd ever laid my eyes on.

I inhaled its aroma with a shudder of ecstasy.

How the heck had it gotten here so fast?

"Well?" Jefferson urged. "Take a bite already!"

Grasping the burger with both hands, the patty's warm juices seeping through my fingers, I leaned in and took a massive bite. *Oh, man.* The combination of perfectly cooked meat, melted cheese, and spicy mayo hit me with one big, divine smack to the face.

"This is…AMAZING!" I blurted out mid-chew. "But how'd it get here so fast? Was it Bones who cooked it?"

Miles shrugged. "Nobody knows who cooks the food here. All we know is that the skeletons take the orders, and that we *always* get Bones."

"Hang on," I said through another bite of burger, "if there's more than one skeleton, how can you tell which is Bones?"

CHAPTER 9

"Simple." Miles's voice suddenly dropped into a whisper. "One time, while he was taking my order, Jefferson here went up behind him and drew an X on the back of a rib with a Sharpie." He grinned deviously as he spoke. I would've probably done the same, if not for the mouthful of burger in my mouth.

"So, Barnaby," Jefferson casually cut in as I ate, "what did your crow bring you in for?"

I nearly choked at the question. Both Miles and Jefferson were now staring at me, eager for my answer.

I swallowed, clearing my throat—which had suddenly become as dry as a desert—and began searching for some sort of reply. Something—*anything*—to tell Miles and Jefferson. Anything but the *truth*. But there was nothing I could come up with that didn't seem too far-fetched.

Should I just tell them the truth? I asked myself. *Maybe it wouldn't be that bad.* Sure, I met these guys like five minutes ago, but they both really seemed like two sound, reasonable guys.

I tried visualizing the exchange in my head.

"So, the truth is...I kinda killed a guy. By accident."

"Wait, no! Don't go! It really wasn't my fault—"

Yeah. No way that was happening—at least not tonight.

"You know, it's still kind of a touchy subject for me," I eventually confessed. "Maybe another time?"

Miles swiftly threw his hands up."Barnaby! Take all the time you need! Just know, if you ever need someone to talk to, we're here for you."

Relief rushed through me upon hearing this. It was weird, having only just met the guy, but Miles's reassurance brought me a real sense of comfort. For the first time since Gallman, I actually felt like someone was trying to help me.

"After all," Miles went on. "You're one of us now—a Lost Boy!"

"Huh? You mean like from Peter Pan?"

"More like Peter Pan got it from *here*," Jefferson offered. "Surely your crow must've mentioned this place's name to you?"

"No," I frowned, feeling yet another prickle of frustration toward Reed. "No, he didn't."

"Well, that's where you are. *Lost Boys High*. That's the name Blackbeard gave this place ever since he started using it to help lost souls like us find our way."

"Lost Boys High?" I repeated, my nose wrinkling at the idea. The label felt heavy and depressing. I mean, just this morning I was competing in one of the nation's biggest fencing tournaments, feeling unstoppable. I was supposed to start high school in a few days. I definitely didn't feel lost.

It seemed rude to dampen the spirits of my newfound companions, so I offered them a small smile, hiding my inner distaste as best I could.

Jefferson smiled in return before looking down at his watch. "It's getting pretty late, Miles. Remember, we've got class early tomorrow." He glanced back at me. "How was the burger?"

I raised my empty plate, licked clean.

"Perfection."

"Got an idea where you'll be sleeping tonight?" Miles asked me.

Surprisingly, the thought had never crossed my mind. All day, I'd been forced from moment to moment without much choice in any of it. I thought about going to ask Reed—he was still sitting at that table with his friends.

CHAPTER 9

"You could sleep by us if you want," Miles offered, taking the silence as my answer. "We've got a spare bed on our ship that you could borrow."

His hospitality amazed me. Ten minutes ago, I had no idea he or Jefferson existed, and here they were, offering me a place to stay for the night. Reed and Roger had left me with a pretty firm impression that I was in poor company here, but perhaps they weren't all so bad after all. In the end, I was really glad the two boys had invited me to their table.

"So, what do you think?" Jefferson asked.

To top it off, leaving without a word would leave Reed clueless about my whereabouts. Imagining him anxiously searching for me all night brought a smile to my face.

"I think that sounds perfect," I responded. "Let's do that."

CHAPTER 10

My first morning at Lost Boys High started something along the lines of this:

"Barnaby?"

"Mrmm…"

"Barnaby, WAKE UP!"

Mmm…wha—what time is it?"

"Ten to seven. Come on now, or we'll be late!"

Irritated, I grumbled as I reluctantly creeped my eyes open. "Why so early?"

Miles shrugged. He was already dressed, donning a pair of dark jeans and a gray T-shirt bearing the sword-and-spyglass Jolly Roger everyone seemed to love around here. *Must be the school logo*, I thought to myself, now noticing the curved cutlass hanging from the boy's belt. It was identical to the ones Reed had been carrying.

"Lessons start at seven on Mondays," he explained to me. "C'mon and get dressed, we've got to hurry!"

I let out another long groan as I forced myself up in bed, my exhausted body wailing in protest. The weight of yesterday's events was definitely taking a toll on me—not to mention that I was still healing from the actual blows I received at Regionals. I glanced around the crew quarters, rows of beds lining the

CHAPTER 10

walls of the ship. The soft creaking of the wooden beams and the gentle sway of the vessel reminded me where I was.

I mean, why am I even bothering to get up? I asked myself. *It's not like I ever agreed to go to class.*

Perhaps it was due to my rising curiosity to see how things worked around here. After all, it's not every day you wake up in a school for pirates.

Rubbing my eyes open, it wasn't long before I noticed the familiar, metallic object sitting on my bedside table. My heart fluttered as I picked it up.

"Oh yeah, that arrived for you after you fell asleep," Miles informed me as I ran a finger along what remained of my saber. "One of the crows came and left it for you."

So, Reed did find me. Who else could it have been?

I was even more surprised to find my saber here. I'd completely forgotten about it, so convinced that it had been left behind on that freeway in Florida. To know that Reed had actually brought it all the way here, well…it didn't completely change things, but it was definitely a start. Having this remnant of my life really lifted my spirits.

Reed had also left me a few other things: a packet of bandages and a small bottle of what I could only assume was the ointment he applied to me back aboard the *Angel's Wings*. Beside the bandages was also a small, folded-up piece of paper, my name scribbled on the front in cursive blue ink.

I reached over, unfolded it, and began to read.

Barnaby,

Hope you enjoyed dinner. Maybe it helped you start to see that things might not be as horrible as you thought.

Head with Miles and Jefferson to class. You're in their year.

If you need anything, I'll be in the mess at lunch.
Good luck on your first day!
Reed

"Well?" Miles probed curiously. "What's it say?"

"It's from my crow. Apparently, I'm going to be in your class in the end."

The boy's eyes lit up stars.

"For real? That's awesome!" He shot me a grin. "I only realized this morning that we never asked how old you are. I guess we just assumed that you'd come along with us until somebody'd say otherwise, but I guess that settles it!

"Yeah, guess so," I replied much less enthusiastically. I still wasn't over the moon on this whole Lost Boys shtick yet. "And speaking of 'us,' where's Jefferson? His bed's empty."

"He's probably already in class. In the history of our time here, I don't think I've ever seen Jefferson late to something." Miles checked his watch. "Which is what we're going to be if we don't leave right now. Quick, get dressed!"

My tummy rumbled. "What, no time for some breakfast first?"

"Breakfast ended five minutes ago," Miles grumbled. "Stupid Jefferson, actually serious about having to wake myself up this year."

A small smile crept onto my face as I reached for my shirt. The dynamic between these two boys was truly entertaining.

Within seconds, I had on the outfit Reed had given me yesterday. I replaced the bandage on my sword wound—when Miles wasn't looking, of course. I also decided to take my broken sword with me. It wouldn't do much good in a fight, but it was still the only form of a weapon I had to defend myself.

"We'll take you to the canteen tonight to get some fresh clothes," Miles assured me. "School swag is a big deal here. Oh, and all newcomers get a free wardrobe."

"Sounds good," I told him, picturing myself in one of those Lost Boys T-shirts. A nice souvenir to take back to Florida with me. "Now, let's get you to class."

At least the weather at this place was great.

Reaching the ship's deck, the island's tropical air greeted us like an old friend. The sun beamed down from a clear blue sky, accompanied by the most delightful breeze. I had to hand it to Reed: if he was going to kidnap me, at least he brought me to a place with five-star weather.

In a hurry, Miles and I scampered across the deck and down the gangplank by the ship's side. The wooden boards creaked beneath our feet as we ran down the docks, eager to put some distance between us and the cobalt-colored vessel that he and Jefferson called home.

That was one of many fun facts I learned about Lost Boys High last night. Apparently, all the students lived on ships, which were divided into several crews and each under the command of a different captain.

All captains—students and crows alike—were appointed by who else but Blackbeard himself.

The captain of this ship, the *Adventure Galley*—Miles and Jefferson's ship—was a girl named Amelia Ash. I hadn't had the chance to meet her yet, but they both spoke immensely high of her. At sixteen years old, she was the youngest captain at the school, nearly two years younger than the average captain's age. Despite Blackbeard's clear confidence in her abilities to lead, it was a move still deemed highly controversial by the bulk of the school.

"Wait. She leads you guys in what?" I asked them.

"You'll see," Miles and Jefferson said, glancing at one another most mischievously.

The ships the students manned were a mix of new and old—and by old, I mean ships that had belonged to *actual pirates*. Miles and Jefferson's ship, the *Adventure Galley*, had belonged to some pirate I'd never heard of named William Kidd. And it wasn't just him. I didn't know almost any of the names mentioned throughout the night.

"Don't worry, you'll learn about them all soon enough," Jefferson assured me as he helped lay fresh sheets on my bed. "Pirate history is the first class tomorrow after lunch."

Pirate history. Of course.

At least I didn't need a history lesson to learn about Blackbeard's ship. Or, I should probably say, ships. His original flagship, the *Queen Anne's Revenge*, was anchored at the far end of the docks and not used for student lodging. Meanwhile, his newer vessel—named the *Queen Anne II*—not only housed his living quarters and the mess where we'd eaten last night, but also contained the teachers' quarters, the classrooms, a medical bay, a library, and, of course, a brig.

I asked Jefferson about the massive vessel's origins.

"That boat's as old as this school," he shrugged. "No one knows where it came from. Well, nobody except Blackbeard."

He did have a little more to offer on another ship I was familiar with. The *Angel's Wings*. But aside from the ship's name, there was one more unique detail of the ship that they revealed to me.

CHAPTER 10

"It's a magical ship," they had told me.

"No kidding."

Jefferson shook his head.

"No, Barnaby. I'm not talking about the whole underwater shtick. That ship will take you wherever you want in the world. Anywhere. All you have to do is grip its wheel with both of your hands and visualize in your head the place you desire."

"Wow," I replied. "That's incredible."

Very incredible indeed...

The *Queen Anne II* was just up ahead from us now, and I followed Miles up onto the ship and down the stairs into its interior. The torch-lit mess lay straight ahead, but just as he had warned, we were too late. The room was devoid of both people and food.

Miles turned in the opposite direction, where another stairwell led deeper into the ship.

"The math classroom is only one floor down," he explained to me as we descended.

His startling comment caused me to halt halfway down the stairs.

Wait. Did he just say MATH?

I'd been expecting something a little more flamboyant for the first class of the day, like pistol training. Could they really be teaching math at a place like this?

By now, Miles was too far ahead for me to confirm with him, which left me no choice but to tail after him and see for myself. Now one floor below the mess, we entered a corridor flanked by multiple doors on either side. Miles only came to a stop at the second-to-last door on the left. Pushing it open, he revealed a quaint classroom with a large, green chalkboard that took up the entire front wall.

Sure enough, scribbled all over it were several meticulous mathematical equations.

I shook my head in disbelief. *Unbelievable.*

The class appeared thoroughly at work on some assignment, but a few curious students threw glances our way when they heard our footsteps. Amongst them was Jefferson, who flashed us a smile and beckoned for us to approach.

"Well, it's about time! Miss Abacus left these for you two." He raised a pair of worksheets off his school desk. "Don't worry, Miles, I explained to her that you might be late because you were showing the new guy around. Which, of course, is *totally* what you were doing." He gave Miles a wink.

"Next time, a simple wake up would do just fine," Miles grumbled.

"Um, I think what you're trying to say is 'thank you'." Jefferson grinned at me. "I already finished my work, want some help with yours?"

I nodded and plopped down in one of the open seats beside him. "Uh huh."

Jefferson handed me one of the worksheets. It was covered from head to toe with complex mathematical problems. From what I managed to understand, they all revolved around using latitude and longitude to measure distances between different points on a map.

"No luck?" he asked, noticing my puzzled expression. "Here, let me show you."

He scooted his chair over to mine and began educating me on all the rules and functions for the problems. I was stunned by the amount of ease it took him to recite them all by memory. I was further flabbergasted when he revealed that they'd been working on this level of math for over two years now.

CHAPTER 10

"What?" he frowned. "Why are you staring at me like that?"

"I'm looking at you this way, Jefferson, because this level of math isn't usually taught until *college*. How can Blackbeard have you guys doing this level of work?"

Jefferson shrugged. "Pirate or not, every sailor needs to understand longitude and latitude to navigate, no?"

"Okay fine, you've got a point there," I admitted. "But still—math? At a school for pirates? I don't know, I guess I was expecting something a bit more…*piratey*."

The spectacled boy offered up another shrug."Well, we've got to learn some form of mathematics if we ever intend on going back."

I felt the pencil slip out of my hand. It bounced off my knee and clattered on the floor.

"Wait. What do you mean, 'go back'?"

It was Miles who answered. His worksheet still untouched on Jefferson's deck, it was pretty clear he'd been eavesdropping on our conversation.

"Upon graduating from Lost Boys High, every student can choose to relocate to the mainland. Most end up going to college around then."

"*Most* students," Jefferson corrected his friend. "Not everyone."

I shook my head, still struggling to comprehend this new nugget of information.

"But I thought everyone here's committed some sort of crime. How can that even be possible?"

"Well, for starters, you're forgetting those who've grown up on Shipwreck Cove, like Miles," Jefferson reminded me. "They have a lot more freedom to come and go as they please. As for the rest… well, I'm not entirely clear on the specifics, but from what I've heard from the older students, when we graduate, most of our records get wiped clean. It's like serving your time and then starting fresh."

He presented it like it was a totally fair deal, but I still didn't see it that way. Not at all.

"So, you just let them take away all these years of your life?" I asked him. "What, don't you like, miss your family?"

The moment the question left my lips, I realized I'd gone too far. Jefferson's face turned bright red as he shifted uncomfortably in his seat.

"Of course I do, Barnaby. But for most of us, *this* is our only way of getting back to them. Maybe you didn't commit such a serious mistake to get here, but many of us really screwed up—myself included."

"You?" My eyebrows shot up in astonishment. "What could you have possibly done that was so bad to end you up here?"

My response brought a wince to the boy's face. *Dang.* I was digging my grave even deeper.

Tugging at his shirt, Jefferson hesitated, visibly wrestling with his thoughts before managing an answer.

"I…may or may not have hacked into a particular government bureau of investigation."

My eyes widened.

"You hacked into the *FBI*?"

"Um, hey guys?" Miles started to chime in, but Jefferson immediately waved him off.

"It was for a bet, all right?" His voice was getting squeaky again, just like it had at supper last night. "My friends swore to me that I wouldn't get in trouble, but sure enough, after school, there were cop cars waiting outside my house. I didn't even get to say goodbye to my parents. I mean, if it wasn't for the crow who helped me get out of there…"

A clear tinge of sadness was in his voice as it trailed off.

Man, I felt so incredibly stupid. How could I judge Jefferson like that? Of course, the boy wanted to go home! That's probably what drove him to work so hard. To him, this probably seemed like his only way to get back.

Jefferson saw the look of guilt on my face and gave me a reassuring pat on the shoulder.

"It's okay, Barnaby. You're still super new around here, and it's totally fine to still have some doubts about how things work. Trust me, we all have them upon coming here. Hopefully, over time, you'll start to see this place's greatness. It's really not that different from any other boarding school. After all, we all get to go home at the end—or most of us do, at least."

But would I be able to? Maybe for hopefuls like Jefferson, it seemed plausible to imagine something like some innocent government hacking being overlooked. But cold-blooded murder…it was hard to feel as confident. I mean, if it were possible, why hadn't Reed mentioned it to me at any point yesterday?

To me, the answer seemed crystal clear.

I wasn't going anywhere.

"Erm, if I may…?" Miles tried again.

"What, Miles?" Jefferson asked, this time turning to face the blond-haired boy. I followed suit, trying to conceal the unease that this conversation had stirred within me.

"Okay. Don't get mad, because I've been trying to let you guys know," Miles said, gesturing to the rest of the classroom. "You guys were too busy arguing to notice."

Jefferson and I glanced around the room. Apart from two

other students in the midst of packing up their bags, the class was completely empty.

"It's all right," Jefferson replied, checking his watch. "Next class only starts in another seven minutes."

"Okay, well, what's next?" I asked the two boys.

Miles's eyes lit up. "Only the best class of the day!"

"On this," Jefferson said, "I actually have to agree with the dummy."

"Well? What is it?"

Miles and Jefferson looked at one another, grinned, and answered in unison:

"Sword fighting."

CHAPTER 11

The Sword Hall was love at first sight.

Stepping into the room, my eyes fixed wondrously onto the arena below. A hardwood floor, spanning the size of two basketball courts, lay before me, evoking serious rec center vibes. Row upon row of benches encompassed all sides of the room except one, where the most beautiful collection of swords I'd ever seen hung. Blades of all shapes and sizes—including a number of fencing sabers—dangled from their place, gleaming in the light. There was just one problem.

"Um, where is everyone?" I asked as we descended. Judging by the looks of Miles and Jefferson as they glanced around, they seemed to be pondering the same thing.

"We were the last ones to leave math," Jefferson said with a shake of the head. "Surely the rest of class should be here by now."

"FINALLY! There you three are!" a voice boomed overhead. We spun around to see a concerned-looking figure burst through the hall's massive mahogany doors, his ponytail messy and coming undone. He hurried toward us, his face flushed with urgency.

"Reed?" I gave the crow a puzzled look. "What are you doing

here?"

"I should be asking the same about you," he wheezed, catching his breath and trying to smooth his tangled hair. "I've been searching all over for you. Barnaby, you were supposed to be on the main deck twenty minutes ago!"

I frowned. "What the heck are you talking about?"

Still hunched over, Reed managed to shoot me a look.

"The tryouts, Barnaby. Didn't your teacher mention them at the start of class?"

"Hold on—the tryouts are *now?*" Miles exclaimed. He spun around to Jefferson. "Jay, you were in class, why didn't you say anything?"

Jefferson shrugged. "I guess I missed it as well. I got lost in that worksheet, man."

Miles shook his head. "For such a smart guy, you can be a real dolt sometimes."

"Hey! We don't have time for this!" Reed waved his arms frantically to regain our attention. "Roberts sent me. He needs Barnaby to get to the deck now!"

Roberts?

Miles stood up straight and nodded, like a soldier given a command. "On it."

Without a warning, I felt a hand snatch onto my wrist and speed me out of the Sword Hall. Miles ran so fast, I feared if I were to slow down for even a second, my arm would be yanked right out of its socket.

"So, these tryouts—what are they for?" I asked him as he dragged me along. "And who the heck is Roberts?"

"He's the Sword Master here," Miles answered plainly, like that answer was explanatory enough. "And the tryouts are for the crews, of course! They're held whenever we get a large group of new recruits. All the captains will be there to get a look at the newest batch of freshies!" He grinned at me as we flew up a flight of stairs. "Which, this time around, includes you!"

"Freshies?"

"It's what we call the newbies around here. Short for *fresh meat*."

"Charming. So, what exactly will I be doing?"

A funny coughing noise suddenly emerged from Miles's mouth. Judging from the boy's exuberant attitude, I think what happened was that he'd tried to laugh but ended up choking due to the lack of air from running.

"Literally what we were going to do in the Sword Hall."

We finally reached the deck of the *Queen Anne II*, which turned out to be jammed with people. Under the bright, blue sky, students of all ages clustered around what appeared to be some sort of long, thin podium. As Miles and I got closer, I made out two figures who appeared to be engaged in a swordfight.

And that's when I realized. This was no ordinary old podium. It was a piste!

Ooooh, boy.

My heart began drumming for what was to come.

The pair dueling looked rather young, their inexperience with swords evident in every clumsy, misplaced attack. Not only were their footing and fighting stances completely off, but even the way they held the swords suggested it was their first time ever handling them.

I stressed this to Miles.

"But they can hurt themselves!" I said. "Those blades aren't toys."

The blond-haired boy shrugged. "And? It'll teach them to be better."

Sure enough, it was only a matter of time before things got out of hand. One of the boys sent a swing so wild, his sword flew right out of his hand and into the crowd, forcing everyone to duck. Miraculously, no one appeared to be hurt.

Meanwhile, his opponent, bewildered and clearly not expecting such an opportunity, awkwardly pointed his sword at the other boy's chest.

"Don't worry, most freshies don't get selected to crews," Miles informed me as the crowd applauded the victor. "There are some ships designated for crew-less students."

"Then why hold these tryouts?" I asked.

"Just in case there's a diamond in the rough," he replied with a wink.

A loud voice approaching the piste caught our attention. It belonged to a middle-aged man with suntanned skin, green eyes, and a neatly trimmed brown beard. His polished boots clunked as he ascended to the top of the podium, stepping forward to congratulate the young boy who'd won. With his short hair tousled by the breeze, he definitely looked to be the person running this event.

"Bravo! Bravo," he applauded, shaking the victor's hand and sending him off. "Well?" he called out, looking at the crowd below. "Who's next?"

"We are!" Miles declared.

No sooner had the words left his mouth did the mass of students before us do a complete one-eighty in our direction. A moment later, the tall man reappeared at the front and flashed us a sparkling white smile.

Blackbeard could learn a thing or two from him about dental

CHAPTER 11

hygiene, I thought.

"Well, well, if it isn't Miles Whittaker! Tell me, who has one of my most *promising* students brought for me?"

Miles blushed at the praise directed at him. Meanwhile, out of the corner of my eye, I noticed Jefferson and Reed emerge from below and turn to watch our interaction with this man.

"I bring you Barnaby Stump!" Miles proclaimed, as if he were my squire. "He's a freshie!"

The man's eyes jumped from Miles and onto me.

"Is that so?" He extended a hand to me. "Bartholomew Roberts, Sword Master at this fine establishment.

Bartholomew Roberts...the name definitely rang a bell. It wasn't long before I recalled it as one of the famous pirates Jefferson had mentioned last night.

"*You're* Black Bart?"

Robert's eyes rose.

"Well, well," he commended. "Boy already knows his history!"

"He also knows how to fight, sir," Miles chimed in. "In fact, Barnaby even brought a sword with him to the island."

Whispers broke out amongst the crowd. I guess this kind of thing must be a big deal around here.

"What, did you really think I wouldn't recognize what Reed left for you with that letter?" Miles teased with a playful nudge.

I said nothing, speechless, and turned back toward Roberts—who was staring at me like he'd just won the lottery.

"I'm simply named after the famous pirate—the conqueror of over four hundred vessels," he explained with unmistakable pride. "Some even say he was the most successful pirate of the Golden Age. But enough about the past—is what Miles saying true? Have ye really some experience in the art of the sword?"

I replied with a short, tentative nod.

"Delightful!" Roberts exclaimed, clapping his hands together. "A real fight then, perhaps?" He called out gleefully to a group of older students, all of them clutching clipboards. I assumed these must be the captains Miles and Jefferson had been talking about.

Without another word, I accompanied Roberts through the crowd and back to the piste. Per the Sword Master's request, Miles joined us there too, and I could only assume why. I doubted there were many freshies my age to duel—let alone one who'd actually held a sword before.

Once we were atop the long, thin podium, Roberts beckoned to see my sword. After much hesitation, I removed it from my belt and passed it over to the Sword Master.

"Marvelous design," he remarked, delicately tracing a finger along the helix-shaped hilt. When it reached the shattered blade, he frowned. "A shame. The blade was of the saber style, correct? For fencing?"

"Correct," I replied, silently hoping that he wouldn't pry further and ask how it got damaged in the first place.

Roberts continued to analyze the blade for some time before finally looking up.

"Barnaby," he began, "I would love nothing more than to give your sword the blade it truly deserves. You may not be aware of this, but while you may have been competing with a saber blade, this hilt was actually designed for the blade of a rapier."

Wait, WHAT.

"Um, are you sure?" I asked, my voice tinged with disbelief.

The Sword Master nodded.

"It's a common mistake," he explained, "as the hilts of the two swords are actually quite similar. Both are crafted in a curved shape to protect the hand gripping the sword. However, whilst the hilts of sabers usually consist of one smooth piece of metal, rapier hilts—such as yours—are more complex and are made up of several curved, metallic strips. Perhaps you've noticed this difference amongst the other fencers?"

Of course I'd noticed. I'd just assumed that it was a design thing. Why did Grandma get me a rapier hilt?

"If you like, I can show you," Roberts offered again, his tone reassuring. "I can restore your sword to its true form. What say you?"

What say I?

Rapier or no rapier, this sword was still my most valuable possession. Was I really going to let a stranger mess around with it, no matter his position at this school?

As if sensing my uncertainty, Roberts added, in the gentlest of tones, "I promise you, Barnaby, no damage will come to your sword. All I want is to bring out its full potential."

I pursed my lips, debating. He sure sounded sincere about fixing it.

It would also be nice to have a REAL weapon for protection, I thought. Decision made, I lifted my gaze to Roberts and gave him a firm nod.

The Sword Master's face lit up with a wide smile. "Splendid! I should have it back to you by the end of this week."

"Thank you, sir."

Roberts scoffed. "Please, it's *my* pleasure!"

"Um, so can we *now* get back to the task at hand?" a familiar voice gawked from the crowd below. I glanced down and, sure enough, there was Roger Riaz, standing amongst the captains—clipboard in his hand.

A noticeable number of students sniggered at Riaz's comment.

"Of course, Captain Riaz," replied Roberts with a graceful nod. "Although. I doubt there's much left the captains need to see from Barnaby after your most grateful *demonstration* with him at supper."

Roger's face paled, clearly taken aback by the Sword Master's comment. I was really starting to like this guy.

"But in case that wasn't enough," Roberts continued, throwing his hands in the air with a flourish, his showmanship on full display, "let's get to it!" He spun around to face me once more. "You'll need a sword now, of course—"

"He can use mine," a voice chimed from below. It came from where the captains were all standing. She was shorter than the rest and looked slightly younger than her clipboard-carrying colleagues, with a freckled face, soft features, and curly chestnut hair. She winked at me as she stepped forward, withdrawing her sword and extending it to me.

"Amelia Ash!" Roberts greeted. "Why am I not surprised? A valuable trait for a captain—the rest of you better watch out," he warned the other captains.

"Thanks," I said as I accepted the cutlass from Miles's captain. I gave it a small twirl. It was definitely a tad lighter than what I was accustomed to, but it would do.

"Good luck," Amelia said to me, before returning to where the rest of the captains stood.

"All right then. Let's get to it," the Sword Master declared. "Fighters, to your positions."

CHAPTER 11

There was no countdown, no clarification of the rules. Roberts wasted no time in getting the match going, barely waiting for both of us to take our positions at either end of the piste before bellowing out "Go!"

Miles exploded out of the gate, charging full speed ahead and swinging his cutlass at me in a wide, diagonal arc. Instinctively, I tried to sidestep the attack, but it was a mistake. I hadn't considered the piste's elevation, and soon found myself teetering on the edge, desperately trying to regain my balance and avoid falling off.

I received a few chuckles from the crowd as I struggled to regain my balance. It seemed pretty clear what they all must be thinking.

Look at the freshie go.

While I eventually recovered, there was zero time to rest as Miles launched another attack. This time, I managed to use my sword to parry, but Miles was too quick for me to deliver a counter-strike of my own. His fighting style perfectly mirrored his personality: fast, energetic, and relentless.

Miles sent a hard lunge at my chest, and I was forced to take a substantial step back.

Despite my retreating, the chuckling below had ceased. Roberts and the rest of the crowd watched on in complete fixation as we dueled. I had a feeling we were giving them their first proper duel of the day.

Well, I better not disappoint, then.

Miles lunged a second time but stumbled just the slightest in his footwork. The hesitation, it was so minute, nobody in the crowd could have noticed it. But I had, and that was all I needed to start turning the tide. I dodged the thrust and used what little recovery he required as an opportunity to swipe my blade at his face.

"Not bad!" Roberts exclaimed from below.

And now it was Miles who found himself retreating, although he showed no dip in his abilities when it came to defense. No, Miles was proving to be quite the swordsman, just as he proclaimed himself to be last night.

But I was still better.

My gut was telling me to show off a little for the captains, for I attempted one of my flashier techniques. Wobbling my legs, I made it look like I'd lost my balance and was once again on the verge of stumbling off the piste.

Miles's eyes immediately widened at this sudden opportunity. Taking the bait, he charged forward, lifting his sword for the deafening blow—

—only to have me straighten up and swiftly point my blade right at his totally unguarded, shock-consumed face.

"Match," I declared, tapping his nose with the tip of my blade.

Miles stared at me, dumbfounded. "Woah."

Below, the crowd of students had fallen into a hushed silence, their eyes wide with disbelief as they gazed up at me. Meanwhile, the captains had gathered in a tight huddle, their whispers frantic as they scribbled away on their clipboards. And as for Riaz, he simply stood frozen, mouth hanging ajar as he stared at me with wide eyes.

Well, there go any thoughts he had of payback, I hoped to myself.

Like any good teacher, Roberts was the first amongst the stunned crowd to shake it off.

"Now *that* was a sword fight!" he exclaimed as he strode back onto the piste, delivering a proud pat on my shoulder. "Well done, Barnaby! Well done!"

CHAPTER 11

As his words of praise washed over me, my eyes continued traveling across the deck. Miles had descended off the piste now and began walking through the stunned crowd toward Jefferson and Reed—both of whom were giggling and grinning like madmen. But it wasn't just them. I also caught their captain, Amelia, shoot me a big thumbs up, which only further boosted my spirits.

Not bad, Barnaby. Not bad at all.

"Well?" Roberts proceeded to ask the crowd. "Who's next?"

It seemed like he was searching for my next opponent. Only, there was no response. Not a single peep from the entire deck.

The Sword Master surveyed the silent scene.

"Nobody wants a go?" he challenged. "What, are ye all scared of the newbies now? Do I detect a case of freshie fever going around?"

No one laughed at the joke.

"I'll face him."

The voice, unmistakably female, cut through the silence like a knife. It seemed to come from behind the captains, who all parted to make way. As she approached, I felt my heart skip a beat.

She was breathtakingly beautiful, with dark red hair cascading down her shoulders like flames dancing in the wind. Her intense gaze held onto mine, holding me in a trance like she'd placed me under a spell.

With a gleaming smile, Roberts hopped off the piste, arms outstretched in welcome.

"Ah, Morgan! What a match this will be!"

The angel-faced maiden named Morgan stepped straight past Roberts and onto the piste, not removing her gaze from me for a second. Now only handful of feet away, I was privy to my best look of her yet:

Suntanned skin and luscious scarlet hair. Dazzling emerald eyes. She wore a stark-white blouse atop a pair of perfectly fitting jeans, baby-blue jeans—and believe me when I say *perfectly fitting*.

Morgan caught me staring.

"Well?" she asked. "Are we going to duel or what?"

"Uh, yeh—yeah," I sputtered, stepping back and assuming my fencing stance.

Morgan raised an eyebrow but followed suit.

"Whenever the two of you are ready," Roberts called out to us, the crowd around him staring, humming with anticipation.

"You got this," Miles mouthed to me from beside Jefferson.

Looking back toward Morgan, I considered charging forward but hesitated. There was something in Robert's voice when he reacted to Morgan's acceptance of the challenge that made me think twice.

Could she be more dangerous than she looks?

"Well?" Morgan suddenly shot at me, beckoning with her cutlass. "What is this, a *'ladies first'* kind of thing? Are you going to make a move or what?"

Now, I'm no fool. It was crystal clear that she was trying to bait me. Yet, for some reason, I couldn't shake off the creeping nervousness. Whether it was her looks, her comments, or eager stares of the crowd below, I could feel a sense of pressure beginning to mount inside me.

"Well?" echoed her voice again, the captivated crowd below waiting for my response.

With a reluctant sigh—and most certainly against better judgment—I charged toward her side of the piste...

Which was when Morgan chose to storm toward mine.

CHAPTER 11

We collided at the center of the stage. Before I could even contemplate where to try an attack, Morgan delivered a swift jab to my ribs—not with her sword, but with her freaking *fist*!

I let out a grunt of pain as I fell back.

"Surprised?" she called out, bringing her cutlass down at my shoulder. "Don't be. You may have learned how to fence. But here at this school, we learn how to *fight*."

I barely managed to parry her next attack. Meanwhile, the side of my chest continued to ache, which had me fearing that Morgan had bruised one of my ribs. Even so, at least she'd missed my wound from the tournament. That would have been bad.

Morgan proceeded to press relentlessly with a flurry of attacks. In a final act of desperation, I tried a quick riposte off one of her lunges. My feet weren't planted when I delivered my counterattack, but there was no time to worry about technique. I parried her thrust and swung my sword at her neck.

Morgan didn't block the attack. No, instead of using her sword, Morgan ducked, leaning back like she was dancing the limbo. My blade missed her completely.

My jaw dropped. Somewhere in the crowd below, someone cried out, "OOOH!"

My blade now light-years away, all Morgan had to do was lift her blade to my neck. She did so slowly, letting the tip nip my chin almost...*flirtatiously*?

"Hmm, what was it again that you said?" she teased. "Oh yeah. *Match*."

CHAPTER 12

For a while, it seemed like my "audition" at tryouts was all anyone would talk about, especially the part where I got my butt handed to me by Morgan. And who could really blame them? Truth be told, I could barely stop thinking about her myself. Her fiery looks and jaw-dropping swordplay lingered in my thoughts for days after the tryouts. I wanted to speak to her about it, but I hadn't seen her since. She basically just vanished after our duel.

But as the week wound down, the buzz shifted toward the imminent reveal of all the finalized crews. Selections were supposed to be finalized by Friday, which meant they could drop at any moment.

Unfortunately, it didn't look like I was going to be one of them.

"Don't count yourself out so easily, Barnaby," Jefferson comforted me between bites of toast at breakfast that weekend. His response came after my retort that maybe it was time for me to move my few possessions to the one of the ships meant for crewless students.

I put my mug of orange juice down and shook my head, unconvinced.

"It's *Saturday*, Jay. Roberts made it very clear that all captains had until last night to welcome any new crewmembers to their ranks. It's time to just face it—I wasn't picked by anyone."

"You know, I bet Riaz is behind this somehow," Miles asserted through a mouthful of scrambled eggs. He angrily waved his fork in the air. "There's no way that none of the captains wanted you. Not only did you manage to take me down—which in itself is borderline impossible—but you went toe-to-toe with Morgan *freaking* Travers. She's like, the best swordsman in her year!"

"Actually, I think it's swords*woman*, Miles," Jefferson corrected.

"Potato potahto."

"Yeah, what's her story?" I asked, trying to sound nonchalant.

"Fifteen years old, in the grade above us," explained Miles. "She's like me, also from Shipwreck Cove, except she grew up at the local orphanage—she was left there as a baby."

"You don't say," I replied, trying to hide my rising interest. *Abandoned by her parents. Guess we have that in common.*

"Uh huh. Besides that, I don't know much, to be honest. Guess you can kind of call her a loner. She spends most of her free time training in the Sword Hall or studying in the library. When she does show up, it's usually to kick butt. She pretty much destroys whoever she duels—"

"And you left *un-destroyed*," Jefferson affirmed with a pat to my shoulder. "That's got to earn you some points with the captains."

"Guess not," I shrugged.

Miles rolled his eyes.

"Always the pessimist, this one," he motioned to me.

"Hey. All I'm trying to do is be *honest*," I defended.

Well, partially honest. Truth be told, I didn't see the big fuss in needing to be part of a crew. *So what if I have to sleep on a different boat with the rest of the freshies*, I thought. *It's not like I planned on staying here any longer than necessary.*

"And all we're trying to say, Barnaby, is don't give up hope so easily," Jefferson said with a soft smile. "Let's just wait and see."

Well, waiting and seeing took longer than everyone seemed to expect. By suppertime, there was still no sign of the results, and nobody seemed to know why.

That's not to say the day didn't pass smoothly. Miles and Jefferson spent the morning working on a book report—their class was reading *Treasure Island*, a pirate classic—that I was exempt from, so I was free to catch up on some much-needed rest. After lunch, Miles and Jefferson decided to teach me how to play Liar's Dice, a traditional pirate game that involved cups of dice, bluffing, and, as expected with pirates, quite a lot of *sailor's talk*. Definitely not for the faint of heart.

As the afternoon waned, thoughts turned to supper—mostly Miles's thoughts—but I had one errand to run. While Miles and Jefferson headed below decks toward the mess, I veered off in the opposite direction to the teachers' cabin, where Roberts awaited me with my new sword.

Earlier in the week, Roberts had left me instructions to find his quarters, informing me that my sword would be ready for pickup by the weekend. Following his directions, I made my way to the second floor. As I ascended the stairs, the lantern-lit corridor revealed itself to be shorter and narrower than the hallway below, and it didn't take long to locate the Sword Master's door.

Eager to retrieve my sword, I rapped lightly on the door

and awaited a response.

"One moment," called out the familiar, exuberant voice from within. Seconds later, the door swung open, and Roberts's smiling face came into full view.

"Come in, come in," he greeted, ushering me inside.

"Thanks," I said, the warmth of the room enveloping me like a cozy blanket. A small fireplace crackled on one side, flanked on either side by jam-packed bookshelves. Two inviting lounge chairs sat in front of the fire, the perfect place to enjoy the warmth of the hearth. On the other side of the room stood a petite kitchenette and a small dining table that looked to be used as a study, judging by the number of books on it. I assumed Roberts took most of his meals in the mess, probably whenever the teachers had their meals.

Roberts guided me toward the fireplace, closing the door behind me as I sank into one of his armchairs. It was just as comfortable as it looked.

"Would you like something to drink?" he offered. "Coffee? Tea? Spice brew, perhaps?"

"Tea would be nice," I replied. I had zero clue what spice brew was.

I sat in silence as Roberts prepared the kettle, the anticipation of receiving my sword building inside me. Once it started boiling, he slipped into an adjoining room I could only assume contained his sleeping quarters.

"So, how's your first week at our esteemed establishment shaping up?" He called out from the other room. "Find any of the classes interesting?"

I had to bite back a laugh at his second question. Interesting" was a total understatement, especially considering the subjects this school taught—they were unlike anything I'd ever seen before. Sure, they might've slapped some familiar titles on the classes, like math, history, and biology, but that's where the resemblance to normal education ended.

For starters, pirate history, as Jefferson had teased earlier, dove into the illustrious and particularly gory legacy of pirates. And biology? Forget about studying the usual things like plants and human anatomy. Instead, we delved into the composition of creatures I didn't even know existed. I mean, who would've ever guessed that there were over twenty different species of mermaids?

But those classes were only just the tip of the iceberg. This place boasted a treasure trove of daring, swashbuckling courses, such as sailing, pistol practice, cartography, and sword fighting. Unfortunately, our slot for the latter had been graciously sacrificed for the tryouts, so I had yet to check it out. But I heard that Roberts was one heck of a teacher.

"It's definitely been quite the ride," I admitted. "Although I've been told I've yet to experience the best class this place has to offer."

Robert's laughter echoed into the den.

"Is that so? I reckon that was Miles's doing, eh?"

I couldn't help but grin. "He may have spoken about it for a word or two."

"Just a word or two? If I know Miles, the only thing he loves more than sword fighting is to *talk about* sword fighting."

A moment later, the Sword Master emerged from the other room. In his hands was a long, thin rectangular case of polished dark wood.

"I'm really glad to see you getting along with your classmates, Barnaby. I always say, coming to this school is like receiving a second family. You have the one you are born into, and then there's the one you can create here. The friends I made here ended up becoming like brothers to me."

"Wait. You were also a student here?" I asked, my curiosity piqued. Meanwhile, Roberts placed the case atop his dining table and returned to the kitchenette to pour our tea.

"I wasn't just born with the title of Sword Master," he winked at me. "I earned it right here, on this very island. And I'm not alone. You'd be surprised how many of the teaching staff are former students."

"Has the place changed over the years?"

"Not so much," he replied. "Blackbeard runs a pretty tight ship—pun intended. Of course, we've had to adapt to accommodate the needs of students returning to the mainland. But the core classes, as well the responsibilities of crew captains and officers, they've all remained quite the same." He paused, a sigh of clear nostalgia escaping him. "I remember my tenure as a captain. My first mate and I did everything together."

After we drank our tea, Roberts returned to the wooden case. With deliberate care, he lifted the lid and withdrew my sword. Instantly, it became crystal clear to me that the Sword Master's initial claim rang true. The slender, pointed blade looked more suitable atop the elegant hilt than the flimsy fencing blade had ever looked.

But what really brought me the most joy was just to see my sword again in one piece. For more reasons than one, I've felt incomplete since the tournament, like there was this tangible void in my identity. And now, as I gazed upon my sword's gleaming form once more, a sense of relief washed over me, filling a part of that void.

"It looks perfect, sir," I said, eyeing the shiny, sleek sword in his hands. "Thank you so much."

Roberts smiled, his eyes twinkling.

Are those the beginning of tears?

"Um…sir?" I asked him, sensing a shift in his demeanor. "Is everything okay?"

"Yes, Barnaby. Everything is *more* than okay," he said after some time before finally reuniting me with my sword. "Being Sword Master, I've come across quite a number of memorable swords in my time—each with its own unique story and journey. I can't help but recall a similar rapier that belonged to another former student."

"Really? Who?" I asked, leaning in.

"A remarkable swordsman, one of the best I've ever seen." Roberts's voice softened, like he was recalling the memory of someone special to him. "He possessed a talent with the sword that transcended mere skill—like he'd been born to wield a blade. Like Achilles, he was nearly invincible, would it not be for one small weakness."

I shone a broad smile, eager to hear more, but Roberts fell suspiciously silent, seemingly lost in thought as he continued to gaze at my sword.

"Are you sure you're all right, sir?" I asked him.

"Hmm?" Roberts blinked, snapping back to the present. "Oh, yes, yes. Ask any of my students, I can get quite fixated for hours on a fine blade such as yours."

Uh huh…

Something felt off about his reply, but I kept quiet. Maybe I was imagining things, but it seemed like the Sword Master was hiding something.

"Thanks again for fixing my sword," I said, still eager to show my appreciation.

CHAPTER 12

Roberts chuckled. "No need to thank me so many times, Barnaby." He gave me a look. "It's like you're saying goodbye or something."

"Just until Sunday," I replied with a grin. "I can't wait to test this baby out."

Little did he know I was saying goodbye for a completely different reason.

What to do, what to do...

Once I was back on the main deck, I drew my sword and attempted a series of swipes and lunges to get a feel for the new blade. To my delight, it performed as well as it looked, enhancing my moves with increased precision, and offering me greater reach with its extended length.

Let's see Morgan take me down now, I thought with a smirk.

Sword in hand, I strolled along the torchlit deck, which was still completely void of people. Below, the clamor of dinner could be heard, but I had other plans. Instead of joining Miles and Jefferson, I made my way toward the gangplank that led to the docks.

I began planning my escape the moment Jefferson told me about the powers of this magnificent white ship. Timing was key, so I waited for every student to be preoccupied in the mess—and until after I retrieved my sword from Roberts. There was no way I could leave it behind.

And now that I had it back, it was time to go.

It didn't take long for me to reach my destination, and as I'd guessed, it was completely deserted. The eerie stillness almost made me laugh, considering the kind of students Lost Boys High attracted. Jefferson had told me that over a third of them were here for pickpocketing or petty theft. And yet, here I was, standing on a dock full of unguarded ships. It was almost funny how much trust this place put in its students to not steal a ship.

Perhaps Blackbeard's words possessed some truth. Perhaps there really was no better place for one of his students than here. The thought lingered with me as I set foot on the *Angel's Wings* where, for the first time all week, I began questioning my plan.

Was I making a grave mistake? Was I really going to throw away everything this place offered me—such as my budding friendship with Miles and Jefferson or the opportunity to learn from a master swordsman like Roberts? Was leaving all this behind truly worth the chance—if any—to reclaim my former life?

Umm...YUP!

Two minutes later, I found myself standing at the ship's helm. I quickly began replaying Jefferson's words from six nights ago, following them like instructions.

"All you have to do is grip its wheel with both of your hands and visualize in your head the place you desire."

I wrapped my hands around the polished wooden grips of the wheel. Inhaling deeply, I closed my eyes and began thinking about Florida. About Grandma. About home.

Suddenly, I heard footsteps.

My eyes popped open. Panicking that I'd been caught, I quickly gave the deck below another scan, but it still appeared empty.

"Um...hello?"

Total silence.

You're probably just hearing things, Barnaby, I told myself. *It's*

CHAPTER 12

just your nerves. Calm the heck down.

But then the footsteps came again.

"Who's there?" I asked uneasily, looking more closely this time. Sure enough, now I thought I could make out a figure at the ship's edge. Maybe they did guard the *Angel's Wings* at night?

Still no answer.

"Everything okay down there?" I asked, striving to maintain a casual tone. It wasn't like anyone could possibly know what I was doing here. Still, I didn't let that stop me from withdrawing my sword as I cautiously approached the ship's bow.

Relief washed over me as I finally made out the figure's identity.

"Oh, it's just you, Jay. Boy, you gave me a fright there."

He must have spotted me from the *Queen Anne II* and only now managed to catch up. Smiling now, I approached my pal, greeting him in a friendly manner.

"I was just checking out that theory of yours. You know, the one about the *Angel's Wings*? Looks like you were right—it *is* like they give its entire exterior a new paint job every twenty-four hours."

Still met with silence, I grew increasingly nervous as I closed my distance to the boy to only several feet. Something definitely felt off.

And that was when Jefferson started to speak.

"Fifteen men on a dead man's chest."

Now, I can't exactly explain it, but the voice that uttered these words from my friend's lips—it *wasn't his*. The soft, squeaky vocals of his voice were gone, replaced by one so sinister it sent tendrils of fear down my spine.

"Jefferson? Is everything okay?" I asked, my voice trembling.

The boy raised his gaze at me, his eyes no longer their usual brown but solid silver orbs, devoid of any emotion.

"Yo ho ho, and a bottle of rum," the boy grunted most unsettlingly.

Then, without warning, he charged at me.

He collided into me with a thud, crashing to the floor intertwined. I tried getting my sword up, but Jefferson had an elbow pinned down on that hand, pressing me down as he reached for his own blade.

Fear rushed through me as I sought to break free, managing to wrestle my arm loose just in time to block Jefferson's vicious swing, his cutlass crashing down on me without a single drop of hesitation.

This guy is really trying to kill me, I realized.

"What's happened to you?" I gasped, hitting the boy in the chest with my knee. Jefferson recoiled from the blow, and I was able to slip out from underneath him. But I was barely able to get to my feet before he attacked me again.

"Drink and the devil had done the rest," he said, swiping at my lower half. Blazing pain sprouted from my ankle as his blade cut into my skin, sending me crumbling to the deck once again.

"Yo ho ho, and a bottle of rum."

WHAT THE HELL IS HE SAYING?

"Jefferson, please!" I pleaded, tears streaming down my cheeks.

"The mate was fixed by the bosun's pike."

The boy was relentless. Like an insect, he started crawling on me, kicking away my sword with a stunning burst of strength. It wasn't long before he had me pinned down again.

CHAPTER 12

I was helpless as he raised his cutlass for the final blow.

He glared down at me with those empty, silver eyes.

"The bosun brained with a marlinspike," the cold voice emitted from his mouth. "Yo ho ho, and a bottle of rum."

Seeing no escape, I closed my eyes and braced for the inevitable.

If only I could've seen my grandma one more time.

CLANG!

The sound of metal meeting metal jolted my eyes open. Jefferson's cutlass still hovered over me, but another was now in its way.

"Go!" Miles yelled at me. "Get out of the way!"

Wincing, I rolled feebly to the side, biting into my lip as I forced myself to stand.

Now it was two on one. Swords pointed at Jefferson, Miles and I refused to let our would-be friend advance an inch.

And then the strangest thing happened. Miles and I watched as Jefferson's mouth suddenly swung open, as if expecting someone to feed him. Then, he began to shake violently, collapsing to the deck in uncontrollable spasms. Miles and I watched on in horror as his entire body continued writhing with no end in sight.

"What the hell is going on!" Miles asked me incredulously, voice filled with fright.

I had no answer for this.

After a minute, the spasms suddenly stopped. Without a word to either of us, Jefferson rolled over and pushed himself up. The veins in his hands pulsed profoundly as he pressed them against the deck.

A second later, he vomited.

"Gross," commented Miles as the boy continued throwing

up for what must've been five minutes. When done, he wiped his mouth and, finally, looked up at both of us.

The milkiness in his spectacled eyes was gone. They were brown again—back to normal.

"Hey, guys," Jefferson squeaked. His mousy voice had returned as well. "Oh, man. That's the last time I have clam chowder for dinner."

CHAPTER 13

"So, let me get this straight," Blackbeard interjected through furrowed brows. "The voice—it *wasn't* his?"

I replied with a nod. "Correct."

As I answered, my eyes darted over to the figure standing beside me. It had been more than ten minutes since we burst into Blackbeard's quarters—completely disrupting his supper in the process—and Miles's eyes were *still* dancing around the room like a kid in a candy shop. It wasn't hard to tell that it was his first time here.

"I've never heard Jefferson speak like that before," I pressed on. "That voice, it was dark and cruel. It was like he was, well—*possessed.*"

Blackbeard's head tilted to the side as he appeared to ponder this. "Is that so?"

I watched as the head of Lost Boys High rose from his seat and began to pace, the massive cutlass at his side casting an imposing shadow. After several laps, he came to a stop and fixed his gaze on the fourth and final occupant of the room. "And *ye* remember none of this?"

Over on the far side of the room, Jefferson shrugged innocently from his armchair.

"I mean, I wish I could. I genuinely have no clue what Miles and Barnaby are talking about." He shifted uncomfortably from beneath the tight layer of rope binding him, and grimaced. "Is this really necessary?"

Blackbeard ignored Jefferson's pestering and resumed his pacing.

"How peculiar," he murmured to himself, stroking his beard in contemplation. "How very peculiar."

No arguments there. This whole thing was getting weirder by the minute. Despite the unsettling events—such as cleaning up Jefferson's vomit and a brief stop at the infirmary for my injured leg—Miles and I had managed to escort Jefferson directly to Blackbeard's quarters without any further incident. And now, as he stood before us, Jefferson seemed as relaxed as he had during the entire journey here. It was as if the dark and violent impulses that had consumed him earlier had simply just picked up and left.

And just when I thought things could turn more for the unexpected, Blackbeard turned his inspective gaze onto *me*.

"Ye said that ye found him on the *Angel's Wings*, correct?" he asked me. "What were you doing there in the first place, Barnaby? Why weren't you at dinner like everybody else?"

I opened my mouth to respond, but it was Miles who spoke first.

"Sir, Barnaby wasn't at dinner because he was meeting with Roberts," he explained. "He went to the Sword Master's quarters to retrieve a sword being prepared for him."

When Miles finished speaking, he shot me a quick nod that read, *I got your back*.

"Okay, but why didn't he head down to dinner afterward?" Blackbeard asked, his intimidating, brown eyes fixated on me once more. "Eh? Why didn't ye go down to the mess for some

CHAPTER 13

food, boy?"

His persistence on the matter had sirens going off in my head. One of his students had morphed into some rambling, rabid animal, and all he cared about was why I missed freaking dinner?

Only one possible reason for this raced through my mind, and it sent a sickening wave of realization through my stomach.

Does Blackbeard know about my plans to steal his ship?

I quickly gulped down some much-needed air and tried to mask my panic as I finally answered the question.

"Um, because I didn't need to. Miles said he'd bring me back a plate to the *Adventure Galley*, which is where I've been staying. After I got my sword from Roberts I started heading back there—and that was when I heard the strange voice aboard the *Angel's Wings*, and immediately went to investigate."

If it hadn't been a complete giveaway, I would've given myself an actual pat on the back for conjuring such a lie. Truth was, it wasn't even a *total* lie, since Miles had actually promised to bring me back some food from the mess.

"Very well," Blackbeard eventually replied, seeming to accept my answer. "Now, ye mentioned that Jefferson had been… *saying things*? Can either of you elaborate on this?"

This time, Miles didn't jump in to answer. No, in fact, he did the complete opposite; he turned and beckoned for me to offer a response. That did make sense though, as I had heard more of Jefferson's ramblings than him.

"Um, it was mostly just nonsense. Things like, 'fifteen men on a dead man's chest…'"

My voice trailed off when I saw the effect the words were having on Blackbeard. From the moment they left my lips, the pirate captain's expression froze over. I tensed as his imposing figure took a large, deliberate step toward me.

"Say that again," he ordered, his signature beard trembling as he spoke. "One. More. Time."

I tugged nervously at my shirt.

"Um, 'fifteen men on a dead man's chest,'" I stammered. "Hang on, I think the next part went something like, "'yo ho ho, and—'"

"'—and a bottle of rum,'" Blackbeard finished. The tone of his voice turned grave as he continued to recite the passage Jefferson had been murmuring while trying to kill me. "'The mate was fixed by the bosun's pike. The bosun brained with a marlinspike. Yo ho ho, and a bottle of rum.'"

He closed his eyes and took a deep breath, engulfing the room in an eerie silence—which Jefferson shattered a moment later.

"You've got to be joking," he said with a laugh. "I think I'd remember saying all of that." His tone shifted when he saw that none of us were laughing. "Come on, this is insane! I don't even know what a marlinspike is!"

"Sir?" asked Miles. "Do you recognize these words?"

Eyes still closed, Blackbeard nodded slowly."Aye. I do."

"Well, that's great then, sir!" Miles went on, eyes sparkling with relief. "That means you know what happened to him!"

Miles proceeded to turn and shoot me a grin conveying a clear message: *cased closed*. And for a moment, it truly appeared that way. Blackbeard had recognized these strange words.

Until—

"I'm afraid I cannot answer that question, Mr. Whittaker."

I frowned. "What do you mean you can't answer? We

CHAPTER 13

deserve to know. The *entire school* needs to know, frankly, so that it can stop this from happening again—"

"I SAID NO!" Blackbeard roared.

The abrupt uproar jolted me from my seat, shattering the illusion of the head's composed demeanor. In that moment, it was as if I had glimpsed the true nature of Edward Teach—the notorious pirate whose legend loomed large over the seas. Like a switch being flipped, the headmaster's calm facade melted away, revealing the fearsome figure lurking beneath.

The air in the room grew heavy with tension as Miles, Jefferson, and I waited in frozen silence. Finally, with a heavy sigh, Blackbeard signaled his return, the storm of his outburst subsiding.

"I apologize for the outburst," he expressed, his tone softer this time around. "But the three of you need to understand that before I can give any sort of statement to the school, all the facts must be carefully examined. The last thing we want is to spread any unnecessary panic around here."

Unnecessary panic? Did he really just say that?

"But, sir," Miles tried once more, but Blackbeard put up his hand to stop him.

"My decision on the matter is final, Mr. Whittaker," he asserted firmly, ending any further objections. "In the meantime, go and get some sleep. You and Barnaby are excused from tomorrow's lessons. I'll ask the teachers to prepare summaries of the classes for the both of you. As for you, Mr. Monroe," Roberts paused, as if selecting his next words carefully, "I'll have quarters prepared for you on the *fourth floor*."

The expression relayed by Jefferson showed he was anything but pleased by this decision.

"I—I don't understand," he stammered. "You're putting me

in med bay?"

"What would you have me do? Let you just waltz back to your ship and your crew like nothing happened?" Blackbeard raised an accusatory finger at my bandaged leg. "That is Barnaby's blood on *your* blade, Mr. Monroe, is it not?"

Jefferson opened his mouth, but no words came out. For the first time all week, the "brains of the operation" couldn't answer a question sent his way.

"Statement or no statement, this situation will be monitored," Blackbeard affirmed. "Mr. Whittaker, please accompany Barnaby to the med bay as well, so that he may get his bandage reapplied. Mr. Monroe, you'll join them there momentarily."

Then, back to us—

"Dismissed."

Miles and I left Blackbeard's cabin without another word.

"Holy cow," I wheezed once we were back out on the deck.

"That actually happened." Miles shook his head in disbelief. "I don't think Blackbeard's ever said a single word to me before tonight. To be honest, I wouldn't be surprised if he hadn't even known that I existed. And when he yelled, man…" He paused, glancing uneasily at me. "I've never seen him that mad before."

I shook my head. "I don't think that was anger, Miles. I think it was *fear*."

Miles scoffed. "Well, ain't that just peachy. If Blackbeard's spooked, there's no telling how bad whatever we're dealing with here is. And how in the Seven Seas does Jefferson not remember any part of it?"

"No clue." I shot Miles a look. "You saw his eyes, right?"

CHAPTER 13

"Uh huh. Milky white. No pupils." Miles ran a hand over his face with a sigh. "I've never seen anything like it."

"I have—in horror movies."

Miles looked at me, the color drained from his face like he'd just seen a ghost. "What the heck is going on here, man?"

I had no answer to give him.

Miles sighed again, rubbing the back of his neck. "As if I didn't have enough going on already."

"What do you mean?" I asked, eyebrows knitting in concern.

"My brother. I haven't heard from him in a while." Miles glanced away, his voice tinged with worry. "I mean, he usually goes AWOL when he's away on missions, but he's always sent messages through other crows. I'm sure he's all right, but it would be nice to hear from him, y'know?"

"Totally," I acknowledged with a nod. "What I wouldn't give to get a letter from my grandma."

Miles and I continued trudging along across the deck, my toes squishing in my blood-filled boot with each step. Like I said, we had rushed Jefferson to Blackbeard as quickly as possible. There hadn't really been much time for a wardrobe change.

"By the way, thank you for covering for me back there," I expressed to Miles. "And about that…"

Miles waved me off.

"It's all good, mate," he said. "It's not like we haven't all been there before."

I frowned. "What do you mean?"

"What? You think none of us have thought about taking that boat for a joyride? Making a spice brew run to Shipwreck Cove? We all have. But no one ever really goes along with it. Because if you did, you would be leaving everyone on this island completely stranded."

I felt my cheeks redden at the last bit, realizing the disaster I had avoided.

We were almost at the end of the deck now—only a handful of feet away from the gangplank—when we heard it: an eerie, blood-curdling scream.

It was coming from back in the cabin.

Miles and I immediately turned and bolted back to the structure. We were mere feet away when the door burst open, unleashing quite the scene onto the deck. A cluster of teachers spilled out—Roberts and Blackbeard in the lead—all struggling to contain a shrieking, writhing Jefferson.

"JAY!" Miles cried out pleadingly.

Jefferson made no attempt to respond; he was too busy thrashing about in the teachers' grasps, resembling a rabid animal. His shrieks pierced the night sky like those of a wounded dog, and he clawed at their hands relentlessly, but not a single teacher loosened their grips.

By now, several students had appeared on the deck, undoubtedly drawn by the commotion. Their faces were etched with the same horror that gripped us all.

"Well, there goes Blackbeard's plan," I muttered. "My God."

Sure enough, it was my voice that drew Jefferson's attention. His head suddenly snapped in my direction, and right away, I saw them. The eyes.

Just as Miles described them.

Milky white.

"And the cookey's throat was marked belike, it had been gripped by fingers ten," the ghastly voice emanated from his mouth.

Miles and I watched in stunned silence as the teachers

proceeded to carry our possessed friend into the bowels of the ship. His final words before disappearing into the depths lingered ominously into the night air.

"Yo ho ho, and a bottle of rum."

CHAPTER 14

As news of Jefferson's "episode" spread like wildfire throughout the school, whispers and murmurs filled every corner, echoing the uneasiness that gripped us all. With each passing moment, the air seemed to crackle with uncertainty, fueling a wave of speculation.

Theories of all sorts began floating around, ranging from the absolutely absurd—like whatever happened to Jefferson was related to the school's *food*—to the more ominous, like the possibility of a mysterious force lurking about and putting us all in grave danger.

But even that didn't seem feasible to me. Miles had made a good point—there was only one way to reach the school, and it meant traveling for miles *underwater*. Surely there was no way someone or something unwanted could've snuck in.

Right?

Nevertheless, precautions were swiftly enacted. Students clung to each other like lifelines, and it wasn't long before all the crews prepared proper buddy charts to ensure that nobody was ever left alone. As for the ridiculous claim about the food, that one died quickly when one foolish freshie began questioning Bones about the quality of the school's produce.

"So, all of a sudden, our service no longer meets your

satisfaction?" The skeleton bellowed at the poor boy in front of the entire mess. "Perhaps you would prefer it if we *didn't take* your orders for a while?" The mass of bones spun its skull around and scanned the rest of the hall. "Anyone else interested?"

Yeah. That basically ended any inquiries relating to the food.

But it was clear to everyone that a disturbance had fallen upon the school, and the only man who seemed capable of restoring order was nowhere to be found. I guess Blackbeard needed more time to assess the situation before making a schoolwide statement.

As for Miles and me, we both slept straight through the next morning. Neither of us were especially eager to leave the safe confines of our beds and rejoin the world—especially a world where our friend was now currently residing in the *freaking brig*. Yeah, that's right. After what happened on deck, Blackbeard believed a more serious relocation was needed.

It wasn't until hours later that we reluctantly emerged and only just to eat. By noon, we dragged our empty stomachs out of bed and took them to the mess.

Walking inside, it was like someone had announced our arrival on loudspeaker. From the moment our feet entered the mess's threshold, we were swarmed by an overwhelming sea of people—students, teachers, and crows alike—all eager to offer their condolences for Jefferson's situation.

The only thing worse was having to endure those who didn't feel sympathy for Jefferson—and there were quite a few of them. Some even found the situation amusing. A handful of such sickening individuals were seated not too far from us at lunch later that week, giggling and making jokes about our friend.

Unsurprisingly enough, Roger Riaz was among them.

"He was probably just drunk," I overheard him say. Catching my eye, he sneered and added, "Did you check under his bed, Barnaby? I bet you'll find that bottle of spice brew he was blabbering about to me."

"Can it, Roger," I snapped, my patience wearing thin.

"Yo ho ho!" His sneer widened as he continued his mockery.

"Don't listen to him," Miles told me, sensing my frustration. He was right, of course. Riaz may be a nuisance, but I'd just be wasting my energy with him. I had bigger problems to deal with.

For starters, there was the realization that I was back to the drawing board in my mission to find a way home. Miles's words from the other night had opened my eyes to the harsh reality that the *Angel's Wings* wasn't a proper option to get me back to Florida. But if that wasn't bad enough, I now had to deal with the increased security around the docks. This became painfully clear later that same day, after supper, as Miles and I strolled past a pair of crows patrolling the deck, each with a cutlass in hand.

"That's new," I pointed out.

"Oh, you didn't hear?" Miles asked. "Blackbeard set up a night patrol across the docks."

"You don't say," I muttered, the newfound information sinking my hopes of home like an anchor.

"Oh yeah." His voice was noticeably more upbeat than it had been in days. "Hopefully that will prevent whatever happened to Jefferson from spreading to anyone else."

"Yep," I answered through clenched teeth—the image of Grandma's heartwarming face spiraling into oblivion. "Let's hope so."

CHAPTER 14

Shoulders slumped, I glumly lumbered after Miles to the *Adventure Galley*, where we were immediately stopped by one of his crewmates, a sullen-faced boy by the name of Travis Bridgewater.

"Barnaby, right?" he asked, his beady brown eyes looking me up and down. "Captain wants to see you in her cabin."

I turned to Miles, who shrugged.

"Maybe she wants to offer her condolences," he suggested.

Maybe. She wouldn't be the first of the day.

"I'll see you downstairs," Miles called after me as I followed Travis to the captain's cabin. When he ushered me in, I found myself facing not only Amelia Ash, but an additional half-dozen members of Miles's crew I recognized to be officers.

"Ah, Barnaby. Welcome!" Amelia smiled invitingly at me. "How was supper?"

"Good, I guess."

"Good...*good.*" The captain's smile widened. "So, Barnaby, I know you've had a rather difficult last couple of days. My officers and I, however, believe we may have some news that might turn things around. A proposition, to be precise."

Her words caused my sunken heart to rise ever so slightly.

Is she talking about what I think she is?

"Apologies for the interruption, Captain," one of the officers chimed in, "but I've got to ask. Are you absolutely certain that this is the right move?" The beefy, olive-skinned fellow who asked the question was Fletcher Cruz, who I knew from Miles to be the crew's ammunitions officer. Whatever that meant.

All eyes in the room turned to Fletcher.

"Riaz was pretty clear with his threats," the muscular boy grunted, running a hand across the fresh crew-cut he sported. "No quarter for whoever takes the new guy." His gaze turned to me next, and he frowned. "Are we sure that's what we want? We're barely ready to compete this year, let alone fend off the defending champs."

For a fleeting moment, Amelia didn't respond. The entire cabin watched on in suspense as she took her time, electing to scan the array of papers and charts on the desk before her.

"Are you scared of Roger Riaz, Fletcher?"

The question was so abrupt and sharp in its delivery, Fletcher's body went rigid as he tried to muster up an answer.

"N-no, ma'am. Of course not."

Amelia nodded. Finally lifting her hazel eyes from the table, she began scrutinizing the expressions of her other officers.

"Are any of you scared of Roger Riaz?"

Not a single officer replied, each clearly too intimidated to do so. It didn't seem to matter though, as Amelia didn't wait around for a response and continued speaking.

"Because if any of you are, I should have Barnaby take *your* spot in my crew." I watched as she slammed a fist on the table before her, a gesture that I swear made Fletcher flinch. "Roger Riaz is a bully who uses fear and force to get what he wants. When Blackbeard made me captain, I swore to him that I would change the narrative around such people at this school. And I see no better way to do so than to make our crew's newest addition the *single person* in this entire school who's had the guts to publicly go toe-to-toe with Riaz."

I couldn't believe what I was hearing.

"Wait," I stammered. "You want me to join your crew?"

"If it was up to me, Barnaby, you'd already be on it," Amelia confessed. "In fact, after your sensational performance at the tryouts, every captain wanted you. That is, until Roger Riaz declared at the next captain's meeting that whoever chose you for their crew would receive no quarter in the raids—even if they surrender."

"Um, raids?"

Amelia's eyes widened in shock. "You've been here for over a week and you still haven't heard about the raids?"

"They're basically the official sport of the school," Fletcher explained to me. "Crews like ours battle one another for control of each other's ship. The first to raise their colors aboard the other ship wins." He shot a look back at Amelia. "That, or if they force the other crew to surrender. But that wouldn't be an option for us against Riaz. No quarter means *no mercy*."

This time, every single person in the cabin flinched as Amelia slammed another fist onto the table.

"If you're already planning on surrendering, Fletcher, then get the heck out of this cabin. I expect us to compete! More than that—I expect us to *win*! We need a replacement for Jefferson, and who at this school is more deserving than Barnaby? I mean, come on—did you not see him at the tryouts? The kid's a natural!"

"I'll second that," a familiar voice echoed from the doorway.

Everyone in the room spun around to find Morgan—jaw-droppingly beautiful as ever—leaning against the doorframe.

Amelia smiled and let out a soft chuckle.

"Perfect timing, Morgan," she said with a nod of approval. "Everyone, I'd like you to meet our new quartermaster— Morgan Travers."

Morgan waved and mouthed a "Hi" in response. The officers around me looked stunned, and it wasn't hard to figure why. The crew's quartermaster was basically the captain's right-hand man. In other words, quite a lofty position for such a young student.

"Sorry I was late," Morgan apologized, shutting the door behind her. "Turns out, transferring crews isn't exactly the piece of cake you'd think it to be. You wouldn't believe the paperwork."

Nobody laughed at her joke. Nearly the entire cabin remained motionless and continued studying the cabin's new addition.

Morgan glanced at Amelia and motioned sideways with her head at me. "Has it been decided yet?"

The captain shook her head. "We were just about to put it to vote." She scanned the room one last time. "Anyone have anything else to say beforehand? Any final concerns regarding Roger Riaz's threats?"

Once again, no responses. Fletcher murmured something to himself, but it was too quiet for me to make out.

"All right then." Amelia folded her arms. "We all know how this works. As captain, I am granted two votes, and I'll start us off by putting both of them toward Barnaby joining our crew. Those in favor?"

My heart did a somersault when I saw that every single member of the cabin put their hand up as well. Even Fletcher had his in the air, although he didn't seem exactly pleased about it.

Amelia nodded, the widening of her smile the purest evidence of her content with her crew's decision. I had a good feeling that her satisfaction wasn't just about me; all her officers just backed a major proposal of hers. Remembering that she was one of the newer captains, I had to guess that display of trust and faith must've felt quite amazing for her.

"Guess it's settled then," she said. "Doesn't look like there's much need to ask who's against. Which means there's only one final thing to say."

All eyes were on Amelia as she walked around the table and approached me, clamping a congratulatory hand onto my shoulder.

"Welcome to the *Adventure Galley*, Barnaby."

CHAPTER 15

I did it. I made a crew!

Heart bursting with joy, there was definitely a skip in my step as I bounded out of the cabin in search of Miles, eager to break the good news to him. Heaven knows we both needed some.

Excitement bubbled within me as I hurried down the stairs to the galley below. I wondered if Miles had already gone to sleep. *Shaking him awake would only add to the fun*, I thought mischievously.

Alas, there was no need for a wake-up in the end. As soon as I stepped off the last stair and turned the corner to the sleeping quarters, there he stood, his signature grin on full display.

"Well?" he asked, anticipation twinkling in his eyes. "What did they decide?"

I smirked. "You already knew, didn't you? That explains your good mood from before."

Miles laughed. "I didn't want to ruin the surprise. I also wasn't sure how the other officers would vote, but I'll take that cheeky look of yours as a yes. Welcome to the crew, Barnaby!"

"Thanks, Miles," I replied, grateful for his heartfelt praise. It felt good to be congratulated by somebody who actually *meant it*.

CHAPTER 15

Despite the warm reception from Amelia, it became clear pretty quickly that not everyone in the cabin shared the same sentiment—which seemed odd, considering that the vote for me to join had been unanimous. Most of the welcomes I received from her officers seemed half-sincere at most.

And if that hadn't been enough, the conversation I found myself having with Fletcher almost confirmed it.

"Don't get me wrong," he'd told me. "It's just that we're risking quite a lot by bringing you aboard. You understand that, right?"

"I do." I replied.

"Okay, good. All doubt aside, Amelia's our captain, and if she wants to give you a chance, then so do we. We trust her judgment—which is why we voted you in. Hopefully, it just won't end with all of us nursing wounds in med bay after going up against Riaz, eh?"

He smiled slightly as he said the last bit, like he'd been joking, but I picked up on the truth in his words. Fletcher and the other officers were skeptical about having me join the crew.

Eager to share the good news with Miles, I bid Fletcher goodnight and turned to leave, only to feel a soft hand stop me at the door.

"So, Barnaby, it appears we'll be working together," Morgan remarked.

"It appears so," I replied, feeling a familiar fluttering in my chest, identical to the one I experienced at tryouts.

"Well, I just hope you won't hesitate in the raids like you did at tryouts," Morgan smirked. "A second's hesitation in battle is an eternity for your opponent to exploit. If you trusted your instincts more, you might've stood a chance against me." She winked, her tone playful yet challenging.

Heat rising to my cheeks, I scoffed and tried shaking it off.

"Thanks for the advice. But don't worry. I know now to play dirty next time."

My retort seemed to catch Morgan off guard, a flicker of surprise in her eyes.

"I guess we'll just have to see then," she responded playfully. With a final smile, she departed in the direction of Amelia, leaving me to wonder about what our little interaction meant.

The whole experience in the cabin left me with quite a lot to unpack, a task I'd tackle with Miles in the days to come. But now, as I sat in the galley with him beaming across from me, a heavier topic weighed on my mind, one that needed to be addressed.

"Listen, Miles," I began, my voice softening with sincerity, "I know that it's Jefferson's spot on the crew I'm taking. I just want to assure you, as soon as he's better, it's his to—"

Miles waved me off.

"Don't even go there," he told me. "It's not like what happened to him was your fault. And I know Jay, and if anyone were to take his position, he'd want it to be someone like you. Someone he liked. So don't feel guilty, Barnaby. Take it for him. Help us win *for* him."

I nodded. "You got it."

Satisfied, Miles nodded, then beamed.

"Ah this is amazing! I can't wait for the *hazing* to begin!"

"Wait...what? Miles, what are you talking about? MILES—what hazing?"

Much like with the news about Jefferson, word of my recruitment to Amelia's crew quickly spread throughout the

CHAPTER 15

school, as evidenced by all the glances I received the following morning at breakfast. And if that wasn't enough proof, well, Riaz's response pretty much confirmed it.

We discovered it after breakfast, when the Crew returned to the ship to retrieve our belongings for class. There, impaled into the mainmast by a dagger, was a parchment with the words *NO QUARTER* scribbled in messy red cursive.

"Oh, now it's *on*," Miles growled beside me. "Violating our ship—the nerve!"

He wasn't alone. Every member of the crew seemed to share his sense of provocation and disgust. I caught snippets of bitter murmurs passing between them, their expressions betraying their outrage. As I glanced around, I spotted Fletcher among the disgruntled group. Expecting him to point fingers and say something about this being my fault, he remained silent, only shooting me a look before leaving for class.

I couldn't shake the guilt gnawing at me. Fletcher and the rest of the crew had every right to blame me. They didn't deserve to take an extra beating in the raids because of me. So, as each day passed, I half expected to wake up one morning and find a notice instructing me to pack my things. But nothing like that ever came. Instead, I received something completely different on my bedside table after roughly a week as part of Amelia's crew.

I furrowed my brow in confusion as I picked up the large, hardcover book.

"Ah," came Miles's voice from the next bed. "Your hazing has arrived."

What? A book report? I couldn't help but think incredulously.

"*The Rise and Fall of Captain William Kidd*," I read aloud to him. "Is this meant to be some kind of joke or something?"

Miles looked genuinely offended.

"Joke? Every single one of us has read that book, Barnaby. It's part of your initiation process into our crew. Amelia wants each and every one of us to know the legacy of this ship and the story of its former captain. He's our patron pirate."

"Um, okay then," I replied, returning the book to the table. I could grasp that logic. No doubt it was considered a great honor around these parts to inherit the ship of such a great pirate captain. Amelia just wanted everyone to understand that.

There was just one problem. William Kidd wasn't exactly what you'd call "great" by any stretch of the imagination. In fact, I wasn't even sure if he could even be considered a pirate!

Now, that's not to say that his story wasn't interesting—I spent an entire weekend devouring it. But the record made it clear that Kidd never intended to enter the pirate business. In fact, he'd actually been sent by his governor to *hunt* pirates, and only after immense pressure from his mutinous crew did he finally attack a civilian ship—and even that was *by accident*! Even more embarrassing was the fact that Kidd was tricked by the same governor to return home where he was arrested and hung for piracy (before the pirates' deal with the mainland).

Upon finishing the book, I was so puzzled, I went straight to Amelia herself for answers. To only further my befuddlement, when I brought up my predicament, the captain just nodded her head right back in agreement.

"Aye, Barnaby. Everything you say is true. William Kidd was, without a doubt, one of the *worst* pirates to ever sail the Seven Seas, and not in the terrifying sense."

"Then why do you urge the crew to learn about him?" I asked, truly perplexed. "Moreover, why did you choose him as your...mascot?"

Amelia chuckled. "Now that's a funny way to look at it. Really, Barnaby, do you think I would actually *choose* Kidd? It was the school who assigned him to me. They like to give the, er...*lamer* pirates to new crews. I mean, this isn't even the real *Adventure Galley* we're standing on—that ship was wrecked in a storm at sea!"

"So then, why make the crew take it so seriously? Surely, you'd want people to forget the connection, no?"

Amelia shook her head.

"I want the exact opposite," she declared. "I want our crew to understand what we've been handed. I want them to take what others might see as a disadvantage and transform it into something powerful. Our crew has something to prove, Barnaby—and I intend to turn that into our greatest strength!"

Boy, did Amelia's words hit home hard. Until now, all I'd done was the complete opposite, and dwell in bitterness about being stuck on this island. But the captain was right: we don't always choose the cards that fate deals us. And if fate decrees returning to Grandma and clearing my name to be unattainable—at least for now—shouldn't I try and make the most of what I *can* control?

So that's exactly what I set out to do. For the first time since arriving at Lost Boys High, I shifted my focus away from getting home and redirected my energy toward other things, such as my classes and bonding with my new crewmates. Miles was always by my side, which proved invaluable, especially amid one night of schmoozing with our fellow mates, when the inevitable question came up:

"So, Barnaby, what brought you here in the first place?"

Miles shot me a knowing look, and without missing a beat,

he deflected the inquiry with a simple, "He's not ready to say." To my surprise, not a single person pressed the issue.

I was beginning to see the true value of being part of one of these crews. It was a blend of loyalty and acceptance, where everyone, regardless of their past, flaws, and past flaws, found a place of belonging. Amelia's insistence on shared meals and gatherings on the weekends only reinforced this sense of unity.

It was in moments like those—sitting atop the deck of the *Adventure Galley* until the late hours, chatting and stargazing—that I found myself reflecting on Blackbeard's words on my first night: people here truly believed in second chances. Lost Boys High wasn't just a school, it was a sanctuary of hope and opportunity—of *freedom*—the very thing the pirates of yore had been craving. And despite my initial feelings, it was getting harder and harder to deny that this place wasn't worth giving a chance.

However, amid all the good vibes, a dark cloud loomed in the form of Riaz and his Sharkheads—a crew known for their brutality and mischief. Filled with some of the school's nastiest bullies and ex-cons, they embraced the legacy of the infamous pirate, Ned Low—even renaming their ship the *Fancy* in his honor. Low's barbaric acts of torture were legendary, like the chilling tale of when he burned a captured Spanish cook alive simply for his own twisted amusement. Yeah, he was definitely one of the folks who gave pirates a bad name.

The feud between our crews was definitely festering—and the teachers knew it. They seemed intent on having us settle our business on *their* terms by having us kick-off this season's raids in the inaugural matchup. The "terrible" Captain Kidd versus Ned Low. Matchup of the century.

I only had three words to say to that.

Bring it on.

With anticipation mounting for the impending battle, the next two weeks whizzed by for my crew. Amidst a whirlwind of grueling practices and countless sword fights, each session ending with our backs drenched in sweat, the eve of our first raid was finally upon us.

As our final practice came to a close, Amelia rallied everyone around the mainmast—the very spot where we had discovered Riaz's little threat. With a commanding presence, she issued orders for a swift dinner and then straight to bed for a good-night's sleep.

"We all need to be energized for tomorrow," she encouraged.

So, as commanded, Miles and I headed to bed after a dinner of some hearty pumpkin soup. Within minutes, the rest of the crew followed suit, and soon the galley fell into a peaceful silence. But sleep didn't come easy for me. I was too anxious and excited for what tomorrow held. Would I be able to step up and help earn a victory for my crew? Or would we end up nursing cuts and bruises as Fletcher had initially feared?

Only time would tell.

As I finally succeeded in dozing off, I heard a slight shuffling sound coming from the opposite side of the galley. I could've sworn I heard some whispering as well, but I just assumed it was some crewmates chatting.

I let out a long yawn, and finally nodded off.

I fell into such a deep sleep, I never even felt them lift my mattress up or carry it to the deck. But I sure as hell felt the water.

SPLASH!

The icy waters of the lake shot volts of energy throughout my body. Eyes popping wide open, I gasped for air as I exploded through the surface and heard my crew hollering from back aboard the *Adventure Galley*.

"To the shore, you two! C'mon!"

You TWO?

I started swimming toward the docks, trying to catch a glimpse of the other figure in the water. After a moment, I spotted them.

Miles?

Reaching the docks, I felt two pairs of hands grip and hoist me out of the water. They did the same for the other guy, dropping them beside me. Only, as I could see now, it wasn't a guy.

Instead, I found myself staring at a soaking, shivering *Morgan*.

"Up, you two!" a familiar voice called out—Amelia's.

I rose, and Morgan did the same. I was wearing nothing but a pair of pajama shorts, while she at least had on a tank top as well. Shivering uncontrollably, we both managed to drag our sopping bodies off the docks and toward the sand bed where the rest of the Crew was waiting.

Carrying torches, they formed a tight circle around us, enveloping us in their glow. Amelia positioned herself directly opposite us, and boy, did she look every bit the part of a pirate captain. Leather boots, jeans, a light linen tunic, and a matching leather waistcoat—all topped with a weathered bandana and a black, three-cornered hat completing her commanding appearance.

With a confident stride, she presented us with swords, their blades gleaming in the torchlight. I recognized one as my own,

CHAPTER 15

and had a feeling the other belonged to Morgan.

"Take them," she ordered, her voice bold and unwavering, "and *defend yourselves!*"

The first attack came from my blindside. I parried my crewmate's strike and ducked under his next one, an act that was all the more challenging by my lack of footwear. With each step, my wet feet turned the sand beneath me into a slippery mush, threatening to unbalance me at every move.

Morgan, fighting alongside me, faced similar struggles. Before long, we were fighting back-to-back, outnumbered and overwhelmed. We'd fend off one crewmate and three more would take their place. Thankfully, our crewmates showed restraint in their attacks, wielding their swords with precision to avoid serious injury. However, they didn't hold back from leaving us with bruises from their strikes with the flat of their swords.

After what felt like an eternity, the flurry of attacks finally ceased, and Morgan and I collapsed on the ground, panting heavily amidst a mix of sweat, sand, and lake water.

A moment later, Amelia approached us.

"You both read the story of Captain Kidd, correct?" she asked us. "Can either of you tell me what led to his downfall?"

Still gasping for air, Morgan and I were too exhausted to reply.

"An unfaithful crew!"

Amelia now spun around to face the rest of her crew. Among them stood Miles, his face brimming with pride.

I wondered which of the bruises I was nursing was of his handiwork.

"To take down the Sharkheads tomorrow, we need unity," Amelia proclaimed. "No scheming, no betrayal. We must trust each other and have faith that together, we can get the job done. Unity is key! Understood?"

When none of the crew responded, it dawned on me that she was directing her words at us.

"AYE AYE, CAPTAIN!" I exclaimed, Morgan echoing alongside me.

Visibly satisfied, Amelia stepped forward and gently patted our backs for us to stand up. I noticed she now carried a bottle in her hand.

"Morgan Travers. Barnaby Stump," she said, lifting the bottle to her lips and jerked the cork out with her teeth. "Drink and join your fellow crewmates of the *Adventure Galley!*"

She took a swig and then passed the bottle to us.

Morgan was the first to drink. I watched as she took a large sip, and immediately winced afterward.

She handed the bottle to me next, and with a deep breath, I slowly brought it to my lips. The mysterious liquid burned my throat as it went down, but I continued drinking because I knew that by doing so, I was officially accepted by the people surrounding me, not only as a member of their crew, but as something else as well—whether I wanted it or not.

A pirate.

CHAPTER 16

The next morning arrived with one final spoonful of drama.

As we ascended to the deck, Miles and I were greeted by an all-too-familiar scene: our crew gathered around the mainmast, their expressions a mixture of apprehension and anger. Sure enough, all eyes were fixed on another note pinned to the mast by a gleaming dagger.

This time around, I don't think Riaz could've been any clearer:

REMOVE BARNABY STUMP FROM YOUR CREW.
DECLARE IT BY BREAKFAST OR ELSE.
FINAL WARNING.

"Not again," I muttered, rolling my eyes.

"Jeez, he must really want you gone," Miles noted. "Riaz has never made a threat like that on the day of a raid. Maybe he's nervous," he added with a smirk, looking over my shoulder. "Here comes Amelia. Let's see how she reacts."

Crossing the deck with a commanding presence, my crewmates and I shifted to make way for our captain. Amelia read the note from Riaz with a calm demeanor, although her clenched jaw betrayed her true emotions. Without uttering a word, she tore off the parchment and crumpled it into a ball.

We stood in silence, watching as she strode to the side of the ship and tossed it overboard. Only then did she finally speak.

"Get to breakfast, everyone," she called out to us. "Most important breakfast of the semester! I don't want to catch anyone with an empty plate—that's an order!"

Her words reverberated across the deck, a firm reminder of the task at hand. Riaz's threats were designed to rattle us, but we couldn't afford to falter. To stand a chance against his Sharkheads today, we needed unwavering focus and commitment to the task at hand. Yet, the tension of the imminent clash hung heavy on us as we made our way to breakfast.

Fortunately for us, we were greeted in the mess by an atmosphere ripe with optimism. Upon our arrival, nearly the entire room rose from their seats and began whooping and applauding us.

"Let's go!"

"Take those Sharkheads down!"

"Well, it's clear who everyone's rooting for," Miles remarked, exchanging high fives with the crowd, clearly enjoying the support. Arriving at our usual table, we found it unusually crowded, with several of our crewmates joining us. I think it was the first time I'd seen our table with more than three occupants.

"Doesn't mean they expect us to win," shrugged Travis as he took the seat to Miles's right. "Riaz's crew is known for their brutality in the raids—they have the highest rate of opponents sent to med bay per raid. And that's *when* they accept the surrender of opposing crews."

"On the way over, I overheard the Henry Morgan crew sniggering, using terms like 'total bloodbath' and 'complete annihilation,'" revealed Nikita, another of our crewmates.

Miles scoffed. "Oh, well, that could mean anything."

There was a collective eyebrow raised around the table, including myself.

"C'mon, guys." he urged, throwing up his hands. "All those grueling practices mean squat if we start second-guessing ourselves. We can take them!"

"Miles is right, though," Fletcher interjected from beside me. I hadn't noticed him join our table, let alone take the seat right beside me. "We need to use every ounce of our training to fight the Sharkheads. Even the smallest slipup could end *catastrophically*."

The weight of Fletcher's words sent a ripple of uncertainty through the table, causing even Miles's optimism to falter. It wasn't long before his smile began to waver, his shoulders slumping as if the gravity of the task ahead had finally hit him.

We weren't just fighting for our pride today. We were essentially fighting for our lives.

So, it should come as no surprise that chatter at the table pretty much died after that, except for when Bones arrived for orders. And when the food arrived, an uneasy silence settled over us, broken only by the clinking of utensils against plates. From an outsider's perspective, it would be hard to believe that we were on the brink of competing in something as exciting as a raid.

And before we knew it, it was time for class.

Being Saturday, having class was certainly unusual, but we'd been given word yesterday that our class was scheduled to have an exclusive one-off sparring session in the Sword Hall with Roberts. Nobody in my class seemed to know why this was, but as sparring time with the Sword Master was rare enough, it wasn't like we were complaining either.

Still, with the raid now only hours away, I did my best to keep it easy with the sparring. I needed to save my energy for the real fight to come. That didn't stop me from successfully disarming my partner twice—all in the span of one minute—much to the delight of Roberts.

"Even when you hold back, with that technique you're still practically unbeatable," he praised me afterward, clearly aware of my intentions to take it easy. I'd volunteered to stay behind and help him tidy up.

I grinned. "Well, it's *your* technique, sir."

Roberts laughed.

"Big day," he noted as I handed him one of the last swords to hang on the wall. "How are you feeling, Barnaby? Nervous?"

I nodded, feeling fortunate that nobody at the breakfast table paid much attention to me. They were all too focused on their own nerves, naturally. But if anyone had looked my way, they'd have surely noticed my heavy breathing and my barely touched plate of food—my nerves all but quenching my appetite.

I glanced up at Roberts and let out a sigh.

"It's just…everybody's eyes are going to be on me. And the risks my crew are taking for having me…how can I *not* be nervous?"

Roberts smiled softly. "I can definitely understand the reason to be nervous. In my first raid, I got knocked overboard by cannon fire. Got my nose bashed in as well. But do you know what the first thing I said afterward to my captain was?"

"What, sir?"

Robert's smile widened at the recollection of the memory.

"Can we go again?" The Sword Master chuckled. "Barn-

CHAPTER 16

aby, these raid exercises are about having *fun*. Yes, they're extremely competitive, challenging, and remarkably violent... but what matters most is that you have fun. After all, that's what's most important. Proving your worth to others is important, but what good is any of it if you're not happy in the end?"

His words struck a chord with me, and I felt some of my earlier doubts begin to fade away.

"I guess," I said with a shrug, "but the Sharkheads are the defending champions. They're not going to go down easily."

Roberts nodded in agreement. "Yes, Roger Riaz's crew went on quite a tear last season. But you know what they say—*all good things must come to an end*. Perhaps that end will come this afternoon, eh?"

He winked at me while saying the final bit.

One could only hope, I thought.

When I returned to the ship, the deck was a whirlwind of activity.

A flurry of excitement and motion, it felt like organized chaos, with raid preparations clearly underway. Crew members scurried around, busy with all sorts of tasks, from tying up rigging to sharpening swords and loading cannons. It was a sight to behold, with everyone pitching in to get ready for the raid.

Eager to join in the fray, I was about to get started on my own responsibilities—assigned to me by Amelia herself—when a curt voice called my way.

"Hey, Barnaby! Over here!"

Turning toward the bow, I spotted the crew's bosun, Brent

Barnes, waving at me. Brent, with his short black hair, warm brown eyes, and round, kind face, was one of the friendliest members on the crew. He was Amelia's go-to for everything related to the storage and logistics of the *Adventure Galley*. Judging by the clipboard in his hand, he also appeared to be in charge of handing out assignments today.

"Where have you been? I've been looking everywhere for you," he asked me.

"Sorry, I was helping Roberts tidy up after class," I explained. "But if you were worried about getting my job, don't be. Amelia already gave it to me. I'm at the boarding party."

Brent's smile faltered as he delivered some unexpected news.

"Don't freak out, but Captain told me to let you know that your position has been switched. You're on defense now."

My heart sank as disbelief washed over me. *Defense?* That wasn't what I'd trained for. I'd trained almost exclusively with the boarding party. I knew nothing about the crew's defensive strategy. But when I voiced my concerns, Brent could only offer sympathy.

"Hey man, I'm just following Captain's orders," he said, his tone apologetic. "If you're not happy with it, you'll need to go and take it up with her yourself. But you better hurry because the raid is about to begin."

And that's exactly what I did. Determined for answers, I marched straight into Amelia's cabin and demanded an explanation.

"Trust me, Barnaby," she assured me calmly. "I put much thought into the change. Just hear me out, alright?"

Arms folded, I said nothing and waited for Amelia to proceed.

"As I was saying, after much consideration, I realized it'd

be much more valuable to leave you on the ship. As you're probably aware by now, the boarding party is more of a *group attack*—less about talent and more about numbers and strategy. On the other hand, seeing as we're going up against the defending champs, who I certainly expect to be aggressive in their attack, I've decided to leave our most gifted fighters aboard the Adventure Galley to protect it. Like Morgan and yourself, for example."

I blinked in surprise.

"M-Morgan's also on defense?"

My captain nodded, a mischievous smile sprouting on her lips.

"You heard me. This isn't 'ship-sitting' I'm tasking you with—I seriously believe that the fate of our crew in today's raid will come down to how we protect our ship. I have faith that you and Morgan can do just that."

Okay, I thought, feeling swayed. *I can get my head around that*.

"Besides," Amelia went on, her smile widening, "you and I both know how much our quartermaster values an impressive swordplay performance. You show up today, that might be what it takes for her to notice you."

My face flushed with embarrassment. "You know?"

"I'm not blind, Barnaby. I'm a girl. I saw the way you stared at her at the tryouts—and that night in my cabin. I know what it's like to have a guy gawking my way. So, what do you think?"

What do I think? Having barged in here to complain, I was on the verge of hugging Amelia for making this change. And I might've just done so had I not been stopped by a loud cry erupting from the deck outside—Brent's voice calling out in urgency a second later.

"Captain! You're needed on the deck!"

Amelia's eyebrows knit together as she frowned.

"Oh, what now," she complained, rising from her chair and hurrying for the cabin door. I followed her onto the deck, where we found the crew huddled around the mast yet again.

Another note, perhaps, I wondered as we approached.

Then I saw the battered body slumped against the mast.

"What in the Seven Seas happened?" There was no break in Amelia's step as she began demanding answers. "Who did this to him?'

"Who do you think?" A hoarse voice replied, and it took us all a moment to realize that the words came from the injured figure himself.

It took me another moment to recognize him as Fletcher.

Leaning against the mast for support, he glanced up at us and revealed the true brunt of damage. His once lean mocha face was bashed in and severely swollen, his eye nearly swollen shut. Blood dripped from a gash in his lips, staining the tattered remains of his shirt.

"Roger jumped me," he told us. "Well, he just stood there and had his Sharkheads do it for him."

"That conniving snake!" Amelia snarled, shaking clenched fists. Always so composed, I don't think I'd ever seen the captain so emotional before. "He did this on purpose, timing it right before our match!"

"So what?" one of our crewmates said. It was Travis. "Let's just tell the Sword Master what happened and disqualify them. They'll give us the win too."

"You do that, Travis," a voice called out, "and you'll just be giving them a bigger victory than any they could hope to achieve in the raid."

CHAPTER 16

All eyes trained onto Morgan as she stepped foot onto the deck.

"Don't you see?" she asked the crowd facing her. Her eyes met mine and I could've sworn I saw her expression soften ever so slightly. "That's exactly what they want us to do. Tattle and lose any shred of a reputation our crew possesses. No one likes a rat."

"Okay, then what are we supposed to do?" a crewmate near me called out. "Fight without our ammunition's officer? We weren't trained for this."

He wasn't wrong. Fletcher was the mastermind behind our crew's cannon team, orchestrating the sequencing and timing of our volleys. Without his lead, our attack would lack the essential coordination we relied on.

Murmurs began to break out among the crew as doubt loomed over our next course of action. The vibrant energy I'd witnessed upon arriving at the *Adventure Galley* was now shifting into an atmosphere of apprehension.

"They're scared of us," I heard Amelia mutter to herself. I watched now as she raised her eyes and leveled them with her crew. "In all my years at this school, Riaz has *never* taken such drastic action against an opposing crew. Threats are one thing, but to actually act on them? Unheard of. So, why now?"

When nobody answered, Amelia went ahead and provided one of her own.

"He's afraid. He doesn't want to face us!" The captain now paused, weighing her next words carefully. "If anyone wants to back out, I understand. But I refuse to back down from this fight, especially with it being my first as captain. I'm sailing out there with whoever's willing to join me. But if anyone wants to sit this one out, that's fine. But now's the time to go."

I scanned the faces of my crewmates. Whatever doubt had been present with them before was now long gone. Nobody made the slightest motion to leave.

An unmistakable wave of relief washed over Amelia's face as she saw that her crew was still behind her. Perhaps she did expect some of them to leave.

"Okay then," she nodded. "Let's see...Barnaby?"

I surged forward. "What can I do to help?"

"I need you to take Fletcher downstairs and help him get to his bed. Attend to him, and if anyone you don't recognize comes down those steps, you take your sword and Fletcher's and you take them down. And don't forget what we talked about." Despite the intense atmosphere and the stakes at hand, Amelia smiled and gave me a quick wink. "Try not to get yourself killed, all right? Time to show *her* what you got."

In the distance, I could've sworn I saw Morgan raise an eyebrow.

"All right, all hands, to your stations!" Amelia proceeded to shout with authority. "Cannon crew, on my word! Quartermaster, weight anchor and hoist the sails! We've got a raid to win!"

Grins spread across the crew as the deck became a flurry of activity. Amidst the chaos of crewmates sprinting to their stations, I felt a brisk tap on my shoulder and saw Miles dart by with an infectious grin.

"Good luck!" he called out to me.

Following Amelia's orders, I hurried over to the mainmast and with a grunt, hoisted Fletcher onto my shoulder. It took all my strength to carry him across the deck to the stairwell.

The next moment happened as if it were choreographed. The literal second my foot hit the first step, Roberts's micro-

CHAPTER 16

phoned voice boomed across the lake, shooting ripples across the water's surface.

"WELCOME, LADIES AND GENTLEMEN, TO THE RAIDS!"

CHAPTER 17

As Roberts's voice boomed above, and Fletcher collapsed atop my shoulder, I stumbled down the stairs and over to the section of the galley where the officer's beds lay.

"Which one is yours?" I panted, unable to carry him for much longer.

"That one," the ammunition's officer mumbled, barely mustering the strength to point a finger at one of the beds. As I lugged him to it, I could hear Roberts carry on with the remaining introductions to the raids.

"THE RULES, AS MOST OF YOU SHOULD BE AWARE OF BY NOW, ARE SIMPLE: THE FIRST CREW TO SEIZE THEIR OPPONENT'S SHIP AND HOIST THEIR COLORS UPON ITS MAINMAST WINS! NOW, REMEMBER, NO SERIOUS INJURING IS ALLOWED, SO…"

Amelia had already gone over the rules during the final practice, so I drained out the noise and kept my focus on the task at hand. Arriving at Fletcher's bed, I slowly lowered him onto it, carefully resting his head onto his pillow.

"Can I get you anything?" I asked him.

"Some water," he gasped as he readjusted on the bed. His eyes were closed shut, although I couldn't tell if it was because of all the swelling, or he was just trying to rest.

Grabbing a cup from my bedside table, I rushed over and flung open the sliding door to the storage room. Once inside, I found the barrel labeled "Water" and ladled a cupful. When I returned, I found Fletcher's sword unsheathed and lying on the bed adjacent to his.

"Take good care of her," he rasped, each word weighed down with discomfort.

Handing him the water, I couldn't help but express my guilt. "Fletcher, I'm so sorry. You were right about all this. It's all my fault!"

Despite his current state, Fletcher managed what looked like a dismissive shrug as he drank.

"I've been through worse than this, Barnaby. And if this fuels the crew to beat those fart heads, it will have all been totally worth it."

I looked at him, astounded.

"I—I don't understand," I stammered. "How can you be okay with this? I mean, you were right all along. I never should have joined the—"

"Stop," Fletcher cut me off. "None of that matters anymore. You want to prove your worth? Take my sword and stand ready for what comes next. We're approaching the *Fancy* now."

My eyes widened. "How can you tell?"

Fletcher gave me a look. "This isn't my first rodeo, Barnaby. I've sailed enough times on this lake to know the feeling of when a ship changes speed. If I'm correct, Amelia's just ordered the sails to be rolled up. We should hear the first volley of cannon fire any second now…"

BOOM! BOOM!

I braced myself against a wooden beam as the ship jolted violently from the cannon fire. Although we didn't use actual ammunition in the raids—our cannons fired rubber balls via a unique spring system—the thunderous blasts still echoed through the air with remarkable force. The exchange of volleys between the two ships, coupled with the resounding impact of the cannon fire striking the vessel's sides, made it seem as though we were caught in the middle of a vicious thunderstorm.

"Head up and keep a lookout," Fletcher ordered as he started to doze off.

Creeping back up the stairwell, I lifted my head barely an inch above the deck and took in the scene before me. Our crew was still firing cannons, but just as Amelia had predicted, the bulk of the battle had shifted onto our deck. It looked like Riaz's crew had been the first to successfully board, and judging by what I was viewing, that wasn't a good thing.

I recognized more people unconscious than those still fighting. Miles was at the bow, and appeared to be holding his own, that is until Sharkheads teamed up to take him down. Amelia was nowhere to be found, but Morgan—*wow*. Her skills unmatched, she held her ground against multiple adversaries, taunting them with each swing of her sword.

"Come on, boys, is that all you've got?"

A sense of admiration washed over me as I watched her, a true goddess of the sword, her beautiful scarlet hair flying in the wind as she struck down her opponents. But even Morgan eventually succumbed to the overwhelming Sharkhead forces.

So...what now?

I scanned the deck and failed to spot any familiar faces amongst the people still on their feet. Did that mean Fletcher

CHAPTER 17

and I were the only ones left? If that was the case, surely nobody—not even Amelia—expected me to take down two thirds of the Sharkheads on my own.

Should I just surrender and get it over with? I debated. Riaz had threatened no quarter, but perhaps if *I* was the one doing the surrendering, Riaz would consider the humiliation of the act enough compensation for our previous squabble. *And it would save everyone quite a lot of time.*

I was still contemplating my next move when a familiar voice called out from across the deck by Amelia's cabin.

"Well, gents, I think that's the last of them."

I scowled, immediately recognizing the voice as Riaz's.

"Sylvie, take Morgan and tie her up with the rest of them. Don't forget to gag her mouth—I don't want her riling up the rest of her crew. Charlie, remind me, how many did you say you counted again?"

"Um, sixteen, sir. Seventeen, including the quartermaster."

There was an uncomfortable pause in Roger's voice as he considered his mate's answer.

"Seventeen? But there's twenty in a crew. Where are the last three? And WHERE'S STUMP!"

Aw, he remembered.

"I—I don't know, sir," I could hear Charlie stammer. "Maybe they fell over the side from cannon fire?"

Another pause as Riaz seemed to mull over Charlie's suggestion.

"Hmm…perhaps. Mattinson, do a patrol around the deck and check the surrounding waters. Charlie, you and Elvis head down below decks and scout out the galley. Everyone else—with me. I think it's time we check out Amelia's quarters. This is *our* ship for the next hour, so me thinks we should have a little fun here, eh?"

I cursed Riaz's name as the chuckles of his Sharkheads echoed above me.

"And whoever finds Stump—bring him to me."

I gulped. Whatever he had in store for me, it couldn't be good.

"Aye aye, sir," chorused his crew in unison before dispersing to their tasks. The sound of boots echoed across the deck as they moved, including the footsteps of the pair of Sharkheads heading toward the galley—toward me. I quickly dashed down the stairs in search of a place to hide.

Last THREE crew members. Well, that had to include Fletcher, of course. But it also meant that someone else was still in the raid. Who could it be?

My thoughts were interrupted by the sound of boots clunking down steps. Desperate not to be seen, I dashed back into the storage area and ducked behind the water barrels.

"Do you think anyone's even down here?" I could hear the boy named Elvis ask. His voice was significantly softer than Charlie's.

I tried pulling the barrel closer to me and prayed that I wouldn't be found.

"Who cares?" Charlie sounded annoyed. "Let's just finish up and go watch Riaz raise the dang flag already. If it wasn't for this Stump guy, this Raid would already be over."

Well, sounds like Riaz has something special planned for me, I thought. *Guess surrendering is no longer an option.*

I couldn't see to be sure, but judging by their footsteps, they appeared to be heading in the opposite direction, toward the sleeping quarters. It wasn't long before they spotted Fletcher.

"Jeez, check out his face," I could hear Elvis point out to

CHAPTER 17

Charlie.

What's there to check out? I thought angrily to myself. *You two know very well what your crew did to him.*

"Oh, man. What happened to him?"

At this, I frowned, puzzled.

I thought Fletcher said Riaz had his crew beat him up?

There was no time to ponder this. The boys were moving on, clearly not identifying Fletcher as a threat. Instead, they headed toward the bathroom. Their footsteps grew faint for a minute or two, then started to get increasingly louder with each step.

They were heading for the storage room.

Time was slipping away, and I had only seconds before they'd arrive. If I wanted any say in how this raid would end, I needed a plan—fast. My eyes raced around the room, desperate for a lifeline. And then, just when I thought that I was doomed to be caught and delivered to Riaz for him to carry out his revenge, I spotted something in the room, and a glimmer of hope emerged.

"Let's finish in here and then head back up," Charlie echoed as they neared. "We'll tell Roger that we scoured the place, but no one was here."

"Sounds good to me," replied Elvis. And the two Sharkheads stepped inside.

I waited, heart pounding, until they passed my hiding spot and ventured deeper into the storage area. Seizing the opportunity, I slipped out from my hiding spot and tiptoed out of the storage room. I clenched my fingers tightly around Fletcher's sword as I prepared myself for what I was about to do.

From where I stood, I was now given a glimpse of the two

Sharkheads on the hunt. One, short and plump with tousled blond hair, stood to the left, while the other, tall and stringy with short black hair, lingered on the right.

"I don't see anyone," declared the short boy, Charlie, while Elvis nodded in agreement. "Me neither," he concurred.

I took a deep, final breath.

Okay. Time for Operation Awesome.

"Ahoy! Can I help you landlubbers with something?" I called out to the two of them, unable to resist a little pirate banter. Roberts said to have fun, so sue me.

Charlie and Elvis spun around in unison, their faces a mix of shock and fury. Without hesitation, they lunged toward me, but I was one step ahead. With a swift movement, I swung the sliding wall shut. Before they could react, I thrusted Fletcher's cutlass blade into the now-revealed crevice at the opposite end, securing it tightly into the slot. Now all I could do was hope it held.

The wall shook once, then again—but it did not give.

"Hey! Let us out!" I heard them call out from inside.

Not knowing how long the sword would hold the sliding wall shut, I knew I needed to act fast. Ignoring the cries for help from behind the makeshift blockade, I sprinted through the galley and out onto the deck for the first time since the raid began. Momentarily blinded by the bright sun shining above, my eyes readjusted just in time to catch the sword-wielding boy charging straight for me.

Ducking under the swinging blade, I swiftly aimed a kick at the Sharkhead's chest. He grunted as he staggered back, and seizing the opportunity, I surged forward, driving the hilt of my sword into his gut. With a groan, he collapsed to the floor.

As the sound of more footsteps echoed closer, I spun around

CHAPTER 17

to confront my next opponent, energized. However, my confidence quickly waned when I found myself facing the remaining half-dozen Sharkheads, Riaz himself leading the pack.

I took in the sight of the battle-worn captain. Heaving heavily, sweat glistened across his face, and a nasty cut that ran down the side of his cheek was still dripping blood. Seeing that he hadn't left his skirmish with my crew unscathed made me feel a bit better.

"Your girlfriend did that to me," he explained dryly, catching my gaze. His plain expression twisted into a cruel smile. "Don't you worry, I got her back."

Anger surged through me. With a yell, I rushed at Riaz, sword raised for an attack. But that's just what the Sharkhead captain wanted. Just as I was about to strike, one of his lackeys stepped behind me and delivered a savage slash to my back. I collapsed to the floor, a familiar wet warmth spreading from the wound.

Amidst the agony, I heard Riaz scold me from above. "How foolish could you really be?" Then he kicked me in the ribs.

I cried out, curling up in pain.

"You humiliated me that night in the mess," Riaz went on. "Humiliation isn't something I take lightly. Respect is everything around here, and I've spent years earning mine. I knew I needed to teach you a lesson then and there, but my men convinced me to wait for the right moment. Well, Barnaby—that moment is *now*."

I winced as the tip of a sword pressed deeper into my shoulder.

"And you know the best part?" Riaz sneered, his voice thick with malice. "There's no one here to save you. Not Amelia, not Morgan, not Roberts—and certainly not that useless crow of yours, Reed. You're all alone, Barnaby. Just as you deserve."

"Um, you sure about that?" a voice called out from the opposite side of the deck.

It took me an absurd amount of strength to lift my head and turn it to catch a glimpse of who was speaking.

It was Amelia, with Fletcher standing right beside her, a wide smile spreading across his face.

I was lost for words, and clearly wasn't the only one. Roger Riaz could barely get out his next command to his crew.

"G-get them."

Two of Riaz's men sprinted toward Amelia, but she was ready for them. Eluding every single one of their attacks, she leaped forward, striking the first with her sword and then the other with her elbow. Both went careening into each other, and then onto the floor—one unconscious, the other clutching his clearly broken nose.

Another Sharkhead rushed at Fletcher, who was swordless. *My bad.* But that didn't seem to stop him. The huge, muscular officer flung himself at the poor boy, aiming a fist straight for his chin. It took me a moment to notice the paintball pistol in his hand, and my eyes widened as he fired at the boy, hitting him at the base of his skull and sending him sprawling backward in a burst of purple paint.

"STOP THEM!" screamed Riaz.

I remained on the floor, watching on as Amelia now parried a quick thrust from another foe. She sidestepped the next swipe at her, ducking as the blade nearly took off her head. When it came time to retaliate, she swiped down with her sword, hitting the girl in the leg with her hilt. The Sharkhead grimaced in pain as she fell to the floor, clutching her injured leg.

Without a word, Amelia stepped over her and continued her march toward Riaz with Fletcher once more by her side.

Time to get up, Barnaby.

Adrenaline coursed through me as I leaped to my feet, wincing as my back straightened. I stumbled over to Amelia, sword tight in my grasp.

Roger Riaz stared at us, utterly stunned. His mouth was open and moving, yet no words came out. He seemed both baffled by the sudden turn in events and terrified of what was about to come his way.

"You all right?" Amelia asked me.

"Never better. So, Fletcher—"

"All a ruse. The black eye was his idea."

I shook my head. "Brilliant. *Insane*, but brilliant."

"I'll take care of Riaz," Fletcher offered, but I shook my head, pointing my blade straight at the *Fancy*'s captain.

"Roger's mine."

The ammunition's officer grinned and nodded.

And then, together, we charged.

CHAPTER 18

One thing I quickly learned about pirates: They party just about as hard as they fight.

For dinner that night, the school had placed us at the victors' table—a massive table placed at the center of the mess that was overflowing with food and drink and had multiple skeletons scurrying about to cater to our every whim. Spirits were high among the crew, and even as people from other tables began to turn in for the night, our feast looked like it would linger much later into the night.

At one point during the festivities, I received a friendly nudge on my shoulder—the undamaged one—and turned around to find Fletcher. The officer looked a lot better since completing his role in our victorious raid. although his left eye still showed signs of bruising, the fake blood had been washed away, replaced by a cheerful smile.

"Here," he said, prodding me with a tall, unmarked bottle. "Go on, have a sip."

Tentatively, I reached for the bottle and brought it to my lips. The burning sensation of the liquid hit me instantly and, unprepared, I recoiled with a massive spray from my mouth. Several of my crewmates noticed and laughed.

"First time having spice brew, eh?" Fetcher asked after a

chuckle of his own. He motioned for me to take another sip. "First sip always burns. Here, try it again now."

Still feeling the burn from the first sip, I hesitated before eventually complying and taking another.

Sure enough, it offered a completely different experience. The burn was still there, although far more subtle now. My palate was overwhelmed by a delightful combination of vanilla, baking spices, and plenty of fresh ginger. It tasted like a sophisticated—and extremely yummy—ginger ale.

I enjoyed it so much, I took another, much larger swig before returning the bottle back to Fletcher.

"Tasty, right?" he asked me. "Spice brew is a favorite around here. It's not exactly 'permitted' to students, but a number of us still manage to get our hands on some bottles. Me, I like to save mine for celebrations."

And tonight definitely qualified for a celebration. We had earned our first victory of this raids season—the first of *any* crew—and against the defending champs at that. It was fair to say that some partying was due our way. I was just about to ask Fletcher for another taste of the spice brew when I felt another nudge on my shoulder.

"The man of the hour!" Miles proclaimed, hopping into the seat beside me. Pumped up, he raised his hand to deliver an exclamatory pat to my back but caught himself. "Sorry, force of habit. How's your back feeling?"

His question brought the dull ache in my back right back into sharp focus.

"All right, I guess."

I was patched up right after the raid. Six stitches and enough painkillers to numb a kraken. Roberts was outraged when he learned of what the Sharkheads did to me, immediately demanding answers from their captain. Word was that Riaz tried to play innocent, blaming it all on the chaos of battle.

"People were running all over the place, swinging swords left and right, sir," he apparently claimed. "I couldn't keep track of every blow my men landed. If I could take it back, I swear I would, sir."

Yeah right.

Fortunately, it looked like justice would be served. I'd heard whispers during dinner that Riaz was facing a suspension from future Raids for his actions. Seems like his excuses didn't fly well with the teachers.

Miles nodded sympathetically at my response.

"Well, I have something that may lift your spirits," he said to me, his voice lowering into a whisper as he nodded toward a nearby table. "Take a look."

Shooting a glance over my shoulder, I spotted Riaz, still sulking over his meal at this late hour. Surrounded by his usual lackeys, he seemed lost in thought, a large vein pulsing angrily on his forehead as he stared aimlessly at his plate.

I wondered what was causing his brooding more: his looming suspension or the manner of his defeat. After finishing with the other Sharkheads, they joined me in cornering Riaz by the bow, where I delivered the pivotal blow—a strike to the chest that sent him tumbling overboard with a large splash. The move that basically sealed our amazing win.

Miles shook his head in disbelief.

"It's just crazy that we're sitting here now—at the victors' table. I know I seemed confident before the raid, but honestly? I wouldn't have believed it if you told me about this a month ago."

CHAPTER 18

I gave him a look. "A month ago, I didn't even know this place existed."

Miles chuckled. "Okay, okay, you win. Imagine if Captain Kidd could see us now." Then he paused. "Or if Jefferson was here."

"Hear, hear."

"He'd probably be going on about our mathematical chances of winning," Miles reminisced. "What's it called again—probability?"

I gave him a look, impressed.

"Well, well! Look who's been paying attention!"

Miles shrugged. "Had to, now that I don't have Jefferson's notes to copy. Speaking of which, you haven't finished next week's history paper yet, have you?"

I laughed, before raising my glass for a toast.

"To Jefferson."

Miles nodded, a flicker of emotion passing through his eyes. Returning my smile, he raised his cup and met mine in a clink, after which each of us took a long sip.

Probably should've gotten some spice brew for the toast, I thought wistfully.

"Um, am I interrupting?"

Miles and I turned to find Morgan standing before us, her presence immediately bringing me a sense of warmth. She was wearing one of her favorite outfits: a pair of denim dungarees atop a plain white shirt. A simple combo, but one that nevertheless looked fabulous on her.

"Not at all!" Miles exclaimed, gesturing for her to join us. "Come, sit! We were just reliving today's incredible victory."

A warm smile befell Morgan's suntanned face.

"Thanks, but I think I'm going to pass. I'm still pretty

drained from the raid and was actually planning on calling it an early night." Her gaze now hovered over to me, her blue eyes twinkling in the mess's lantern light. "With that said, I was wondering if there was a chance I could steal Barnaby away for a quick chat?"

Her request caught me completely by surprise. I glanced at Miles for guidance, unsure how to respond. The look he shone my way said it all:

Go get her.

"Sure," I replied with a smile. "How about I walk you back to the ship."

"That would be lovely," Morgan replied, her widening smile sending butterflies fluttering in my stomach.

She actually wants to go on a walk with me.

I owed Amelia big time.

A cool evening breeze greeted us on the deck of the *Queen Anne II*. The sun set hours ago, leaving us with a clear sky adorned with a blanket of twinkling stars, like tiny diamonds sparkling in the night. You couldn't have asked for a more peaceful night—especially for a lakeside stroll with your crush.

"So, um…" I cleared my throat, trying to sound confident as my nerves did somersaults inside of me. Let's just say I never had the best of luck with girls in Florida. Maybe it had something to do with all the bullying. Yet here I was, strolling beside the most incredible girl I'd ever met, as skilled with a sword as she was stunning. I didn't want to blow this chance. "What do you want to talk about?"

"Your performance in the raid, obviously," she said with a grin. It didn't seem like she was aware of my nervousness. "You're really starting to make a name for yourself here."

I shrugged, hoping she couldn't see me blush.

CHAPTER 18

"Please. It was all Amelia and Fletcher. Their plan got us the win, not me."

Morgan winked at me. "They weren't the only ones in on the plan."

My eyes widened. "You were in on it too?"

"Who do you think got Fletcher looking like that? I was the one who got the ingredients for the blood. I was also responsible for…um, *high fiving* Fletcher in the face—but only because he insisted."

I shook my head in amazement. "I had no idea. But if you were in on it, can you tell me where the heck Amelia was hiding the whole time?"

Morgan's grin widened. "That's right, you were already down below when she climbed up. Amelia hid in the crow's nest right before we set sail."

I gave her a round of applause. "Genius!"

Morgan chuckled appreciatively. "Thanks, Barnaby. I should probably be saying the same for what you managed to do below decks. I heard all about your little move with the sliding door. Brilliant!"

I shrugged, feeling a mix of pride and humility. "It was all I could do to help. Honestly, I felt like such a coward hiding down there. I wish I'd been up on the deck, fighting with you guys."

Morgan's response was a firm shake of the head.

"No, you obeyed your orders and did exactly what we needed from you. If you were with us above, you probably would've been taken out like the rest of us. Who knows if Amelia and Fletcher would have been able to take out the rest of Riaz's crew without the element of surprise you helped provide."

"That's a good point," I agreed as we reached the end of the deck and started making our way down the gangplank. Save for the occasional teenager on patrol, the docks appeared to be completely empty. The silence it offered was extremely soothing, especially after a hectic day like today.

"So," Morgan went on, "what do you think your parents would say if they saw what you accomplished today?"

"Oh, yeah. My parents. Um…" I shifted uncomfortably. "I never knew them. They left me with my grandmother when I was a baby."

Morgan's hands flew to her mouth, her face stricken with guilt.

"Oh my god, I'm so sorry. That was so dumb of me to ask!"

"No, it's not. You couldn't have known." I gave her a reassuring smile. "It's really fine. Honestly, my grandma did such a great job raising me, I really don't give it so much thought. Please don't feel bad."

"Okay, thanks." Morgan slowly brushed a strand of scarlet hair out of her eyes. "I'm not sure if you know this, but I never knew my parents either. I grew up in the orphanage on Shipwreck Cove. All I have from them is this."

She pulled out a thin gold chain with a wavy, rectangular charm.

I squinted. "Is that…a pirate flag?"

Morgan nodded. "It's the Jolly Roger of Jack Rackham. Or, more accurately, Anne Bonny. She was the one who designed it, after all."

I watched as Morgan touched the charm fondly.

"She was his girlfriend, right?" I recalled. "She left her abusive husband to go pirating with Jack. They're like the most famous pirate couple in history."

CHAPTER 18

Morgan smirked. "I see you've been paying attention in history. But here's something they don't tell you in class. Before they died, Anne and Jack had a child together."

Her grip on the charm tightened, making everything click into place.

"No way. You're a descendant of Anne Bonny and Jack Rackham? That's insane!"

Morgan's smile softened. "The lady who ran the orphanage told me about my heritage on my tenth birthday. She also gave me this necklace, saying it was passed down from Anne herself. She said it was mine to have, a reminder of where I come from and the legacy that I carry."

As the weight of her incredible ancestry sank in, I recalled something Miles had told me after my match with Morgan at the tryouts.

"Is that why you push yourself so hard?" I asked. "All the hours training in the Sword Hall and studying in the library. Do you feel the need to live up to their legacy?"

Morgan bit her lip, then looked up to me and nodded slowly.

"Can you blame me, Barnaby? For all I know, I'm their last living descendant. Honoring their legacy is up to me. Who am I if I don't try to live up to it?"

I nodded in understanding. I could probably relate to her struggle more than most. All I've ever wanted to do was make my grandma proud. Fencing quickly became my way of restoring the legacy my parents had left in tatters. It seemed like Morgan had that same drive, wanting to live up to the lives of her famous ancestors. Maybe that's why I felt such a spark when I first laid my eyes on her.

"I was watching you, you know?" I suddenly blurted out. "From below. You gave Riaz's crew quite the fight. Quite deserving of their legacy if you ask me."

For a moment, I worried that I'd overstepped. But Morgan quickly dismissed my praise with a wave of her hand.

"It was nothing, really," she insisted.

"Are you kidding? You were amazing. You were outnumbered like crazy—and it took them forever to stop you!"

"Still wasn't good enough," she mumbled.

"So then, what *is* good enough?" I asked.

Morgan stopped walking and contemplated the question.

"I guess I—look, there's a lot of pressure with joining a crew, something you probably know a thing or two about yourself."

"Do I ever," I scoffed.

"Exactly. But coming in as quartermaster—the *youngest in school history*, no less—multiplies that pressure by a million. Add that to being a Lost Girl at *Lost Boys High*, where I'm constantly proving myself, and it feels like no matter how hard I work, there's always still more I could do."

"You want to know what I think?" I asked, to which Morgan nodded, intrigued. "I think you've been reading too many of Riaz's letters."

Morgan laughed, and gave me a light punch to the shoulder that was more playful than serious.

I suddenly noticed how close we were standing to one another. The scent of Morgan's perfume, a mix of lilacs and lavender, filled my senses. It got my heart racing.

"Speaking of the devil, the reason I charged at him was because of what he was saying about you," I admitted. "He talked about hurting you to get even with me."

Morgan's eyes widened. "Is that why…"

Her voice trailed off, but by the way her eyes moved to my shoulder, I knew what she was referring to.

CHAPTER 18

"Yeah," I confirmed. "He wanted payback from that time I embarrassed him in the mess."

"What a jerk," she muttered, her gaze meeting mine. "That was really stupid of you, Barnaby. You shouldn't have done that for me."

I said nothing and simply shrugged.

Morgan stepped closer, her hand finding mine.

"But it's probably the sweetest thing anyone's ever done for me," she confessed, her green eyes glittering in the moonlight.

I couldn't tear my gaze away from hers. My heart was racing, and I was close enough to Morgan to notice that hers was as well. With a deep breath, I closed my eyes and leaned in to—

"AYEEEEEEE!"

Morgan and I separated at once. The chilling sound echoed through the night, sending goosebumps rippling through me.

"What in the Seven Seas was that?" she asked, her face pale. "A banshee?"

"It came from the end of the docks." I looked at her. "You don't think—"

She finished the sentence for me, her expression now blanched with dread.

"The *Adventure Galley*!"

We both turned and sprinted in the direction of our ship, our feet pounding against the wooden dock. Memories of Jefferson aboard the *Angel's Wings* replayed in my head.

"Is anyone aboard the ship?" I asked as we ran, my ears still ringing from the horrifying sound.

"Amelia!" Morgan responded quickly. "She left the feast early to catch up on some homework."

Unease flooded through me like a rising tide.

Oh, no. Not again. PLEASE—NOT AGAIN.

"We need to hurry," I expressed with urgency, increasing my pace. Morgan followed suit.

Finally reaching the ship's deck, another bone-chilling shriek pierced the night, shattering our eardrums. My heart raced as I prayed that the sound didn't belong to our beloved captain.

"That came from Amelia's quarters," whispered Morgan, her voice barely audible over our pounding hearts. Fear gripped us both as we exchanged worried glances.

We turned toward the cabin, its door hanging off its hinges, swaying in the night breeze. The sight sent shivers down my spine.

That can't be good.

Together, we darted across the deck and into the room. Morgan's gasp filled the air as we took in the chaos. Furniture lay overturned, clothes strewn across the floor, and papers scattered everywhere. Everything was a mess and out of place—everything, that is, except for the bed. It stood in the far-right corner, perfectly made sheets a stark contrast to the rest of the room. And on the bed, a single figure lay.

Amelia.

At first glance, she appeared unharmed—but I knew better than to approach. Morgan, however, began to cautiously approach the bed.

"Morgan, wait," I called out, but the quartermaster ignored me and continued to approach the still-bodied captain.

"Amelia? It's your first mate, Morgan. Are you okay? What's happened?" Morgan's voice trembled with concern as she reached out toward Amelia.

But as Amelia spoke, the voice twisted into a sinister, all-familiar growl. And with it, those same, wretched words.

CHAPTER 18

"Fifteen men on a dead man's chest."

Suddenly, Amelia's hand shot out, seizing Morgan's neck. And I watched in horror as it began to squeeze.

CHAPTER 19

"Morgan!" I cried, rushing to her aid. I drew my sword as I ran and brought its hilt down hard on my captain's hand. The blow got her to release Morgan—who collapsed upon the floor, gasping for air.

"Captain, stop this!" I yelled. "This isn't you!"

Amelia didn't respond, her expression unreadable. She didn't scream from the blow or appear to be in any sort of pain. Her head just turned toward me, agonizingly slow, and when her eyes met mine, that's when I saw them—liquid silver, just like Jefferson's had been.

"Yo ho ho, and a bottle of rum."

A sword materialized in Amelia's hand as she rose from the bed, her movements now fluid and menacing. Slashing at me, I managed to leap back just in time, the rush of air from the cutlass grazing my skin.

Regaining my footing, I gripped my sword and braced for her next attack. But it never came. Instead, Amelia's gaze turned elsewhere—back to the still-reeling Morgan.

"An' there they lay, all good men. Like break o' day in a boozing ken."

"NO!"

I tore at Amelia and leaped on her. We must have looked

ridiculous—my arms wrapped around my captain's torso as she swatted at me like a bothersome fly. But I held on tight, determined to protect Morgan at all costs. As her strength waned, I felt her knees buckle beneath us, and we crashed into her work desk, sending a wave of pain shooting through my back.

Grimacing, I tried to get myself back on my feet, but Amelia pinned me down, her hands moving in the direction of my throat.

"Yo ho ho, and a bottle of rum."

Struggling to breathe, I squirmed in her grip in a desperate attempt to break free. But Amelia wouldn't let go, her grip as unyielding as the dark force manipulating her.

"Am-el-ia, pleeezze!" I wheezed, tears streaming down my face. "Don't do this!"

No response. Amelia's hands continued to squeeze down on my throat. Her lifeless, milky eyes told me everything I needed to know.

CLANK!

Amelia recoiled from what had struck her, and I took the opportunity to free myself from her grasp. Glancing up, I found Morgan, cutlass in hand.

"Had to return the favor," she shrugged.

Free at last, I rolled onto my chest, gasping for air. Chest heaving, my lungs were on fire, like my throat hadn't known air in eons. Doubling over, I made it to my knees just in time to vomit.

And that's when it happened. Mid-puke, a strange sound by the broken door snapped me out of my misery. I lifted my eyes and saw him—a dark, cloaked figure dashing across the deck. I couldn't believe it.

Anger and adrenaline surged through me. Without hesitation, I wiped the remaining bile off my lips and leaped up in pursuit.

"Barnaby!" Morgan's cry echoed behind me, but I ignored it. There was no way I was letting this guy get away.

I chased him across the entire ship. He had a good head start, but his cloak was starting to slow him down. By the time we reached the docks, I was only a few feet behind. That's when I decided to make my presence known.

"HEY!"

Hearing my voice, the cloaked figure hesitated in his plight, stumbling as he tried to pick up speed. But it was the glance over his shoulder that sealed his fate. It slowed him down just enough for me to tackle him.

THUMP!

If I thought the last tumble had been painful, this one was a whole new level. Wincing, I felt the damp stickiness of my wounds reopening. But all I could focus on was the mysterious stranger lying beneath me.

"Who are you?" I demanded as we wrestled. The hit I delivered had knocked his hood off, and I pivoted myself to get a glimpse of his face. Or should I say, what was *covering* it. He was wearing a mask of some sort—a smooth, silver one with just two eye slits for him to see.

Silver, just like the eyes.

"Why are you doing this?" I asked him. "Why are you attacking students?"

No response came from behind the mask. It was clear he had no intention of speaking. I needed to try something else.

"Help!" I cried out. "HELP! I'VE GOT HIM! IT'S THE ONE WHO ATTACKED JEFFERSON!"

CHAPTER 19

Surely, someone must be around, wandering the docks at this hour—a returning student or a crow on patrol. Someone *had* to hear me.

Beneath me, the stranger continued to resist, his fingers wrapping around my wrists in a desperate attempt to break free.

When he did, the strangest sensation washed over me. I suddenly felt eerily tired, like I was crashing after drinking a case of energy drinks. Only the feeling, it wasn't just exhaustion. It was something deeper, like my mind was being drained of everything that made me who I am—my thoughts, memories, even the pain in my back.

The wooden planks beneath my head felt strangely comforting, like the softest pillow in existence. The world started spinning around me as I struggled to hold on, but my fingers slackened, and I lost my grip on the stranger's cloak.

No! He's getting away! I told myself, urging my body to go after him. But I was too tired, my body too weak...

As darkness closed in around me, I caught one last glimpse of the intruder staring directly at me, his silver mask gleaming in the dim light.

And then, everything dissolved into darkness.

Waking up was a mission in itself.

I felt like I'd just gotten out of a coma. Drained to the core, a relentless pounding echoed through my head, making even the simplest movements feel like I was climbing a mountain. I felt so weak, I couldn't even muster the strength to massage my throbbing temple. Frankly, it took everything I had just to keep my eyes open, which at least helped me figure out where in the Seven Seas I was.

The massive mahogany desk. The throne-like chair pushed in behind it. I was back in Blackbeard's cabin.

A few minutes passed before I heard the cabin door creak open. I was still too weak to roll over and face the newcomer, but I didn't need to; Blackbeard's unmistakable voice gave him away.

"Remarkable, isn't it?" Blackbeard said, seemingly aware of my awakening. "You've been here less than two months and already garnered more attention from me than any other student in the last fifty years. What have ye to say to that?"

"Uh...thanks?" I mumbled weakly.

Without warning, the pounding in my head intensified, causing me to wince. Swearing under my breath, I finally managed to clutch my temple. Blackbeard, meanwhile, pulled up one of the armchairs beside the bed.

"What happened to me?"

"You were attacked," Blackbeard explained, "by the same culprit responsible for the attacks on Mr. Monroe and now, unfortunately, Captain Ash."

A lump formed in my throat.

"So...am I...like them?"

Blackbeard rolled his eyes. "If you were, would I be keeping you in my cabin to rest?"

I blushed. "No, you wouldn't. But I'm not back on my ship either." I locked eyes with Blackbeard. "You don't know what to do with me yet, do you?"

Blackbeard grunted what I could only think meant "correct."

"Unlike the others, you have yet to show any of the symptoms. Only time will tell if you've truly avoided their fate."

"And what about Morgan?" I asked, my voice laced with

concern.

Blackbeard nodded and I let out a massive sigh of relief.

"I've just come from visiting her. She's in med bay being tended to. She's still shaken up from tonight's events, but she'll be fine. Just a few bruises around her neck to attend to, and she'll be good to go."

Thank God.

I felt guilty about leaving her back on the ship to deal with Amelia on her own, but hopefully she understood why I'd done so.

Another bolt of pain shot through me, this time from the fresh trail of stitches in my back. Whatever pain relief they gave me must've worn off.

"I wanted to offer my apologies for the actions of Captain Riaz and his crew," Blackbeard expressed. "Rest assured, we are devoted to inquiring further into the incident."

I appreciated the gesture but quickly shook my head.

"I appreciate the gesture, but I'd prefer if you allocate those resources toward finding the culprit behind these attacks. Riaz's actions mean nothing to me," I stated firmly. Pausing for a moment, I debated whether to voice my suspicions. "Unless Riaz is somehow involved in this."

Blackbeard raised an eyebrow. "You suspect Captain Riaz of committing these attacks?"

I shrugged. "It wouldn't be beneath him, considering everything else he's done. He's hated me since the day I arrived, and it's my friend and my captain who've been attacked."

"Do you have any proof to support your claims?"

I hesitated. "Not exactly. But I did spot him earlier at dinner. He seemed…irritated, to say the least. He could be up to something."

"Maybe," Blackbeard agreed. "But I've actually already questioned Riaz about any potential involvement in tonight's attack. After all, he did suffer a major defeat to Captain Ash herself. But he was still in the mess when it happened and appeared to have no knowledge of the attack."

"He could still be involved," I persisted. "He still wants revenge. He still wants to cause harm. I honestly don't understand why you allow him to be captain."

Blackbeard leveled me with an intense gaze, causing me to second-guess my words.

"Believe me, Barnaby, there's a reason Roger Riaz is one of our captains," he assured me sternly. "Not everyone in this school is as friendly and easygoing as that curly-haired pal of yours. I stand by what I said that night you barged into my cabin. We take in *anyone* who deserves a second chance, no matter the circumstances. But some of our more...*aggressive* students require specific mentorship that only someone like Captain Riaz can provide. They see themselves in him and respect him for what he's managed to achieve for himself. He's worked extremely hard to earn their respect and helps keeps them in line for us."

This information struck me by surprise. I'd only ever seen Riaz as a bully, but perhaps there was more to his cruel demeanor than met the eye. I couldn't help but wonder what in his past had shaped him to take on such a role.

"Okay, so if Riaz isn't behind the attack, then who is?" I asked.

"That," Blackbeard went on, "is the other reason why you're here."

The realization hit me. "You want to know if I saw him. If I recognized him."

CHAPTER 19

Blackbeard nodded in silent confirmation.

I bit my lip. "I'm afraid I didn't see much, sir. He was wearing a cloak from head to toe. To be honest, I'm not even sure it's a 'he' we're dealing with."

"You didn't catch a look at the attacker's face?"

I shook my head, downcast. "I'm really sorry, sir. But I'm afraid whoever it was had it covered with a mask—a *silver* mask."

The moment the words "silver mask" left my lips, Blackbeard erupted from his seat. With a thunderous roar, he flung the armchair across the cabin. I watched the whole scene speechless.

"SILVER! Of all things!" His piercing gaze bore into mine, demanding certainty. "Barnaby, are you absolutely sure that the mask was silver?"

His urgency gripped me.

"Aye, sir, I'm sure. But what does it mean? Does it have something to do with the color their eyes turned?"

Blackbeard let out a dark laugh. "Oh, Barnaby. It means so much more than that."

Without another word, Blackbeard began pacing frantically around the room. The eyes of the most legendary pirate to ever sail the Seven Seas were ablaze with what astonishingly appeared to be dread.

"This mask, it's a symbol," he explained with urgency. "A symbol known to every pirate of yore. The mask you described belonged to someone named Davy Jones."

He spoke the name with a thundering intensity, like the nine letters could be used as a weapon.

"You mean the guy with the tentacles on his face?"

Blackbeard frowned, confused. "What?"

"Never mind," I replied quickly. "So, what's the big deal with this guy?"

As soon as the question escaped my lips, an icy chill enveloped my body, sending shivers down my spine. The cabin suddenly plunged into darkness as a frosty gust of wind swept through, extinguishing the room's lantern light and casting the room with shadows.

Chill out, Barnaby, it's just some wind, I told myself in an attempt to calm my rising sense of unease.

"According to the ancient legends," Blackbeard's voice cut through the eerie silence, "the devil himself once appointed a man named Davy Jones to ferry sailors' souls to the afterlife. Some believe he guided them gently, while others claim he ripped their souls from their bodies with his bare hands. But one thing remains consistent in all accounts—that wretched, silver mask."

The wind outside howled against the windows with increasing ferocity, drowning out my thoughts. Summoning every ounce of courage, I pressed on with another question.

"And what about those words they keep saying? You seemed to recognize them that other night."

"They stem from an old sea shanty known as 'The Derelict,'" Blackbeard explained, his tone grave. "It recounts a harrowing tale of a shipwreck, where each sailor met a gruesome demise in their own unique manner. It used to be sung by pirate crews all across the Seven Seas."

A shudder racked my body from this revelation. "So, you believe this shanty's got something to do with Davy Jones?"

Blackbeard's gaze met mine, his response grim. "Legend is that he wrote the damn thing."

I held his gaze steadily.

CHAPTER 19

"That's why you were taken aback that night," I deduced. "You suspected Jones might be behind Jefferson's attack, didn't you?"

"I didn't want to believe it," Blackbeard responded, nodding. "You have to understand, Barnaby—nobody's seen Davy Jones in *centuries*."

"Why?" I asked. "What happened to him?"

Blackbeard paused, as if choosing his next words carefully.

"He disappeared. According to the legends, Jones grew corrupt and started using his powers for himself. Reanimating corpses with the souls he stole, he eventually collected enough to create a *crew of the undead*. But then, one day, the sightings of him just…ended. Nobody's seen Jones in over four hundred years. Until tonight, I always thought all of it to be nothing but stories. But now…"

Blackbeard gripped my shoulders, urgency in his voice. "Barnaby," he went on, "you must promise me that you won't tell anyone what we've discussed tonight. It was one thing for students to find out about Jefferson, but if they hear about this—it could be the *end* for things on the island. Promise me, you will not tell anyone about what you've heard tonight."

I took a deep breath, knowing quite well the weight of such a secret. I also knew the power of the person standing before me requesting it.

"All right, Blackbeard, I swear. I won't tell a soul."

CHAPTER 20

Per Blackbeard's strict orders, I spent the remainder of the night cooped up in his cabin. He also excused me from all morning classes to grant me more time to recover, informing me that the stitches in my back would only be removed on Thursday. That news stunk, as it meant no sword fighting until then.

Like the last time I was in this situation, I tried to use the opportunity to gain some extra shuteye, but the lack of blinds on the cabin windows thwarted my plans. The room was flooded with sunlight by breakfast, so I gave up on sleep and headed down to eat.

Maybe I'll see Miles there, I thought wistfully. I needed to share everything Blackbeard and I discussed last night.

However, to my dismay, I found our usual table in the mess empty.

Oh well. Guess I'll have to tell Miles another time.

Yeah, yeah, I'm well aware that by confiding in Miles, I'd be breaking my promise to Blackbeard. But I made that promise with the understanding that my friend deserved to know what was going on. After all, it's his best friend sitting in the brig. It just didn't feel right to keep him in the dark.

Bones arrived as I sat down, and I ordered scrambled eggs

and toast. The food came quickly, along with a hefty bonus serving of bacon, which I devoured eagerly. My body craved nourishment after such a draining night.

"Well, you definitely look better than expected."

The voice was lower than Miles's and devoid of his signature enthusiasm. Looking up, I found myself locking eyes with my crewmate Travis.

"I beg your pardon?"

Travis tucked his hands into the pockets of his jeans. "Word is you were attacked last night by an animal or something," he explained. "The crow who heard your cries for help and found you barely breathing, and said that your back was coated in blood." His brown eyes narrowed pryingly. "So, what *really* happened?"

"Erm..." I hesitated, glancing around the mess, spotting tables from other crews looking our way. Clearly, he wasn't the only one curious.

Dang, does the whole school really know?

Not wanting to fuel their suspicions, I replied with a quick, casual nod.

"I slipped on a wet part of the docks. Reopened the wound in my back from the raids. Honestly, it looked worse than it really was."

Travis cocked his head to the side skeptically, his long black hair falling over his eyes. "You just...*slipped*?"

"What, you don't believe me?" I challenged him, rising from my seat to confront him head-on. More eyes around the mess turned in our direction.

Travis quickly took a step back, the stark red flushing on his face a contrast to his pale skin. "No, I—I'm sorry. It's just that...you know what, never mind. I just came over to see if you were all right—and to tell you about the vote this afternoon."

Now it was my turn to be curious.

"Vote? What vote?"

Travis's expression softened. "For interim captain. Surely you've heard by now about Amelia?"

Of course I had. But I shook my head, eager to hear what the rumor mill was churning out.

"No, I haven't. I must've missed it after my fall—I was out for a while. So wait, what happened?"

Travis bit his lip. "So, nobody seems to know for sure, but the talk is that she came down with some kind of illness. They took her away last night and we haven't heard from her since."

An illness, huh? Well, that's one way for Blackbeard to keep Amelia "quarantined" as long as he needs, I thought.

I continued to play along, dropping my jaw in feigned shock. "What! But the raids!"

"I know!" Travis threw up his hands, expressing disappointment. "As if losing Jefferson wasn't enough of a hit! Anyways, the vote's happening on the *Galley* right before lunch. Blackbeard gave us all the period off to hold it. Don't be late!"

Believe me, Travis, I wouldn't miss it for the world.

Travis left soon after that. With the vote for interim captain now looming, I decided to spend the rest of the free morning I had left on a walk and clear my head.

I winced as I stepped outside, the bright, blinding sun piercing through a scatter of clouds. Before long, I was off the *Queene Anne II*, embarking down the very path I'd taken with Morgan just hours ago. Just thinking about her and the moment we shared—or *almost* did—was enough to turn my mind to jelly.

CHAPTER 20

Boy how the difference of a few seconds could've changed everything. I knew how I felt about Morgan, and last night, I was on the brink of discovering if she felt the same way. But now...all I could do was wonder:

Did she really feel the same way about me?
Was she really going to kiss me back?
And what was I supposed to say when I saw her next?

That would most likely be at the upcoming vote, now taking place in less than an hour. Gosh, I needed to come up with something fast.

And then, as I passed the place on the docks where Morgan grabbed my hand, it hit me. The perfect solution.

Why don't I just vote for Morgan to be captain?

It made perfect sense. Morgan had just opened up to me with regards to how important it was for her to succeed, to honor her ancestors' legacy. Voting for her as interim captain, it wouldn't just put her on the path to do just that, but it would also show how much I believed in her abilities to succeed. And so, it was decided: I'd vote for Morgan and, afterward, tell her how I felt about her—if I could even muster up the courage to do so. After all, it would mark the first time I ever told a girl I liked her.

A sudden uproar seized my attention. It came from the lake, where a sloop of freshies was departing for a sailing lesson. It wasn't difficult to tell that they were freshies—the violent, clumsy swerves the ship was taking resembled the veering of someone driving a car for the first time.

I couldn't help but compare their efforts to my first experience in sailing class. While my entire class arrived prepared with paper puke bags, I found myself remarkably comfortable at the helm, guiding the vessel across the lake with surprising ease. When asked for an explanation by the teacher—who was just as stunned as my classmates—I just shrugged. The wheel, it just felt as natural in my hands as a sword. It was like I'd been born to steer a ship.

Pausing to observe the scene on the lake, I took a moment to also marvel at all the iconic vessels dotting the shoreline—the *Queen Anne's Revenge*, the *Adventure Galley*, the *Fancy*, and plenty of others I'd studied in history class. It was truly incredible, the treasure trove of naval history that was nestled into this lake. I'm not sure even a dozen museums would be enough to house them all.

I looked back to this tranquil moment—peacefully wandering the school grounds, thinking of various ways to impress a girl I liked—and wished I savored it just a bit more, for I had no idea the avalanche of events that were cascading my way.

I had no idea that such a sunny, beautiful morning was about to turn into one of the worst of my life.

It all started with the vote.

Arriving at the *Adventure Galley*, I could see that the majority of the crew had already arrived. They all sat on their beds, so I followed suit, smiling when I spotted Miles by his.

"Hey, buddy! Missed you at breakfast today. There's so much I've got to tell you!"

I waited for Miles's response, eager to catch up with him. But for whatever reason, he seemed distant, his eyes staring blankly ahead. He remained unresponsive until I waved a hand in front of his face.

"Earth to Miles—everything okay?"

"Huh? Oh, yeah...everything's fine," he finally replied. But

CHAPTER 20

something seemed off. His usual cheerfulness was gone, and he sat slouched over with clenched fists, barely acknowledging me.

Before I could ask what was wrong, Fletcher called for silence to get the meeting going.

"All right, so..." The ammunition's officer's voice trailed off and he looked uneasy. He struggled to speak, and I could tell he wasn't the only one having a tough time.

The celebratory energy encompassing everybody was long gone. There were no smiles or laughter, just a somber mood throughout. I heard sniffles, and when I looked over, I saw Brent, our bosun, being comforted by friends.

Maybe this is why Miles seemed so upset, I thought.

After a while, Fletcher managed to start again.

"Um...you all know why we're here. I know nobody's feeling great about this, but we've got our next raid in two weeks, and in order to compete, we need a captain to lead us. Of course, once Amelia recovers from her...*illness*, she'll immediately reclaim control, but in the meantime, we need someone to take the helm." Fletcher paused as he anxiously glanced around the room. "So...who would like to nominate themselves for interim captain?"

Glancing around, only now did I realize that Morgan was missing. According to Blackbeard, she should've been released from med bay by now. Whatever the reason for her absence, it was definitely throwing a wrench at my plans.

All eyes in the galley darted around, waiting to see who would speak first.

Imagine my surprise—and everyone else's—when Miles was the one to stand up.

Miles for captain? Is THAT why he seemed so tense?

I watched as Miles cleared his throat. "I'm not nominating myself for captain," he began, turning to Fletcher. "But there's something I need to say to the crew before we go any further."

Fletcher hesitated, clearly caught off guard by Miles's request. He wasn't alone. Judging by the looks around the room, no one seemed to know what to expect. Something was clearly wrong.

"Um, sure, Miles. The floor is yours."

Miles nodded his thanks and took a deep breath, as if gathering strength for what he was about to say. When he spoke, his usually lively voice was now monotone, his smile replaced by a somber expression.

"My brother is dead."

The four words hit the galley like a bomb. Gasps rippled through the room as hands flew to cover gaping mouths. Without hesitation, Fletcher and I rushed from our spots to offer Miles our support, but he immediately brushed us off. And he wasn't done speaking yet.

"I was informed of his passing after supper last night by a crow returning from the mainland. As some of you already know, my brother himself was a crow, and had been off the grid for some time. It's not something uncommon amongst crows, but after a while, several of his friends got worried and felt that it was time to look for him. It was one of them who gave me this."

Holding our breaths, we watched as Miles withdrew, of all things, a newspaper from his jacket. Slowly unfolding it, a twist of nerves gripped my stomach when I spotted the logo at the top—the *Miami Herald*. As I peered closer, my heart lurched when I found my own face staring back at me from the front page.

CHAPTER 20

Right away, I realized what was happening.

No, it can't be. There's no way...

Knots formed in my stomach as Miles raised the paper and began to read.

"FUGITIVE BOY STILL ON THE RUN. Officials are continuing their investigation into the disappearance of local boy Barnaby Stump, age thirteen. Witnesses reported sighting him on the outskirts of his hometown suburbs, accompanied by a second, older delinquent, allegedly armed with razor-sharp swords. Stump was en route to the county police precinct, where he was to be detained and questioned regarding his involvement in the assault and murder of another boy at a local fencing tournament. The victim, identified as Mason Whittaker, age nineteen, was on a student visa from Bermuda—"

My insides melted when Miles stopped reading and looked at me. His eyes glared a scorching red, undoubtedly from a sleepless night of mourning.

"Since the day you arrived, I've had your back," he spat bitterly at me. "When the crew asked about your past, I was the one who told them to mind their own business. After all, you never told *me*." Miles shook his head incredulously. "But now I see...you kept it a secret for a reason."

"Miles," I interjected, my voice trembling with a whirlwind of emotions, "I swear to you, on my *grandfather's grave*, that I never meant any harm to your brother. I was the one who was attacked, and Mason had a mask on at the time, so there was no way—"

"LIES!" bellowed Miles. "The article states that nobody saw him move against you, only witnessing *you* standing over him with a bloody sword. And to think...I praised your swordsmanship..."

He spat on the ground.

Desperate, I took a step forward and tried to reach out for the boy I'd considered one of the greatest friends I've ever made. Everything I'd built in the last month was crumbling before my eyes.

"Miles, you have to believe me—"

"GET AWAY FROM ME!" he shrieked. Suddenly, Fletcher appeared at my side, gently but firmly holding me back.

"Give him some space, Barnaby," he whispered in my ear.

Jeez—where was Amelia when we needed her?

"What in the Seven Seas is going on here?"

I whirled around, and a whole new array of emotions flooded through me when I found Morgan standing there.

"I just got released from med bay," she explained, "but I heard your shouting all the way from the docks. What are you guys yelling about?"

Not saying a single word, Miles walked past me and handed the newspaper to Morgan. Eyebrow raised, she accepted the paper with confusion—and gasped after five seconds of reading.

"Is this true?" she asked me.

"Morgan, I can explain," I hurried to say. "It's not what you think."

"Not what you think?" Miles demanded. "You killed my brother!"

"So...what do you want us to do about it?" one of our crewmates chimed in—Travis, of course.

Fuming, Miles marched over to Travis and fixed him with a piercing stare.

"I want him off this ship."

CHAPTER 20

A hushed silence enveloped the galley. And then, one by one, all eyes shifted toward Fletcher. It seemed like everyone was waiting for his response. He had been the one leading the meeting, after all.

Suddenly, Fletcher's grip on me loosened. I watched, crestfallen, as he crossed the galley to stand with Miles.

"Fletcher," I sniffled, tears now streaming down my face. "I'm not a killer. You have to believe me—"

For a brief second, Fletcher seemed to hesitate. But after a short sigh, he continued crossing the floor, laying a hand on Miles's shoulder when he reached him.

One by one, my crewmates abandoned my side, aligning themselves with Miles. Tears continued to cascade down my cheeks as I watched them go.

Now, it was just Morgan and me on my side of the galley.

"Morgan, you have to believe me," I pleaded. "I would *never* kill someone. Please, search your heart, you have to see this!"

Morgan met my gaze, and I could see that tears now glistened in her eyes as well.

"I know you wouldn't, Barnaby," she reassured me softly.

For a moment, hope shimmered within me.

"So don't believe that's the reason I'm doing *this*."

And, without another word, Morgan stepped across to Miles's side of the galley.

Miles stared at me, a fiery vindication in his eyes.

"Barnaby Stump, you are hereby removed from the *Adventure Galley* for the murder of my brother," he declared, satisfaction in his words. And then, under his breath, I heard him hiss, "Just wait until the rest of the school hears about this."

CHAPTER 21

It was official—I had hit rock bottom.

The vote aboard the *Adventure Galley* plunged my life into a whirlwind of turmoil, like a scene from those romcoms where everything goes wrong for one of the movie's characters. You know, the ones where they look so sad and alone?

That was basically my life now. One miserable series of events after another.

First, there was my walk of shame off the *Galley*, my former crew watching in silence as I carted my belongings off the ship. Fortunately, I didn't have that much, so it was pretty brief—just my sword, backpack, and the linens and clothes Miles had gathered for me. Unsure if it was mine to keep, I left my copy of *The Rise and Fall of William Kidd* on the ship. Hopefully it will impact its next reader as much as it had me.

From that moment on, my nights were spent aboard *The Leaky Bucket*. Its amenities were as drab and depressing as its name. Painted a monotone gray, it was home to all the crewless students, mostly freshies. But even there, it wasn't long before I was all but excommunicated. Word traveled fast, and by dinner, everyone knew of my role in the death of Miles's brother.

CHAPTER 21

The hits just kept on coming. In class, nobody wanted to work with me, let alone talk to me. The same thing happened in the mess hall, where I ended up eating alone every day.

But what could I expect? To everyone, I was a murderer, and the evidence against me seemed insurmountable. I felt I had no choice but to swallow the pill and move on. The isolation was hard, but I could handle it—I was used to being an outsider. What really ate me up was the guilt I felt every time I saw members of my crew. I could see it in their eyes—they saw me as not only a killer but a downright liar as well.

It didn't help that I couldn't join them in the raids anymore. It was torture to watch them get defeated by, of all crews, the Gentleman Pirates. Finishing last in the standings for three straight years, their patron pirate, Stede Bonnet, was as a wealthy landowner who got bored and turned to piracy. He was also known for being, quite literally, the lamest pirate in history—I'm not even sure he ever even successfully raided a ship. Losing to a crew like that made it feel like all the momentum from the victory over Riaz had all but completely evaporated.

All thanks to me.

And if that guilt was bad, being around Miles was even worse. Just knowing he wanted me dead kept my insides twisted inside out. I caught him glancing my way several times, but any attempt to speak to him was met with silence. He'd just jerk his head away, denying my existence.

And rightfully so.

But with Miles all but out of my life now, I needed to find a new sparring partner. The following Monday, Roberts asked the class if anybody would be willing to pair up with me. Sure enough, there wasn't a single volunteer.

"Very well," he nodded curtly. "I guess Barnaby will be sparring with me then."

Hearing this, my spirits rose higher than they had in over a week. *Training with the Sword Master himself?* Was I finally catching a break?

Alas, sparring with Roberts proved to be a trial unlike any I'd faced at the school thus far. Roberts fought with a finesse and speed that surpassed every opponent I'd faced in his class and the raids. What made matters worse was Roberts's stoic silence, speaking only when absolutely necessary.

"Again," he commanded, when I stopped once to catch my breath after fending off a relentless barrage of attacks. "Your opponent will never allow you to rest."

When the lesson finally came to an end, I was caked in sweat from head to toe. I opened my mouth to say something to Roberts, but he was already halfway up the stairs toward the exit. Defeated, I let out a resigned sigh and I gathered my belongings to leave as well.

"Hey, Barnaby," a familiar voice called out to me in the hallway.

A mixture of emotions surged through me as I turned to face her. "What do you want, Morgan?"

Morgan seemed taken aback by my bluntness, hesitating before answering.

"Well…" she began tentatively, "I was wondering if you'd like to hang out today? We could skip class and take a stroll around the lake. What do you say?"

What do I say, Morgan? I'm not sure you want to hear what I REALLY have to say.

For now, however, I kept it to myself and responded with a terse nod.

CHAPTER 21

"Thanks for the offer, but I think I'll pass."

Without waiting for Morgan's reaction, I turned and briskly walked off toward my next class.

"Wait—Barnaby!"

Despite her calling after me, I refused to slow down. It wasn't until halfway down the stairs to the next level that I felt her hand grip me. Morgan stood a couple of steps above me, breathing heavily.

"What, Morgan?" I snapped, finding it hard to mask my true feelings.

Morgan flinched at my response.

"I—I just wanted to see if everything was all right with you," she confessed.

Boy, was I close to letting it all out there. And no, I'm not talking about the guilt I felt toward Miles—I'm referring to the betrayal I felt that day on the *Adventure Galley* from *her*. I'd been moments away from affirming my feelings to her, more than hopeful that she felt the same way. But apparently that wasn't the case. Afterall, how could it be if she hadn't even been willing to hear my side of the story?

And where the heck were you this past week when I've been all alone, I asked myself bitterly. *Where were you when I needed you?*

"I'm fine," I said through gritted teeth. "I'm just...busy."

I watched as Morgan's shoulders slumped, her disappointment on full display.

"Oh, okay. Another time then...when you're not...*busy*."

"Ah, don't look so glum, Morgan," sneered a voice to our left. It was Riaz. "If the *murderer*'s too busy to take you on a walk, I'll happily volunteer."

"Oh, shut up, Riaz," Morgan shot back, her cheeks crimson

with anger. "You don't know what you're talking about."

Riaz shook his head disapprovingly at Morgan. "I honestly expected better from you," he admitted. When Morgan didn't respond, Riaz raised an eyebrow at her, feigning skepticism. "What, you don't find it one bit suspicious that just a week after Barnaby here arrives and befriends Jefferson, the poor boy turns up all zombified? No? Not even after it happened *again* when he joined your crew?" Riaz made a *tut-tut* sound. "Poor Amelia, putting all her faith in Barnaby Stump. Look where it got her—a cell next to Jefferson in the brig."

All around us, people had stopped walking to class and began watching the scene unfolding before them.

"Amelia's just sick," Morgan insisted, although the tremor in her voice betrayed her claim. "You don't know what you're saying."

Riaz scoffed, dismissing Morgan's answer with a wave of his hand. When he spoke, his voice was low so only we could hear him. "C'mon, Morgan, you and I both know that's just a lie Blackbeard made to stop this place from turning upside down. You saw her with your own eyes. You know there's a reason she's locked up with Jefferson. And I think the very reason is standing next to you." Riaz's eyes locked onto me now, his gaze sharp and accusing. "The only plague to strike our school is you, Barnaby Stump."

Morgan's lips pressed into a thin line as she struggled to produce a response. Meanwhile, I'd reached my breaking point. I could live with Miles loathing me, Morgan rejecting me, and Roberts's silence, but Riaz was crazy if he thought I was going to take any flak from a punk like him.

With a swift motion, I unsheathed my sword and lunged at the Sharkhead captain. About a dozen people gasped as I

CHAPTER 21

closed in on him, but just before I could land a strike, Riaz dodged the blow with a quick sidestep.

"Finally, a rematch!" Riaz taunted, drawing his own sword in response. But before either of us could make another move, we were forcefully restrained. Riaz was pinned to the wall by none other than the Sword Master himself, while *Reed* of all people held me back on the other side.

"Don't do it, Barnaby," my crow urged me. "It's not worth it."

Meanwhile, Riaz was getting an earful from Roberts.

"Enough, Roger! I expect better from a captain such as yourself!" he admonished the boy sternly.

"But he deserves it!" Riaz's voice turned shrill. "I'm just trying to look out for my crew. Barnaby here's brought nothing but disaster to this school."

"A wild accusation. Unless you want Blackbeard to hear about it, I don't want to see you anywhere near this student!" Roberts cast a warning glance at me as well. "The same goes for you, Barnaby."

"Come on, Barnaby," Reed pleaded, tugging at me. "Time to leave."

"Don't you all have class!" Roberts called out to straggling onlookers. "Move along!"

Reed began pulling me away but was stopped by Morgan. The crow motioned for her to stay back.

"He clearly needs time away from all this. Can you respect that?" Reed asked, his voice soft but firm.

Still shaking from the ordeal, Morgan managed a brief nod, her concern still etched on her face.

"Thanks." Reed said to her.

Escaping the remaining disquieted stares in the stairwell,

Reed led me back up to the floor of the Sword Hall and the mess. Once we were a healthy distance away from any prying eyes and ears, he stopped and turned to me.

"What the heck is wrong with you!" he demanded. "Do you have some desire to get yourself thrown into the brig or something?"

I threw my hands in frustration. "What does it matter, Reed? At least there, I'd have Amelia and Jefferson for company."

"You don't actually mean that," Reed insisted.

"I do!" I exclaimed. "Heck, I'm even more imprisoned here! Everybody hates me and won't speak to me—and I couldn't even freaking leave if I wanted to!"

Reed paused and bit his lip.

"Well," he began slowly, "what if you *could*?"

My eyes widened, and now it was Reed being seized by the shirt and shoved into the wall.

"What are you talking about, Reed?"

Reed swallowed hard. "I'm saying that I—I feel bad about all of this. I truly thought that bringing you here would make things better for you. And for a while they were, but now…this is just unfair. You can't live like this forever."

"So? What is there to do about it?" I pressed.

Nervous, Reed's head darted around to ensure that nobody was listening in.

"The crows—they're leaving again for the mainland on Saturday morning. If you want, I can try to sneak you aboard the *Angel's Wings* and take you back to Florida. Most of the guards are friends of mine. Once in Florida you'll be on your own but at least you'll be home. And you'll have your grandma, I guess."

I was stunned. With the *Angel's Wings* so profoundly

guarded, I'd thrown out any idea of attempting to go back. My chances of seeing Grandma in the near future seemed next to none. Was Reed really offering me a ticket home?

"Um, I'll have to think about it," I sputtered in reply, a million thoughts buzzing through my mind.

Reed nodded understandingly, using the opportunity to slide out of my grasp.

"I understand," he said. "Way I see it, you've got a bit more than a day to decide. I'm sorry I can't give you more time. But when you're ready, tell me what you've decided."

And with that, he turned and left.

CHAPTER 22

What to do...what to do...

The question continued to pinball through my head, echoing louder each time. Alone in the aftermath of supper, with the final diners trickling out of the mess, the weight of my impending decision pressed down on me.

My brain had been in overdrive ever since Reed dropped that bombshell on me. The knowledge that there existed a potential way home, and that I had only a little over twenty-four hours to decide, consumed me as I tried to find my bearings and make the right choice. I even went ahead and skipped class for some solitary focus time. But despite all of that, I was still no closer to a decision.

I'd laid out the pros and cons countless times. Accepting Reed's offer meant returning to Florida, but it also meant confronting the mess I'd left behind, with no guarantee if it could be resolved. Leaving would also mean forfeiting everything I'd come to cherish—the exhilarating sword fighting classes, the pulse-pounding raids, and the bonds forged with my crewmates, even if I was currently lacking in that department. Was the allure of seeing my grandma again worth sacrificing the life I had begun to build here?

CHAPTER 22

I sighed, frustration bubbling within me as I wrestled with my indecision. Lost in my thoughts, I failed to notice the skeleton approaching to collect my untouched plate—the bombshell dropped by Reed all but robbing me of my appetite.

A small smile tugged at my lips when I spotted the tiny X etched on the skeleton's ribcage. It soon faded when I recognized the next table Bones went to clear. Despite all the laughter and stories I shared with Miles and my former mates at that table, it felt wrong to sit there now. It seemed Miles felt the same way, as he now opted to take his meals elsewhere. The table now lay unused, as if deemed *cursed* by the school.

Not unlike how they saw me.

I swore under my breath as a wave of loneliness crashed over me. Until now, I'd managed to sidestep this feeling, but with no one to lean on for support, the weight of solitude bore down on me. With no grandmother to turn to, no crewmate or Sword Master to call upon for advice, I was truly left to untangle this mess alone

Well, and Morgan, a voice unwelcomingly chimed in my head. She'd seemed more than willing to help, but even if I was ready to forgive her—still a pretty sizable "if" —I wasn't sure if this was the right conversation to have with her. Especially when she was technically one of the reasons to stay.

So then...if not Morgan, then who?

As I let out another hopeless sigh, my gaze fell on another skeleton passing by. Unlike Bones, there was no X marked on his ribs, but something else caught my eye—a rusted manacle encircling its shinbone. Imagining whatever murky cell this poor soul must've spent his last days in sent shivers down my back.

But as I pondered this, a spark of realization lit within me. There *was* one person I hadn't considered. The road to reach them wouldn't be easy though. I'd need to be smart about it—and have plenty of luck.

But what did I really have to lose?

An hour dragged by before I found myself back aboard the *Queen Anne II*. Anticipation built in my chest as I descended flight after flight of stairs. Eventually, I reached a small, unmarked wooden door, a lone lantern hung above to illuminate the small landing.

I quickly recognized the brown-eyed, curly-haired guard on duty. It was the same crow who'd called out to Reed in the mess, way back on my first night at Lost Boys High.

"Can I help you?" he asked as I approached.

I nodded, trying to keep my nerves in check. "I'm here to visit a friend of mine. She's been staying down here for about a week now. Ring any bells?"

Recognition flicked in the guard's eyes. Unfortunately, he shook his head at my request.

"I do, but entry into the brig is forbidden without written permission from a teacher. Do you have that?"

"Nope."

"Then I'm afraid I can't let you in," he stated matter-of-factly. "Sorry."

I shrugged like it wasn't that big of a deal—even though my heart was racing.

Keep it cool, Barnaby.

Without another word, I lowered my bag and reached into it. Sensing danger, the guard's hand twitched toward his sword,

CHAPTER 22

but he froze when he saw the unmarked bottle I withdrew a moment later.

"Would you consider *this* as written permission?" I proposed.

Nodding so fast his head was basically a blur, the older boy eagerly shot out a hand to accept the bottle, but I quickly yanked it out of reach.

"Uh uh." I wagged a finger at him. "First let me in, and then you can have your reward."

Without missing a beat, the guard produced a ring of keys and inserted one of them into the door. As he swung it open, he shot me a cautious glance.

"To be clear, you were never here."

"Wouldn't have it any other way," I reassured him as we entered the brig.

The scene before me was surprisingly cleaner and brighter than I imagined it to be. No smelly sewage or nibbling rats in sight. Just another well-lit, wooden-walled hallway.

I did notice some differences to the rest of the ship. The hallway was narrower, and instead of the doors like they had above for classrooms, metallic meal ports were evenly spaced along the walls. Still, there was nothing grim or horrifying about the place at all.

I was led over to the third meal port on the right.

"Your captain's in there," he said, gesturing to the space. "Now, the bottle please."

I shook my head. The spice brew was my only leverage. I wasn't giving it up until I got what I came for. "Open up first."

With a sigh, the guard selected another key and inserted it into a small, almost invisible hole in the wall. With a quick twist and a push, the section opened inward like a secret door.

"You've got fifteen minutes," he instructed me. "Also, I've got to lock you in. If anything happens, well...*yell*, I guess. I should get to you in time—hopefully."

"Reassuring," I noted, handing over the spice brew after stepping inside. "Thanks."

His response was a curt nod before slamming the door in my face.

Turning around, I got my first look at the cell's interior, which was way above expectations. Instead of a dreary prison cell, the room resembled a small single-room apartment, furnished with everything from a table and chairs to a wardrobe full of clothes.

The lone occupant didn't look too shabby either. Clad in shorts and a dark gray sweatshirt emblazoned with the Jolly Roger of Lost Boys High, she sat comfortably on her plush bed, a book opened in her lap.

"Barnaby," Amelia closed her book and greeted me with a smile. "So good to see you."

I couldn't help but smile at my former captain's welcome. It had been so long since somebody had actually seemed happy to see me.

"Treating you well down here, I see," I commented, motioning approvingly at the cell's interior.

Amelia shot me a bemused glance.

"Well, what were you expecting? Rats and sewage?"

Good guess.

"So, who else gets brought down here?" I asked out of curiosity. "Besides for, you know—"

"Those displaying sudden urges to strangle their crewmembers?" Amelia offered wryly.

I blushed, shrugging sheepishly.

CHAPTER 22

"I'm just messing," she said. "I understand why they brought me and Jefferson here. And to answer your question, the brig is typically used for students who cause...*excessive trouble* at school. But such cases are so rare it's nothing you need to worry about."

It took me a second to realize what she was referring to.

"Don't worry, Barnaby, it would never get to that," Amelia reassured me again, seeing the effect her comment had on me. "Even now, I can see it in your eyes—there isn't an ounce of a killer in your body. Whatever happened must've been some kind of accident."

Her words washed over me with a wave of relief I hadn't felt in days.

"T-thank you," I stammered, tears welling in my eyes. "For believing in me. It's been a tough week."

Amelia nodded, her smile warm and understanding.

After wiping my eyes, I cleared my throat and changed the subject.

"So...you and Jefferson are doing all right down here?"

Amelia shrugged. "As well as one can down here. They have Jefferson in the cell before mine. We get three meals a day from the mess, and Blackbeard's even arranged for our teachers to prepare us some work to keep us in pace with our classes as much as possible. The only difference is Jefferson's bookshelf compared to mine. I swear, the library must be working overtime to fulfill all of his requests."

I let out a chuckle, my first in over a week.

"Well, that's Jay for you."

"I had no idea, and I'm his captain," Amelia confessed. "It was only when we started doing homework together that I began to see. At first, I offered to help him with his projects, but now *he's* helping *me* with my essays. He's even shown me some ideas for future raids that, mind you, are nothing short of brilliant."

"Well, I'm happy to hear you guys are getting along," I expressed.

Amelia's eyes twinkled. "Indeed, we are. Now, Barnaby, an explanation please: What are you doing here, and how in the Seven Seas did you manage to get in here?"

I matched her mischievous gaze. "I may or may not have stolen a bottle of Fletcher's spice brew before I left the *Adventure Galley*."

I watched as my former captain's eyes widened to the size of gold doubloons before proceeding to give me a round of applause.

"Well, well. And so his pirate career begins," she teased. "But you must have quite the reason for coming if it cost you a whole bottle of Brew. You didn't just come to chat, did you?"

"No, I didn't." I took a deep breath and let Amelia in on my current predicament. "I have to let Reed know by tomorrow night," I explained to her. "And I've got no idea what to do."

"I see." Amelia shifted her place on the bed so that she was now facing me. "Well, let's start with the obvious. Say you do return to Florida. What would be the plan—just throwing your fate into the police's hands? Telling them that you were kidnapped and brought to a school run by pirates?" She chuckled. "Yes, I bet they'll believe that."

"Well, it's better than remaining here in exile," I countered. "And at least I'll have Grandma to defend me."

"That may be true, but it's still quite risky. I mean, truly think about it for a second. How do you plan on spending time with your grandmother when you'll be busy serving time for murder?"

I opened my mouth to respond, then closed it. As much as I hated to admit it, Amelia had a point. It was a massive risk to take.

Amelia must've noticed how hard her words hit me because a moment later, I felt her hands grip my clenched ones. When she next spoke, her voice was much softer, and filled with concern.

"I'm sorry to be the bearer of bad news, Barnaby. I can't imagine how much you must want to go home. I just don't want you throwing your life away."

"What life?" I snapped, shaking my head. "I haven't got one here anymore. I'm no better off here than I'd be back in Florida!"

"That's not true. Look at me—*look* at me, Barnaby." She lifted my face to hers. "I know it doesn't seem like it right now, but I think this school can actually offer exactly what you're seeking. In fact, it's been offering this very thing for centuries."

"Oh yeah? And what's that?"

Amelia straightened, her eyes steady and serious. "The core of every pirate's belief. Something so fundamental to life, yet nearly forgotten by the world until *we* reintroduced it: *redemption*."

I almost laughed. "Didn't you hear me, Amelia? Nobody will even *talk* to me. How on earth can I redeem myself if everyone acts like I don't exist?"

Amelia's voice was steady and firm, like she truly believed in every word that came out of her mouth.

"The same way a guy like Roger Riaz got named captain of his own crew. The same way Anne Bonny and Mary Read—

two women in a time of male prejudice—become two of the toughest and most respected pirates in the Seven Seas. The same way a former slave became the *greatest pirate of all time*. You work and give your all for it. You *earn* it."

I frowned. "Earn it? How?"

Amelia shook her head. "That, I'm afraid, I cannot tell you."

I stared at her in disbelief. "What do you mean you can't tell me? How the heck am I supposed to figure it out without your help?"

"Barnaby, it wouldn't count if I just handed it to you. You alone need to decide if the chance for redemption is worth giving up this chance—if you could even consider it one at that—to return home."

Before I could respond, Amelia rose from her seat and started moving toward the door. My eyes widened when I realized what she was doing.

"Wait, Amelia!" I cried. "Please, not yet. I still need your help!"

Stopping before the door, Amelia turned to face me, her expression warm but stern.

"I'm sorry, but this is your path to choose, Barnaby. I can't pick it for you."

And with that, she reached for the door and rapped lightly.

Just as he'd promised, after around half a minute, the door creaked open, and the curly-haired teenager stuck his head inside.

"Yes?" he asked. "Everything all right?"

Amelia shook her head.

"Everything is most certainly *not* all right! I don't know why you let Barnaby into my cell to begin with, but if you don't remove this freshie right this second, I fear that I may go into a murderous rampage—and we don't want that happening on your watch, now, do we? People might start asking questions—*black-bearded people*, in particular."

The guard gulped.

"No, we certainly wouldn't want that to happen," he agreed hastily, before turning to me with a stern expression. "Well? You heard the lady. Out."

"Wait, I just need one more—"

"Out!"

Dismayed, I bowed my head as I made my way to the door. Just before I stepped outside, I paused and shot one last, desperate glance at my former captain. What I saw baffled me.

A *smiling* Amelia.

"Goodbye, Barnaby Stump," she winked at me. "I sincerely hope this isn't the last time we speak."

CHAPTER 23

Defeated, I left Amelia's cell without a single complaint.

Well, what now?

That was the dilemma I found myself facing as I was marched through the brig by the guard. I'd been so sure that Amelia held the answers I needed. Yet, here I was, still nowhere closer to having an answer for Reed.

"This is your path to choose, Barnaby. I can't pick it for you," Amelia's words echoed in my mind.

I rolled my eyes at the thought of her reply. If I'd known what to choose, I wouldn't have come down to the brig for answers in the first place!

Approaching the exit, we passed by the cell I now knew belonged to Jefferson. Call it desperation, but something came over me at that moment, causing me to stop.

"Jefferson?" I called out. I even went as far as to open his cell's meal port and lower my face to the narrow opening. "Jefferson, can you hear me? It's Barnaby."

Nothing but silence came from within the cell. But, then again, what else was I supposed to expect from *Miles's best friend*? If Amelia had heard about what happened, then he had as well, which meant all I was doing was making a complete fool of myself for not knowing where his loyalties would lie.

"Come on, buddy," the guard impatiently prodded me in the back. "I really don't want to have to drag you out of here."

Apologizing, I straightened up and followed him out. As he sealed off the brig once more, I could literally feel him closing the door on any potential closure I'd hoped to find by coming down here.

"Oh wait, before you go—somebody came by and left you this."

I was already one-third up the stairs when he handed me a small, crumpled note. Sure enough, when I turned it over, I spotted my name scribbled across the side. The handwriting was unfamiliar.

"Did you see who left it?" I asked the guard.

I received a simple shake of the head in response.

"Whoever it was," he explained, "they came and dropped it off while I was escorting you to visit Amelia. Don't worry, I didn't read it," he added a second later.

Well, whoever had left it certainly caught my attention—and my curiosity. I stuffed the note in my pocket before thanking the guard and darting up the stairs. Only once I was out of his sight did I stop to read it.

The note was brief, and only contained nine words:

Library: Row sixty-five. Shelf eight. Third book. Chapter one.

While its motive was still unclear, at least the note gave me a destination. Fortunately, the library was located only a single floor up, so it wasn't even that much of a journey. With renewed purpose, I made my way to the library, the anticipation of this sudden scavenger hunt quickening my pace.

As I crossed the empty hallway, I continued contemplating

the identity of my mysterious messenger. As far as I'd been aware, nobody even knew I was heading down to the brig in the first place.

So then, who could it be?

The intrigue only deepened as I arrived at the library. Passing through the room's large doorway, the school's emblem inscribed above—a subtle reminder of academic pursuits and a warning against the allure of students *getting cozy* in between the books—I found the interior completely deserted.

What on earth is going on? I wondered.

Venturing further inside in search of answers, I passed the student workstation area, which was eerily empty. It was rather unsettling to see all the tables and armchairs, usually bustling with chattering students, now totally bare. The sight also stirred a wave of emotions as I recalled all the hours Miles and I had spent down here, working on projects and discussing raid tactics. Those times seemed like a distant memory now.

After the workstation area, it was onto the books. Zigzagging through them like a corn maze, the search for the sixty-fifth row led me deep into the history section and, upon finding the aforementioned row, my heart sank like a stone in my chest.

There was nobody there.

If I wasn't currently in a room where silence was more precious than gold, I would've screamed. I was sick of the emotional rollercoaster this night was taking me on.

With a long sigh, I located the specified shelf and began counting titles.

Pirates: A Renegade Democracy
The Cutthroat History of the Cutlass
Pirates of the Far East

CHAPTER 23

Treasure Island

I froze. *What was this book doing here?* I've never been the biggest reader, but even I knew about *Treasure Island*. My class had done a book report on it earlier in the year. It's also like, the most famous pirate story of all time. But as far as I was concerned, it was a work of fiction. So, what the heck was it doing in the history section?

Could it have been left here by accident? I wondered. I chose to check the next book on the shelf, just to be sure.

Sails: A History.

Nope, definitely not an accident. Someone had intended for me to find this book.

But why?

Hope rekindling within me, I pulled the book off the shelf and ran my fingers across its leaf-green leather cover. Engraved on the bottom were the words *First Edition—1883.*

My eyes widened upon reading this. Now aware of the book's age, I handled the tome with utmost caution, turning to the first chapter with the gentlest of movements. My heart, however, raced wildly. Unsure of what I might find, I began reading, and it only took two pages before I encountered something that sent shivers down my spine.

Fifteen men on the Dead Man's Chest.
 Drink and the devil had done for the rest.
 The mate was fixed by the bosun's pike,
 The bosun brained with a marlin spike.
 And Cookey's throat was marked belike,
 It had been gripped by fingers ten.
 And there they lay,
 All good dead men.

Like break-o'-day in a boozing-ken,
Yo ho ho and a bottle of rum!

I slammed the book shut, refusing to believe what I had just seen.

What the heck was "The Derelict" doing in a children's novel?

My mind raced with theories. Perhaps the author—labeled *R. L. Stevenson*, although I had no clue what 'R' and 'L' stood for—had heard the creepy song simply by chance? Or maybe he was aware of the legend behind the poem's writer?

I tried reading a bit more of the chapter to try and find a connection to Davy Jones. Not a single mention. No matter how much I read, there wasn't one detail alluding to the ghoulish ferryman of souls.

After awhile, I gave up, shutting the book with a long flurry of curses. The answer to this place's creepy, supernatural dilemma felt like it was right here in these pages, and I just couldn't see it. But somebody had left that note for me to find. Somebody on this island had a reason for me to find this book. Who could it be, and why?

I pursed my lips, debating what to do.

Even if I *did* plan on leaving—which was still a pretty considerable *if*—there was a chance I could finish the book in time. With that said, Reed said he didn't need an answer until tomorrow night, so I might even have enough time to go and investigate any potential leads I picked up. Worst case, I'd just pass along the book and any newfound discoveries to Blackbeard. I'm sure he'd find it useful—if he didn't already know about it.

Satisfied with my newfound plan, I stuffed the handwritten note back into my pocket, closed *Treasure Island*, and carried it out of the library. Hopefully I didn't need a library card to do so.

CHAPTER 24

Stifling several yawns as I made my way off the ship, I barely set foot onto the top deck before running smack-dab into the last person I wanted to see.

"Well, it's about time you showed up," Morgan smirked from two feet away, having jumped aside to avoid a collision. "I was beginning to think you were planning on spending all night in the library."

I froze. "Wait...*you* left the note for me?"

"Bingo! Finally starting to put the pieces together, eh?"

"Not really," I admitted. "How'd you know I was going to visit Amelia tonight?"

A sheepish look crossed Morgan's face—the look of someone who'd done something they knew they shouldn't have.

"I...may or may not have eavesdropped on your talk with Reed," she confessed. "And where else were you going to go and get advice to make a decision like that?"

I was too stunned to get mad. I didn't know whether to yell at her or applaud her for being so clever. It didn't matter though because Morgan kept speaking.

"Anyways," she went on, "I finally cracked it, and I think I know where he's hiding. Let's go!"

"You cracked what, Morgan?" I demanded, frustrated by all

the riddles and half-answers. "I'm not going anywhere until I get some answers."

Morgan's cheeky expression vanished.

"I don't understand," she said. "Didn't you figure it out? Surely you read the book? Both our grades had to do reports on it?"

"I never did the report," I replied. "Is that going to be a problem?"

Morgan shook her head. "Nope. It just means I have a bit more explaining to do than I thought."

I shrugged. Sure, I was still quite vexed by her actions aboard the *Adventure Galley*—or lack thereof—but I was willing to spend all night with her if it meant getting closer to saving Jefferson and Amelia and ending these horrible attacks. Besides, I could use a break from trying to figure out what to tell Reed.

"I'm in no rush," I told her. "Let's hear it."

Morgan nodded softly. If she sensed my bitterness, she didn't show it.

"Okay, well, let's start with the backstory. The basic idea is that there was once a pirate named Flint. Over the years, Flint accumulated a dangerous mix of greed and mistrust in his crew—a deadly combination, as you can imagine."

"More than just imagine," I grumbled, though Morgan didn't seem to hear.

"Eventually, Flint's paranoia got the better of him. He decided to take all the treasure his crew had collected and bury it on a hidden island. He even went as far as to kill all those who'd helped him so that he could be the only person who knew of the treasure's location."

"Sounds like a nice guy."

Morgan chuckled lightly. "Yeah, totally. Anyway, the book actually begins a few years later, when a boy named Jim Hawkins discovers the lone map to the treasure. He forms a crew to go after it, not realizing it includes former members of Flint's crew. They know he has the map and eventually overtake the ship to claim the treasure for themselves. A massive battle breaks out on the island, and in the end, Jim and his friends manage to leave unscathed with the treasure. The end."

"The end," I repeated, giving Morgan a slow, sarcastic round of applause. "Well, that was quite the tale, Morgan. But what the heck does it have to do with attacks on our friends?"

Morgan gave me a look like my head was hollow.

"I thought you said you read chapter one! It's right there—the words they were both saying—"

"Yes, but that could be a total coincidence," I argued. "What proof is there that *Treasure Island* has anything to do with the attacks?"

"Just let me finish!" Morgan exclaimed, clearly losing her patience.

Frankly, I was losing mine too, but I motioned for her to continue.

"In the book," she explained, "Jim Hawkins discovers a marooned man who'd been living on the island. He tells Jim he was once a member of Flint's crew and was left there by another crew after failing to deliver the treasure to them."

I folded my arms. "And this is relevant how?"

"I'm getting there, Barnaby. Jim finds this man living in a cave he'd made into his home. It's a secret cave that the other pirates missed. Well, what if everyone missed this cave just like in the book? What if this is where the attacker has been hiding all along?"

I wanted to roll my eyes. *This was her big revelation? The attacker was hiding in a cave just like there's one in the book?* After everything she'd put me through, I expected a better built claim than that.

"Why here, Morgan? Of all the islands in the world, why do you think we've been sitting on Treasure Island all this time?"

For a moment, it looked like I had finally silenced her. But then, without a word, she reached into her dungarees and withdrew a piece of paper, unfolding it to reveal a map roughly the size of a book page.

"Because Robert Louis Stevenson, the author of *Treasure Island*, is a former student of Lost Boys High."

She held up the paper, and goosebumps rippled through my entire body. It was a map of Treasure Island, with the title in an old-fashioned, squiggly font. But what caught my breath was how familiar the island's unique formation was—from the length of the jungle to the number of mountains, even the large lake in the middle.

Lost Boys High and Treasure Island were one and the same.

Morgan's hand trembled as excitement filled her voice. "Barnaby, the map, the song—it all fits! Stevenson must have found the cave during his time at Lost Boys High! This must be where Amelia's attacker has been hiding all this time!"

The theory definitely seemed more compelling now, but I still had some doubts.

"It's definitely a possibility, but it still doesn't explain how he got Jefferson and Amelia chanting 'The Derelict' and acting like that."

Morgan's eyes suddenly narrowed.

"I never told you what the song was called," she said. "How

did you know that?"

"I-I read it somewhere," I quickly lied, swallowing nervously. *Idiot! How could you slip up like that!*

I couldn't help but bite my lip as Morgan studied me suspiciously.

"You're hiding something," she deduced. "Come on, spit it out. What is it?"

"N-nothing," I lied again. After another minute of her staring at me like that, I couldn't help myself and blurted out, "I can't tell you, Morgan. I promised Blackbeard that I wouldn't tell a soul."

"Oh, come on, Barnaby!" Morgan stomped her foot on the deck. "Are we really going to do this? I've been working on this theory all week. I wanted to tell you earlier today—I think we're close to catching this guy!"

I felt my mouth open, ready to divulge everything I knew about 'The Derelict', Davy Jones, and these attacks. But then, at the last possible moment, something came over me and I stiffened.

"I...I don't know if I can trust you anymore."

Morgan's lips drew into a puzzled frown. "What's that supposed to mean?" she asked. When I said nothing, her expression shifted. "Wait, this isn't about the whole Miles situation, is it?"

Well, the cat's finally out of the bag, I thought. But I was in no mood to have this conversation tonight. Electing to remain silent, I turned and started making my way to the ship's gangplank.

"Barnaby, wait! I'm sorry!"

"Bit too late for apologies," I muttered, thinking I was out of earshot, but Morgan caught my murmuring.

CHAPTER 24

"What's that? Barnaby, you need to believe me—what I did wasn't personal."

I halted mid-plank and spun around.

"What part of it wasn't personal?" I demanded. "The part where you voted me off the ship or the silent treatment you gave me for almost an entire week? I totally get it, Morgan. You had to protect your family's legacy. Just don't tell me it wasn't personal."

Morgan's face flushed red, and her eyes flashed with anger.

"Did it ever occur to you that maybe I was taking the time to come to grips that you killed someone?" she shot back. "I mean, come on, Barnaby. Don't act like you're so innocent. It would've been kinda helpful to know that you murdered Miles's brother."

My face drained of color.

"It's…more complicated than that," I stammered.

How am I on the defensive here?

I stormed down the rest of the gangplank and onto the docks. It wasn't until I passed a dozen ships before I felt Morgan grab my hand, tugging me backward. I'd forgotten how soft her hands were…

No, Barnaby. You're not letting her hurt you again.

Shaking away the thoughts her touch put in my head, I yanked my arm away and continued down the docks. I didn't hear from Morgan again until I was a ship or two from the dock's end. Beyond where the wooden landing ended, a rough, manmade trail wound into the shadow-clad trees of the island's jungle.

"Barnaby, wait! You'll never find the cave on your own. You don't even have a light."

I ignored her and pressed on, plunging into the pitch-black

jungle. I wanted to show her that I didn't need her help, but sure enough, I was tripping with nearly every step on the rough, jagged ground.

"Did he cry out for mercy?" she suddenly called out. "Or did you kill him quickly and quietly?"

I slowed my pace, the blood leaving my face.

Don't listen to her, Barnaby. She's trying to get under your skin, Barnaby.

"I bet you enjoyed it too. You were probably smiling throughout it all."

What on earth—

Her logic was so flawed, but I couldn't contain my anger any longer. I'd suppressed it all week, and now it erupted like a volcano. Spinning around, eyes blazing, nostrils flaring, I grabbed Morgan by the arms and—*finally*—just let it rip.

"YOU DON'T UNDERSTAND!" I bellowed, the uproar startling birds into flight from their nests above.

"Then make me!" Morgan cried, the tears in her concerned-stricken eyes illuminated by the lantern in her hand. "Make me understand, Barnaby!"

I shut my eyes tightly, forcing the tears back, and took a massive breath.

"Whatever you think happened between Miles's brother and me, what everyone is saying—it's not true. He attacked me. I acted in self-defense. I *had to*…it was my life or his. I've got no way to prove it to you, so you're just going to have to take my word for it. Or don't—I actually don't care anymore. I'm done here."

Once more, I turned to leave. But once more, Morgan reached out for my hand.

"Barnaby," she whispered softly. "Why didn't you tell anyone this?"

"I tried. But no one believed me. *You* didn't believe me."

Morgan bit her lip, appearing to accept this harsh truth. Her smooth, unblemished fingers slowly interlocked with mine.

"Well, I'm here now, Barnaby," she told me. "Can you give me one more try? After everything we've been through?"

I hated to admit it, but she had a good point. I never considered how tough it must've been for her to open up with me that night after the raid.

If she doesn't believe you, Barnaby, I thought to myself, *nobody will. And then you'll have your answer to give Reed. Two birds with one stone.*

Swallowing hard, I took one final deep breath before I began. Morgan listened intently, as if the world depended on it.

"It happened during our match at a fencing tournament. I'd just scored the first point when—"

My voice trailed off as I heard something strange in the distance. Something oddly...*familiar*.

"Then what happened?" Morgan asked me impatiently. "What happened next?"

Trying to listen, I waved my hand at her to be quiet, but she totally took it the wrong way.

"Stop it Barnaby! Why can't you just open up and tell—"

I didn't let her finish, shooting a hand over her mouth. This infuriated Morgan even more, as she started squirming fiercely. I felt her mouth open to say something, and once again, I signaled her to be quiet.

In a whisper, I asked her: "Did you hear that?"

Now *that* got her to shut up. For a moment, neither of us spoke, simply listening to our surroundings. For half a minute, there was nothing—save for the gentle tickle of some nearby stream.

Then, out of nowhere, a gruff hissing sound came from several feet away. It sounded like a geyser prior to eruption and appeared to come from the direction of the stream—two signs of something extremely dangerous that I was all too familiar with, thanks to my upbringing in Florida.

"Morgan, be quiet and run!" I whispered to her. "Run—NOW!"

And then, behind us, the alligator charged.

CHAPTER 25

One thought kept repeating itself in my head as we ran:
I should've just gone to sleep.

The sharp, pointed tips of the ankle-high grass bit my legs while my arms repeatedly smacked into various vines and tree branches. Both extremely annoying experiences, but neither remotely close to slowing me down.

A few cuts and splinters over becoming gator food? Pu-lease.

A few feet to my left was Morgan, who I noticed was beginning to struggle to keep up. She was easy to spot, thanks to the bobbling glare of her lantern. The weight of the clanky lantern definitely had an impact on her pace, however. I almost yelled at her to toss it, but then remembered that alligators are strong nocturnal hunters as well, so throwing it away would really just be casting us at a further disadvantage.

Together, we stumbled, tripped, and dashed through the overgrown jungle as fast as our bodies allowed. After what felt like forever, the bloodthirsty thrashing of the alligator finally seemed to disappear in the distance.

Reaching a place to stop, Morgan dropped the lantern and collapsed to her knees, huffing and puffing like she'd just run a marathon.

"How—how did you know," she asked me, still bent over. "How did you know that it was a freaking alligator?"

Still catching my own breath, I managed a small smile. "In Florida, we have an alligator-warning class every year in school. There are over a million of them in the state."

"Seven Seas," she gasped. "So, you don't like to read but know all the proper signs of an alligator approaching."

"I'm more of a hands-on guy."

"No kidding." From the ground, the quartermaster raised the lantern to take in our new surroundings. "Where are we?"

"I can't say for sure, but I think we reached the mountainside."

I motioned to our left, where up a small dirt incline, a rigged wall of stone jutted out from the ground. The end wasn't visible—it continued on way past the leafy treetop.

Reclaiming her lantern, Morgan shined it on the large slab and gasped.

"Barnaby—do you see what I see?"

I glanced up to where Morgan was pointing. There, about a hundred feet to our left, was a thin opening in the rocky parapet.

"You don't think…" her voice lingered.

"Only one way to find out," I replied, taking the lantern from her before making my way up to the cavern.

"Be careful," she called out to me. "You don't know what could be waiting inside. Or *who*."

Appreciating her concern, I gave Morgan a small nod before continuing my approach. I couldn't reveal it to her, but I was secretly dreading the same thing. What if there *was* someone waiting inside? Or more specifically—what if Davy Jones

CHAPTER 25

himself was inside?

Even so, I proceeded forward. I owed it to Amelia and Jefferson to investigate this cavern. The key to saving them could be somewhere inside.

"I think I see some sort of engraving on the cave wall," I called down to her. "I'm going to go inside and get a closer look."

"Okay, I'm right behind you."

I took a step into the mouth of the cavern which was so narrow that I had to begin squirming sideways to pass through. When there was finally enough room, I straightened up and raised the lantern at the wall. I found myself looking at an array of small, uneven lines etched into the stone—a diagonal dash crossing through every four of them.

"It looks like some sort of tally…but for what?"

"Maybe for counting time?" Morgan's voice came from much closer this time, and I turned to find her sliding through the cave's entranceway. She too began staring in awe at the carvings. "Years spent marooned on this island?"

My eyes widened. "Are you saying what I think you are?"

"Only one way to find out," Morgan said, taking the lantern from my hands before venturing further.

The walls continued to grow farther and farther apart as we pressed on deep into the cave. Suddenly, we found ourselves stepping into a large, circular landing. My hand swiftly flew to my sword when I spotted several large shadows hovering nearby. However, as I got closer, they revealed themselves to be nothing but pieces of rotten, wooden furniture.

"I can't believe it," I heard Morgan gasp from beside me. "It actually exists."

I couldn't help but smile. "Well done, Morgan. Anne Bonny

would be proud."

"Gee, thanks," she replied, her cheeks visibly glowing from the compliment. Her ears had begun to ting a bright pink as well, the sight of which immediately sent a blast of warmth through me.

I felt my face redden as my hand brushed against hers. We were so close to one another, the air between us charged with an unspoken but clear connection. Neither of us quite seemed to know what to say next.

I cleared my throat, reluctantly breaking the moment. "Um, w-we should probably split up to save time," I suggested, trying not to stumble over my words.

"Yeah, sounds good," Morgan replied quickly, her eyes darting away from mine.

Faces red as tomatoes, we slowly stepped apart and each took half of the room to investigate. Morgan chose the front half, which included the narrow entranceway and the bed area. I took the rear, which meant the closet and table.

A thought popped into my head as I inspected my part. Sure, the furniture was old—the table crumbling into dust the moment I placed a finger on it—but there was no way a maroon could have built any of it. Even the closet, which I moved to next, possessed a level of craftsmanship beyond that of a basic scavenger. Which could only mean one thing:

Somebody had to have brought it here.

As Morgan moved to examine the bed, I continued going through the closet. I began rummaging through the drawers, which, to my surprise, possessed not a single speck of dust. Not only that, but they were brimming with clothes—and fresh ones too.

Looks like someone's been here recently, I thought.

CHAPTER 25

I started sifting through the garments, quickly realizing that they were all men's. Basic and ordinary, they unfortunately bore no name tags or any distinguishing features. With a deep sigh, I started returning them to their place in the drawer and was just about to move on when one particular item stashed in the side caught my eye.

Between all the plain black and white tops, I almost missed it. Pulling it out of the drawer, I unfolded it to get a better look. My mouth went dry when I realized what it was:

A striped, black-and-white shirt. A *referee* shirt, to be precise.

And that's when the terrifying realization came crashing through me.

No...

How could I have been so blind?!

How could I have been so stupid?!

Dust erupted into the air as I stumbled back into the bed, stunned by the chilling discovery. My body tensed even more when I noticed how quiet the cave had gotten. I couldn't hear Morgan searching anymore.

"Um, Morgan?" I called out tentatively.

I spun around and found her standing at the cave's entranceway, her back to me. I started to approach but came to a gut-wrenching halt when I caught sight of the pistol aimed at her head. A vortex of rage and fear swelled inside of my chest as I met the gaze of the person holding it.

"You two shouldn't have come here," Reed said, his voice low and menacing.

CHAPTER 26

Reed's frown deepened, his pistol trained steadily on Morgan. With his free hand, he motioned toward me.

"Quickly now. Come stand behind your girlfriend and drop your sword to the floor, or I'll put a bullet between her eyes."

"Don't listen to him, Barnaby!" Morgan cried out, only to have Reed press the pistol against her forehead.

"Silence," he snarled at her.

"Wait, stop!" I shouted at Reed. His menacing glare shifted back to me as I approached, arms outstretched.

"Look, see? I'm doing exactly as you said. Just, please, Reed, don't hurt Morgan. *Please.*"

As I neared, I shot a reassuring glance at Morgan before withdrawing my rapier and letting it clatter onto the cavern floor. Gun still raised, Reed bent down to retrieve my sword and slipped it into his belt. A flash of metal from the other side of his waist confirmed he'd already taken Morgan's weapon.

"Start walking," he ordered, the cold barrel of his pistol now digging into my back.

Morgan led the way. In a single-file line, we squeezed through the cave's narrow entrance and descended the mountain's rocky slope. At first glance, it seemed like an opportunity to escape, but Reed kept a close distance, his pistol never straying far from my back.

"No funny business," he warned as we entered the jungle. "You had one outburst tonight that gave you away. The next one will be your last."

It was clear he was referring to my earlier outburst at Morgan. I made a mental note to slap myself in the face when this was all over.

Must've also been what got the gator's attention. Great going, you idiot.

For a while, Morgan and I obeyed Reed's commands. We trudged through the jungle in silence, the only sounds coming from our heavy breathing as we struggled to maintain our footing across the rugged terrain. But eventually, curiosity got the better of me. Still walking, I turned my head and asked a simple, two-worded question.

"Why, Reed?"

His cold voice wavered as he appeared to be wrestling aside a stubborn bundle of vines.

"You want the short story, Barnaby? Money—and *revenge*."

I frowned, stepping over an exposed root, narrowly avoiding a nasty fall in the process.

"Um, revenge for what?"

Judging by the sharp intake of breath I heard behind me, Reed appeared to hesitate at my question. Recovering quickly, his acidic tone sent chills down my spine.

"For abandoning me on the mainland. For leaving me to starve and suffer for *two years*, without any support or aid. And for you, Barnaby, for killing my best friend."

And just like that, the pieces of the puzzle finally began coming together—and I couldn't help but shake my head at all the signs I missed.

"You're talking about Mason Whittaker, aren't you?"

Reed's initial response was an exaggerated *"Pfft."* Then he said, "Well, it's about freaking time! Honestly, Barnaby, how in the Bermuda freaking Triangle did you not put it together already? Two crows at the same silly fencing tournament, in *suburban Florida* of all places? Come on!"

My cheeks reddened at his accurate, albeit harsh, remark. Afterall, I should have seen it coming.

How hadn't I?

Reed. He'd played the role perfectly. A ruse capable of winning an Oscar. His shy, insecure demeanor had convinced all of us—Blackbeard included. Letting Roger toss him around for the whole school to see was just the cherry on top.

"So, let me get this straight—you're being *paid* to attack students? Quite the line of work you've got there, Reed."

My snark comment earned me a sharp thwack to the head from the barrel of Reed's pistol.

"Are you really that naïve? If I'd been paid to do that, do you think *only two* would've been attacked by now? No, I came back to steal the only thing of actual value in this wretched place. I came back to steal the *Angel's Wings*."

"What!"

The bright beam of the lantern shot upward as Morgan's hands flew to her mouth. It was the first time she'd spoken since we left the cave.

"But that's our only way back to the mainland and to Shipwreck Cove. You would be trapping everyone here!"

Reed snorted. "So what? I've been promised *half a million* to retrieve it. Well, *we* were. Mason and I." His voice started to waver. "We were going to split it."

CHAPTER 26

None of us spoke for a while after that. We continued our trek through the jungle, the silence only broken by our breathing and the occasional rustle of leaves. As we neared the first speckles of artificial light, I realized we were getting close to the docks.

Yet still no escape route, I thought troublingly. Scrambling for a shred of an opportunity, I tried to stall Reed with more questions, hoping to buy Morgan and me some more time.

"You who turned Miles against me with that newspaper," I said, gritting my teeth. "Didn't you?"

A brief silence passed between my question and his answer.

"You took my best friend away from me. Only fair that I should do the same, no?"

"But Mason attacked *me*, Reed," I argued. "What I did was in self-defense."

"LIES!" Reed exclaimed from behind me. His spare hand latched onto my shoulder, whirling me around to face his enraged, murderous glare. "You can try lying to the rest of the school, Barnaby, but you won't trick me. I was there! I gave the countdown to that match! And while I don't know what sort of witchcraft you used to freeze everyone back there—no doubt the same trick you used to find my cave—I will avenge his death!"

Reed's words were quickly followed by the sudden cock of his pistol, and I looked over in the direction he was now pointing it. There, half a dozen feet away, was Morgan, trembling in fear.

"Nice try, but if you take one more step, I'll blow Barnaby's brains out. I'm sure the alligators would love to have them."

The pistol's cold steel yet again pressed against my head as Morgan's shoulders slumped in surrender. Wordlessly, she waited as Reed dragged me over, and we set off once more.

Twenty steps later, we reached the jungle's edge. Morgan brushed aside a pair of bushes, revealing the brightly lit docks. Any thoughts of making a run for it were instantly terminated by the cold steel prodding in my neck.

"If either of you utters a single sound, you're both dead," Reed warned. "Now, do you two see that pathway bending around the lake? That's where we're heading—*now*."

Signaling for me to take the lead, I pushed aside the shrubbery and stepped through. Without a word, I headed left, where the docks ended, and another beaten path continued.

"Reed? I have a question," Morgan said, her voice no more than a whisper.

Reed grumbled. "Make it quick, Travers."

"What exactly *did* you do to Jefferson and Amelia?"

A curt burst of laughter escaped the would-be crow. "Funny you should ask—I was just about to show you."

We continued down the dirt path until a small rowboat came into view, resting on the shore near a grove of palm trees. A figure sat beneath them, illuminated by Morgan's lantern as we approached.

It was Riaz.

Reed's snarky tone resurfaced as we stared, stunned, at the sight of the Sharkhead captain.

"I believe you both know dear Roger here?"

At the sound of his name, Roger began squirming about in the grass, two bundles of rope restricting his movements and muffling his speech. His manic, bloodshot eyes widened when they spotted us approaching.

Reed motioned to another pile of rope lying nearby. "Guess it's a good thing in the end that I brought extra. Go and tie yourselves up."

Not having much of a choice, we did as we were told.

"Reed, why is Riaz here?" I asked. "Your beef is with me, not him."

Reed shook his head. "See, that's where you're wrong. Not everything I told you was a lie. This cretin made my life miserable for years. And like I said, I came back for revenge."

Morgan and I watched as he proceeded to withdraw a pair of shiny, silver gloves from his jacket pocket. The moment I saw their color, I knew what was happening.

"My benefactor told me how to find these. I'm sure you're both aware of the legend of Davy Jones? These were the source of his power. Watch."

Reed stepped over to Roger, slipping the gloves on as he approached. He lowered his hands toward the rope covering his mouth, which sent the Sharkhead captain in a frenzy.

The former crow stopped and eyed him darkly. "Roger, if you don't shut up, I'll cut out your tongue and feed it to you."

Roger silenced immediately. Reed produced a knife, cutting the rope over Roger's mouth before tugging at the older boy's sleeves, revealing his wrists. With a deep breath, Reed grabbed them, and the most bone-chilling scene unfolded before our eyes.

First, Reed's gloves began to glow. Their shiny, metallic sheen brightened to a ghastly, pale white. It was the same white that had emitted from Jefferson's and Amelia's eyes—and now Roger's.

And that's when the shakes began.

They began as light tremors but quickly escalated until Roger's entire body was convulsing like he was suffering from a seizure. Immediately, I was reminded of Jefferson's quakes that night aboard the *Angel's Wings*. But those had led to the end of his...*possession*, and I feared Roger was suffering an opposite fate.

"Reed, stop! You're hurting him!" Morgan pleaded, but Reed ignored her. His iron-clad grip remained on the spasming Roger until the gloves' brightness vanished, and the Sharkhead captain slumped over.

Reed stood up and brushed the dirt off his jeans.

"Roger Riaz, report for duty," he proclaimed.

Without a second of delay, Roger's head shot up, his eyes as silver as the moon.

"Fifteen men on a dead man's chest. Yo ho ho, and a bottle of rum."

I looked up at Reed with sheer horror. "What—what did you do to him?"

Reed looked at me, a devilish twinkle of darkness in his eyes.

"I took his *soul*, Barnaby. You see, Davy Jones didn't just transport souls of sailors to the afterlife—he could also store them in these gloves to possess their bodies. His crew was full of obedient, soulless, cutthroat killing machines."

Reed now turned back to Roger and cut off his second bind of rope. "Go and put the boat in the water."

The Sharkhead captain did as he was told, mumbling the all-too-familiar, hair-raising chant. When he was done, Reed's next order was to put Morgan and me in the rowboat. He followed right after us, pistol raised the entire time, and once everyone was seated, Reed ordered Roger to start paddling.

If it wasn't for the grim circumstances, I would have loved to enjoy a night like this. Along with the full moon, the clear night sky was a blanket of twinkling stars, reflecting off the lake like a million diamond points. It was the perfect night to

CHAPTER 26

spend with someone special, like Morgan.

Alas, if only we weren't so preoccupied.

Once the rowboat reached the center of the lake, Reed had Roger cease with the oars. He then handed him one of the three swords in his possession—Morgan's by the look of it—and ordered him to kill us if we tried to escape.

"You won't get away with this," Morgan shot at him. "Blackbeard will stop you."

Reed responded with a short, scornful laugh.

"Blackbeard's a relic," Reed sneered. "The sooner you all wake up from your brainwashed delusions, the better. He leaves his crows stranded on the mainland, providing no support. He lets his students engage in brutal violence without a shred of intervention. And don't kid yourselves—he's fully aware of the chaos unfolding, the very chaos I've brought to this island—and has done nothing to stop it! And do you know why? Because he's powerless to act—so long as I wield the power of Davy Jones."

"So, what now?" Morgan asked. "Are you going to kill us?"

"You? I hope I don't have to. Barnaby's a whole other story. But as for you…I'm happy to let you go after you just explain how you and Barnaby found my cave."

Reed waited for Morgan to respond, but when she remained silent, he sighed.

"I really don't want to kill you, Morgan. I'm not the villain you think I am."

Morgan looked at him like he was daft. "You've stolen the souls of two of my friends, manipulated them, and driven them into madness. Please explain how you aren't a monster."

Reed shrugged. "Look at the facts. I haven't killed anyone. Not Jefferson, not Amelia—not even the police officer I rescued Barnaby from. Nobody at this school needs to die—except for Barnaby, and that's because he deserves it."

"Nobody ever deserves to be killed," Morgan countered.

"Murderers do," Reed reasoned. "Ever heard of the death penalty? Now please, answer the question: How did you and Barnaby find the cave?"

I sat there and watched as Morgan took a deep breath. Her eyes met Reed's, and she opened her mouth as if she was going to speak—only to shoot a large glob of phlegm directly into his face.

Bullseye.

Wiping saliva off his nose and cheeks, Reed shook his head.

"It's a shame, really," he said. He pointed up at the sky. "So much bloodshed on such a pleasant night. You know, full moon and all."

Any vindication I felt from Morgan's spit spectacle quickly vanished as, without warning, Morgan's side of the boat rocked violently. I glanced over to find her pale as a ghost, shaking, her eyes wide with fear.

"You wouldn't dare," she gasped, the fear in her voice unmistakable.

"What, Morgan? What is it?" I asked her. "What's—"

I never got to finish my next question because, at that moment, Reed ordered Roger to cover my mouth with his hand.

"So, have you had a change of heart?" Reed asked Morgan.

Morgan hesitated—then began to stammer up an answer."The—the map, it's from *Treasure Island*. I-I took it from the library, r-r-ripped it from the book. That's what led us to your cave."

With a massive heave of strength, I managed to free myself

from Riaz's grasp.

"There," I said to Reed. "She gave you the information you wanted. You have me now too, so do as you promised. Let her go."

Reed said nothing to me. Deep in contemplation, his eyes stayed on Morgan. After a moment, he shook his head.

"No, no, no," he said. "Do you really expect me to believe that nonsense? That you found it with a map from a children's book?"

Morgan gulped again and nodded frantically. "It's the truth, Reed! I swear!"

"Oh yeah? Then show me."

"I…I can't," she confessed. "I dropped it when we were running from the alligator."

"So, what? You just happened to stumble upon my cave by chance? No way. Stop lying, Morgan."

"I'm not! Reed, I swear—"

"I said, stop lying!" Reed bellowed, furiously waving his pistol at her. And then, suddenly:

CRACKOOM!

"NO!" I shouted, leaping from my seat toward Morgan, but it was too late. Accident or not, the bullet's impact had propelled her over the side and into the dark waters below. She was gone.

Anger coursed through my veins, and with a barbarous roar, I leaped out of my seat at Reed, but Roger had already taken hold of my arms, pulling me back.

"YOU MONSTER!" I roared, tears streaming down my face. "She didn't deserve to die!"

With an unnervingly calm face, the former crow looked at me and nodded. "You're absolutely right about that, Barnaby.

She didn't. But you do."

Suddenly his pistol was pointed at me, cocked for the second time in a minute. And before I could get out another word—
CRACKOOM!

A sharp pain ripped my chest, sending me overboard. The cold waters of the lake consumed me, extinguishing the starry night's light and replacing it with complete darkness.

CHAPTER 27

"Barnaby Stump," a gentle, feminine voice echoed around me, starting as a distant whisper that drew closer until I could feel the warmth of her breath. "Open your eyes."

I hesitated but obeyed.

My surroundings were a murky, dark blueness, rippling like waves on a pond. And there, directly across from me, floated two beautiful girls.

"Beautiful" felt like an understatement. They looked almost celestial, with sapphire blue eyes and long, elegant hair cascading like silk over their shoulders. But that's where their similarities ended. One had fair skin dusted with freckles and curly, sandy hair, while her friend's skin was olive-toned with glossy black hair.

Their flawless complexions captivated me, not a single blemish in sight. Even the freckles on the blonde girl only added to her charm. I found myself staring, almost entranced, feeling all my panic and frustration melt away in their presence.

"Am I dead?" I finally asked, breaking the spell.

Both girls shook their heads, the blonde giggling lightly and flashing me a mischievous smile that warmed my heart like sunshine on a chilly day.

"Well, if I'm not dead," I pressed on, "where am I? And who are you?"

The smile on the freckled girl's face widened, revealing a pair of perfect dimples.

"My name is Melody," she replied softly. "And I think I can answer your questions with two simple words: Look. Down."

Doing as I was told, I lowered my eyes. I needed a double take to confirm what I was seeing. Below the girl's sleek green tunic, where her legs should have been—there was a large, blue-tinted fin. A tail, to be precise.

I met Melody's face again in a mix of awe and fright.

"You're a-a…" I sputtered. "You're a mermaid!"

Still smiling from dimple to dimple, the ethereal half-human, half-fish nodded.

"Melody the mermaid," I repeated, amused by how it sounded. Suddenly, another realization hit. "Wait, if you're a mermaid, then that must mean I'm—"

"Not dead. And still in the lake, yes. Oh, and where are my manners! This is my friend, Harmony."

The olive-skinned mermaid gave me a small, shy wave. I quickly noticed that while the scales on Melody's tail were a clear sky blue, Harmony's were a dark forest green. Both colors perfectly complemented their complexions.

"Um, are the names musical themed on purpose?" I asked.

Melody nodded, her expression turning serious. "The two of us belong to a group of mermaids known as the Sirens. Our kind originated in the Mediterranean Sea, but a small group made the journey here centuries ago. You might have encountered our ancestor's stories in Greek mythology."

"Yes, I know of you," I admitted, recalling the lessons we had on sirens. "Your kind is known to lure sailors with songs, drown them, and then eat them." I gulped, my face draining of color. "Um…are you two going to eat me?"

At this, both girls broke out into giggles, their razor-sharp teeth on full display.

"Nah. You're too cute to eat," Melody teased with a wink.

I felt myself blush—a total turnaround from the fear I'd felt moments ago.

"I'm not lying, Barnaby. You're *way* cuter than most of the pirates we've come across. Tooth decay and scurvy are total turn-offs."

"Plus," Harmony added, biting her lip innocently, "we kinda need your help."

"My help? What could two beautiful mermaids need my help with?"

I hadn't planned on saying the "beautiful" part, but it slipped out. Maybe there was some enchantment at play here. Regardless, both girls giggled in a charming, almost seductive way.

"You're *literally* the sweetest," Melody cooed. "If only I could, I'd keep you and your marvelous hair down here with us forever. Sadly, we can only create temporary air bubbles for humans. It's part of our predatory nature, you know?"

"Yeah, totally," I replied, trying to sound like I understood. "So, what exactly do you two need my help with?"

Upon hearing my question, Harmony's expression turned serious, although she still managed to make it look fashionable.

"A terrible crime has occurred," she explained to me. "A former student from your school found our master's instruments and defiled them. But you already know about this, don't you?"

I nodded, realizing who they meant by "master." "You're talking about the gloves, right? Davy Jones was your master?"

The olive-skinned mermaid nodded. "We've had many masters over time. The enchantments encompassing this island originally belonged to an angel tasked with ferrying sailors' souls to the afterlife. The silver gloves, the ability to reanimate the dead, that legendary white ship you arrived on—they all were created to aid him in his task. But eventually, the angel grew tired and sought a successor."

"From that moment on, as these artifacts continued trading hands, we vowed to safeguard them and prevent them from falling into the wrong hands," Melody explained. "For if they ever did, the consequences for this world would be catastrophic. Unfortunately, Blackbeard doesn't seem to trust us and hid them away himself."

"What? Why wouldn't Blackbeard trust you guys?" I asked.

Melody and Harmony exchanged sheepish glances.

"We…may or may not have eaten several of his crew," Harmony confessed. "But it was over *four hundred years ago*. You have to understand, Barnaby, it was a different time, and a full moon—"

I raised my hand to stop her. "Wait, did you say full moon?"

Harmony nodded. "Yes, it's our primary hunting night. Why do you ask?"

Hunting night. That explains why Morgan panicked.
Wait. MORGAN!

"I have a friend who sunk down here as well," I explained to the mermaids. "She was shot by the person who took your master's gloves. Do you know anything about her? Is she okay?"

"For now," Melody answered with a frown. Her tone was

noticeably less cheerful now. "Our healers are working to save her. The bullet missed her heart by a hair. Your wound was easier to treat."

Relief flooded through me.

Thank goodness! Morgan's still alive!

"Okay, so let me get this straight. You want me to retrieve Davy Jones's gloves for you?" My expression turned sour. "Ladies, I'm not sure I can do this. The last time I faced Reed, I almost lost my soul to him. What makes this time any different?"

"This time," Melody told me firmly, "You have us on your side."

I watched as Harmony dipped her hand into the water, revealing a large, ordinary-looking seashell inside the air bubble. I couldn't make out any distinct details—it looked just like any shell you'd find on a beach.

"The next time you face Reed, place this on the ground and crush it underfoot. Our sisters will take it from there. But it must happen above the lake, or we can do nothing."

I nodded, taking the shell from her. "Thank you."

"No, it's us who should thank you," Melody said. "There's no amount of gratitude we can offer for the task you're about to undertake. When the time comes, we will repay your kindness. Now, we must return you to the surface. Your air bubble is nearly depleted, and it is time to act."

"Will Morgan come with me?" I asked, disappointed when Harmony shook her head.

"We need assurance you'll use that shell to complete your mission, Barnaby. Get us the gloves, and we'll release Morgan to you."

I couldn't help but notice how upset the mermaids sounded

when mentioning Morgan.

Could they possibly be...jealous?

"Wait," I pleaded, shaking my head. "Please. I need her help. Everyone else at this school—they all hate me."

"I'm sorry, Barnaby, but this is our way to ensure you keep your word. Besides, she needs more time to heal."

Pouting, I waved my hands in the, um, bubble. "How am I supposed to convince anyone to help me then?"

The mermaids surprised me with their response. Without warning, Melody fluttered over and kissed me.

WOAH.

Kissing Melody was unlike anything I'd ever experienced before—maybe because it was my first kiss. Her lips tasted like saltwater taffy, bringing sensations of a tropical paradise. First, sitting on a beach with a cold drink, then laughter and joy swimming through clear blue waves with friends. Finally, it was the starry-eyed feeling of holding hands and watching the sunset over the water with someone who looked a lot like Morgan.

It was the exact opposite of how I'd felt when Reed attacked me with Davy Jones's gloves. Instead of darkness, I felt warmth. Instead of weakness, strength surged through my veins.

After who knows how long, Melody pulled back and smiled.

"There. If anyone doubts your intentions, show them the Sign of the Mermaid. That kiss is your proof."

"Wait, what? What sign?" I asked her. I didn't see or feel anything different about me.

Melody said nothing and snapped her fingers. Suddenly, I felt the floor of the air pocket start to rise and me with it.

"Wait!" I yelled. "I still don't see any sign! What am I

CHAPTER 27

supposed to do?"

Melody smiled, but her words were lost in the rising air bubble. It ascended higher and higher until I could barely see Melody and Harmony below.

With a sigh, I turned my gaze upward. The bright, sunny surface of the lake came into view. When I went under, the lake had been showered with stars.

Jeez, how long had I been underwater?

Suddenly, the area around me erupted in a large splash, and I was flung through the air, falling face-first into hot sand.

CHAPTER 28

Time to get moving, I told myself.

The sun blazed overhead like a ticking time bomb as I pushed myself up from the scalding sand, spitting out a glob in the process. There was no telling how much Reed had accomplished during the night—how many students and teachers he now had under his control. He might have even run off with the Angel's Wings by now.

What if the mermaids were wrong? What if it was already too late?

A quick glance across the shimmering lake quelled my doubts. There, anchored in its usual spot, was the ethereal white ship.

Not wanting to waste another second, I started up the beach toward the man-made path. I passed the grove of palm trees where Reed had performed his ghastly ritual, a hard lump forming in my throat when I spotted the rowboat lying nearby.

Despite the mermaid's assurance, I cast a hopeful look at the water, where nothing but a crushing emptiness met me—as I should've expected. Afterall, Harmony's terms had been crystal clear: retrieve the gloves to see Morgan again.

So why was I still looking?

Because I blamed myself for what happened. If I hadn't

CHAPTER 28

let my emotions get the better of me, Reed would never have heard us in the jungle. If I hadn't been so self-centered, Morgan might still be...

Quit it, Barnaby, the voice in my head urged me. *She's not dead yet! Get moving!*

Pushing the toxic thoughts to the back of my mind, I pressed on with my trek up the beach. It wasn't long before solid ground replaced the loose, powdery sand that'd been infiltrating my boots with every step. From there, it was just a two-minute sprint to reach the edge of the docks.

Along the way, I tried to settle on a plan of action. I didn't need anyone to tell me that heading straight to Blackbeard would be the safest move. He already knew about Davy Jones—probably more than he let on—which would make him the easiest to convince of what was really going on at Lost Boys High. But who knew how long it would take him to muster up enough force to confront Reed—especially if he now had more than just Riaz under his control.

To stop Reed, I needed numbers, and I needed them fast. And that's when option number two presented itself to me. It was certainly faster than its predecessor, but it was also ten times as risky. *Bodily harm* risky.

But the true allure of option number two wasn't its speed. It was the potential for redemption that if offered.

Redemption and saving Morgan. I liked the sound of that.

Decision made, it set my course for the *Adventure Galley*.

They might not even be aboard, I realized as I dashed toward the blue ship. I still had no idea of the current time, and for all I knew, my former crew might be in class now. Nevertheless, I was only two boats away now, so there was no reason not to check.

With my expectations recalibrated, I reached the ship and hurried halfway up the gangplank—and there they were. Two dozen of my former crewmates clustered together in casual conversation. Judging by their sleepy banter and the occasional yawn, it seemed they had just returned from breakfast.

"Um, hello," I greeted them, trotting onto the deck.

Instantly, all heads on the ship swiveled toward me. The once lethargic-looking crowd stared at me with bloodshot eyes, as if they each had just downed a dozen shots of espresso.

"What is *he* doing here?"

"I dunno. Didn't we kick him off the crew?"

"Ooh, boy. Does anybody see Miles? He is gonna—"

I didn't catch the rest of what that particular crewmember claimed Miles was going to do to me. Instead, at the sound of his name, my eyes scanned the deck for my curly haired former ally. Sadly, he didn't appear to be present. It seemed like my *real* redemption would have to wait.

Beside the central mast, a stir of movement caught my attention. The crew parted, and Fletcher stepped through.

"Barnaby?" He looked flabbergasted to see me. "What are you doing here?"

He appeared to speak for the rest of the crew, who all fell silent at the sound of his voice.

"Jeez, you look like a mess." Fletcher pointed warily at my chest. "Why are you covered in sand?"

"I promise, I'll explain on the way," I told him. "But right now, I need you and the crew to come with me to the *Angel's Wings*. Someone's going to try and steal it."

"Someone?"

"Reed," I clarified.

CHAPTER 28

Fletcher scratched his buzzed head, his frown unwavering. "Um…who?"

I muttered a quick curse at Reed before replying.

"My crow. Oh, and he's the one who attacked Amelia and Jefferson."

Now *that* got the crew's attention—just as I'd intended. Whispers flooded the deck, and Fletcher's raised eyebrows mirrored the concern etched across his face.

"Well, that's quite the accusation, Barnaby," he said. "Do you have any evidence?"

I glanced down at my body. Even after brushing off all the sand, I was unable to find the mark Melody had been describing. Defeated, I shook my head.

"I don't, unfortunately. But ask yourself—would I really come back here if I wasn't telling the truth? I swear, Reed's been behind everything!"

A loud, unexpected guffaw followed my plea. I traced it to the source and found Miles emerging from the stairwell.

"Thought I heard your voice," he shot at me. "You've got some nerve showing up here."

"Here we go," I heard that same guy from before whisper again. I wanted to hit him.

Meanwhile, Miles approached the scene with visible disdain.

"What does *he* want?" he asked, turning to Fletcher for a response.

"Barnaby claims his crow's behind the attacks on our crew." Fletcher's gaze slowly returned to me. "And I think it's safe to assume that you want our help in stopping him?"

"Exactly," I affirmed, silently pleading with Miles to truly consider my proposal. After all, it was his best friend who was locked up because of Reed.

"So now you're selling out your own crow, Barnaby?" Miles shook his head. "Jeez, who are you going to throw under the bus next?"

"What? No, Miles, you don't understand," I interjected, urgency creeping into my voice. "Reed's been using Davy Jones's gloves to steal souls. He's planning—"

My words were cut short by Miles's sudden laughter.

"Sorry," he managed between chuckles, his clear amusement belying any sincerity in his apology. "But come on, how can you expect us to buy into this? You hid my brother's death from me for weeks. Weeks! And now you expect us to believe that your crow, of all people, has been busy conjuring up pirate magic to attack our school?"

"Yes," I insisted. "I also know that he was the one who gave you that newspaper with the article on me. It's all part of his plan, Miles—taking away every single person close to me. Jefferson, Amelia, you…and now Morgan."

"Hang on," a voice called out from the crow. It was the ship's bosun, Brent. Stepping forward, his coffee-brown eyes locked onto mine. "Did you just say *Morgan*?"

I nodded firmly. "Reed took her. He's also got Riaz under his will."

I didn't see the point in causing widespread panic by saying that Reed had shot her, dumped her body in the lake, and now she was being kept hostage by mermaids. Nevertheless, I needed them to understand the stakes at hand.

Gasps broke out as the news sank in. Brent turned to Fletcher, his expression grave.

"We never mentioned anything about Morgan to him."

"Oh, please!" Miles scoffed from several feet away. "You've

CHAPTER 28

got to be joking. Barnaby could've heard about that from anyone. Everyone knows she's been missing for more than a day now."

More than a day?

Dread swelled inside me as I grabbed onto the bosun.

"What day is it, Brent?" I asked, my voice trembling.

Clearly confused, the bosun blinked twice before answering. "Um…Saturday?"

The realization hit me like a hurricane. I knew exactly when Reed was planning to strike.

"Reed's going to take the ship when the crows leave for the mainland this morning," I exclaimed. "We've got to go!"

"No, Barnaby!" Miles snarled at me. "I've had enough of your lies. The only one who needs to go is *you*!"

"But, Miles, what if he's right?" Fletcher asked. "What if Reed is really going to steal the *Angel's Wings*?"

"He's not. Barnaby is making all of this up."

"I actually think he's telling the truth," Brent firmly chimed in. His eyes met mine, and he gave me a curt nod. "And if he's got a lead on saving all three of our crewmates, then we owe it to them to investigate."

To my relief, several other members of the crew began murmuring in agreement as well.

"No!" Miles stomped on the deck. His face was redder than lava. "How can you consider believing this liar, this… MURDERER! I won't have it!"

Ignoring his fellow crewmates' cries, Miles launched himself at me, his arms aimed at shoving me down the gangplank. I braced myself, hoping to hold my ground, but Miles's frustration fueled his strength, and I began to feel myself slip. My feet were seconds from giving way when—

"What the heck!" Miles gasped suddenly, releasing his grip on me and leaping back. His face was a mixture of revolt and shock.

He wasn't alone. The entire crew stared at me, mouths agape in silent astonishment. Fletcher's face had turned white. Beside him, Brian held a hand over his mouth, the other resting on a cannon for support. Eventually, he managed to raise it and pointed at my side.

I let out a yelp when I saw what he was pointing at. My left sleeve had gotten yanked up in the tussle, revealing my forearm, which was now glowing a bright, aquatic blue. Within the glow, an image appeared to be materializing on the skin—a ring of fish scales.

"My god," Fletcher whispered. "Is that—"

"It is," Brent confirmed with a nod. "The Mermaid's Mark."

"Mermaid's Mark?" a crew member asked, her voice tinged with confusion. "We never learned about such a thing in biology."

"You wouldn't have because it's always been thought to be nothing but a myth," Brent explained, his eyes fixed on my forearm. "Legend has it that mermaids give it to those they deem as allies—something extremely rare, considering humans and merpeople have never really been on the best of terms." He gave me a look of sheer wonder. "How on earth did you get one, Barnaby?"

That's when I told them everything. I explained how Morgan had left the note for me, how her findings in *Treasure Island* led us into the jungle. Then, with great discomfort, I told them about Reed's arrival and his actions afterward by the lake. Finally, I told them about my strange encounter with Melody and Harmony in the depths of the lake.

CHAPTER 28

Nobody, not even Miles, interrupted me as I spoke. Even his stubbornness seemed to falter when I described Reed's deadly blow to Morgan aboard the rowboat.

"Listen," I told them at the end, "what do any of you have to lose by coming to check with me? Well, now you all know what you could lose if you don't."

"He's right," Brent said, nodding. He wasn't the only one. Virtually everyone aboard the *Adventure Galley* appeared to agree with my logic—everyone that is, except Miles. "We owe it to everyone to check this out."

Fletcher proceeded to clamp a hand on my shoulder—just as Amelia had done the night I joined the crew.

"The crew is behind you, Barnaby," he assured me. "Let's go take Reed down."

Two minutes later, after everyone aboard traded their backpacks for swords and pistols, we marched down the gangplank and headed for the *Angel's Wings*.

As we crossed the docks, I kept glancing at my left forearm, where the scales remained etched like a tattoo. Their bluish glow had faded, but the markings still lingered, making me begin to wonder if they were permanent.

A sudden nudge on the shoulder jolted me from my thoughts. Looking up, I found Miles walking beside me.

"You know, this doesn't change anything," he muttered to me.

"Miles," I began, but he was already striding away.

Sighing, I pulled down my shirtsleeve and turned my focus on the large white ship coming into view. Teenagers, all a year or two older than anyone on the crew, bustled about on the deck, attending to the rigging and cargo.

I spotted our target the moment we boarded the ship. Standing casually by the helm, Reed was chatting cheerfully with his friends. I watched as he laughed at something one of them said, his carefree demeanor infuriating me.

"Reed!"

The deck fell silent as the mass of crows took note of the disturbance. Up above, Reed spun around, his face paling at the sight of me. I could have sworn I saw him mouth "Impossible."

Ever the actor, Reed's shock vanished quickly. Within seconds, he was back to adopting his unsure, awkward persona, going as far as stumbling down the stairs and colliding directly into another crow. Worst of all, his ploy seemed to be working. I saw several of my former crewmates exchange skeptical glances. I could only imagine what they were thinking.

This is the guy who's responsible for all the attacks on our crew?

Beside me, Fletcher stepped forward and greeted Reed with a wave.

"Hello, Reed," he said. "Mind if we have a word?"

Reed extended his arms welcomingly.

"Of course," he replied, his tone calm and friendly. "It's Fletcher, right? What can I do for you?"

"You can explain to us where our first mate is," Fletcher demanded sternly.

Reed frowned, his expression one of genuine confusion.

"I'm sorry, I don't quite know what you're talking about."

The moment those words left his lips, members of my former crew began reaching for their swords. Miles had said it himself—everyone at Lost Boys High knew about Morgan's disappearance.

Reed had made his first mistake.

"Her name is Morgan," Fletcher explained, his tone growing sharper. He must've picked up on this as well. "Barnaby says you had something to do with her disappearance."

All around us, crows listened intently. Seeming to notice, Reed's eyes began darting around the deck.

"Morgan? I've never even met her. What makes Barnaby think that I'm involved?"

"Because I was there!" I yelled, stepping forward with my fist clenched. I was seconds away from charging at him, but Brent stopped me, urging me to let Fletcher handle it.

"Look, Reed," Fletcher continued, "I'm on your side. It's highly unlikely you had anything to do with her disappearance. But as her fellow officer and friend, it's my responsibility to find out anything I can about her whereabouts."

"Of course." Reed nodded reassuringly. "I want to help. What do you need me to do?"

Fletcher paused, choosing his next words carefully. The whole deck watched in suspense.

"I think we should take this to Blackbeard and see how he wants to deal with it."

At this, Reed shook his head. "I'm sorry, but I'm afraid I can't do that. The ship's scheduled to leave for the mainland in eight minutes. If I were to go with you, I'd miss the voyage."

"Oh, I'm sure Blackbeard would agree to postponing it for such an *important* meeting," Fletcher urged with a smile. "So, come on. What do you have to lose? Prove Barnaby wrong and show us you're innocent."

My heart skipped a beat as I realized what Fletcher was doing. He was calling Reed's bluff. I watched victoriously as

Reed's lips started to twitch.

"I...I can't let that happen," he murmured. "I'm sorry, but we're supposed to leave now."

"Hey, Barnaby?" A voice shot out from behind me, cutting through the tension. All eyes turned as Travis, of all people, stepped forward and wagged a finger at Reed. "Isn't that *your* sword under his jacket?"

Reed's hand flew to his side, but not before every single person on deck had enough time to notice the silver, helix-shaped bell guard hanging from his waist.

"I don't freaking believe it," I heard Miles mutter in disbelief.

Dead to rights, Reed froze, his face bright red. His eyes flicked, racing from Travis's raised hand to Miles, and finally to me.

"This is your fault, Barnaby," he sneered. "Everything that happens from this point on is entirely on you."

Before anyone could react, Reed drew a pistol and aimed it at Travis. The loud crack of the shot echoed across the deck, and Travis collapsed in a spray of red.

And then all hell broke loose.

CHAPTER 29

"YOU MONSTER!" Miles roared, flinging himself at Reed.

The former crow timed his response perfectly. Ducking under the wild slash of Miles's sword, Reed spun around and grabbed the back of his head. With a swift, practiced movement, he slammed Miles's face into the deck. Miles barely moved after that, letting out only a weak, wet moan.

To make matters worse, by the time Reed had straightened up, he'd slipped on the silver gloves again. Panic surged through me as I realized what was coming.

I opened my mouth to shout a warning, but before I could get anything out, Reed raised his hand and snapped his fingers.

My former crew and I watched in horror as every single crow on the deck suddenly stirred, as if awakened from a long, deep slumber. They shuffled into rows behind Reed, their unblinking silver eyes fixed on us. There must've been every crow at the school on the ship's deck.

Several of my former crewmates gulped as Reed pointed in our direction—and the crows charged. Swords drawn, they ran at us, chanting lines from 'The Derelict' as they came.

"FIFTEEN MEN ON A DEAD MAN'S CHEST. YO HO

HO, AND A BOTTLE OF RUM."

Jeez. As if hearing that wretched song from one person had been bad enough; hearing it chanted in unison by so many was truly terrifying. Their sinister growls echoed across the deck, making my blood run cold.

"Brace yourselves!" yelled Fletcher. His voice wavered as he did his best to maintain order amongst his frightened crewmates. "Remember, the crows aren't your enemy. They're being manipulated by Reed. Fight to disarm only!"

As this was happening, Travis remained motionless on the deck, a growing puddle of crimson surrounded the upper half of his now-limp chest. Unfortunately, nobody was able to go and check on him, lest they wished to join him on the floor.

The crows charged, and it wasn't long before a blade was thrust in my direction. It was the same boy Reed had bumped into on the stairs. Instinctively, I shoved him aside, not looking for trouble. Besides, I wasn't in any shape to fight—not with my rapier still in Reed's possession, leaving me completely unarmed.

And speaking of the devil—*where was he?*

My eyes skirted through the skirmish and found him by the stern, using the unfolding battle as cover to reach the helm.

A loud grunt emanated from my right, and I turned to discover Brent fending off the same crow I'd just shoved away. I'd been too focused on Reed to notice him charging again. If it hadn't been for the bosun, I would've been toast.

I watched as the two interlocked swords, each pushing with all their might. Teeth clenched, veins bulging in his forehead, Brent let out a brutish yell and drove the crow over the railing.

"Thanks," I told him as a loud splash followed a second later. "We need to stop Reed. He's going for the helm."

CHAPTER 29

"Well then, what are you just standing around here for?" Brent shouted back over the chaos.

I showed him my empty hands. "Reed's got my sword, remember?"

The bosun nodded, understanding. "Then let's clear you a path."

Together we rushed forward, directly into the heart of the battle. Crewmates and crows rushed past us, engulfed in combat. Fletcher surged right past us, screaming at the top of his lungs as he swung *two* cutlasses at a crow. Hopefully, he was still keeping to his "disarm only" command.

We did what we could to help turn the tide of the battle along the way to Reed. Brent gave a hand to Patrick, a young crewmate who was being overwhelmed by two crows near the mainmast. With a quick maneuver, Brent managed to disarm one crow and distract the other long enough for Percy to regain his footing and rejoin the fight.

Meanwhile, I stopped to aid Cindy, a brown-haired girl that Morgan was close with. An older girl had her pinned to the side, but with her back turned to us, it wasn't too difficult to grab her and flip her over the side.

Back across the deck, Fletcher seemed to see how I'd handled the crow and promptly called for the rest of the crew to follow suit. Before long, he had the entire crew pushing the crows to the edges of the deck, a symphony of splashes following as more and more were shoved off the ship.

As we finally reached the helm, Brent and I devised a plan to trap Reed by taking separate stairwells, cutting off any potential escape routes. However, as I approached the top, I found myself alone in confronting Reed directly. Three steps from the helm, I glimpsed Brent engaged in a fierce struggle with another adversary—Riaz, by the look of it.

Well, at least *that* explains where he went.

Praying that Riaz wouldn't prove too much for Brent to handle, I continued for the wheel, where Reed was standing. Eyes closed, hands gripping the wheel, he appeared to be deep in thought—concentrating, no doubt, on his desired destination. Given our hectic surroundings—and the amount of time it was taking him—it must've been quite the difficult task, but I was no more than two feet away when the deck suddenly shook, and the ship started moving.

I was running out of time.

Determined to seize the moment, I crept closer, clenched my fist, and aimed a punch at his face, reminiscent of our last encounter aboard the *Angel's Wings*. But before my blow could connect, Reed spun around with lightning reflexes, delivering a preemptive strike. I staggered back, clutching my gut as pain seared through me—and Reed spat at me.

"You really are a cancer, Barnaby. You go ahead and kill my best friend, make me murder an innocent girl, forever ruin my reputation with my fellow crows—and you still can't let me have even *this*?"

The punch landed hard, sending a wave of pain through me, but it had a silver lining. With Reed momentarily distracted and his hands off the wheel, the ship came to a stop. I had halted him—for now.

"You lost the right to worry about your reputation when you sold out everyone at this school for a quick payout," I shot back, my voice cutting through the tension. "You once told me this place offered so much to people like us. Was that just a lie?"

For a moment, Reed seemed genuinely struck by my question, as if memories of his time at Lost Boys High flickered in his eyes. But any trace of hesitation vanished, replaced by a venomous glare.

"They abandoned me, Barnaby. I starved out there as a crow. I slept in parks, ate from trash cans. I was left to die."

"But you could've come back," I countered. "You could've called for the *Angel's Wings* the same way you did when you found me."

Reed laughed bitterly. "And let Riaz ridicule me? Nobody returns without a recruit, Barnaby. I would've been humiliated. It would've been worse than death. And that's when I realized the truth. Blackbeard doesn't care about us—he only cares about controlling this place. He deserves what's coming to him, and it starts by me leaving with this ship."

"Then fight me for it," I challenged, my voice steady despite the throbbing pain in my gut. "Avenge your friend the same way I took *his* life."

Reed's face contorted with fury, his chest swelling with rage. Despite his anger, I thought I saw a glint in his eye that suggested my challenge resonated with him.

"Very well," he muttered through gritted teeth, tossing my sword back toward me. "Let's finish this once and for all."

I ducked under his first attack, the blade slicing through the air where my head had been moments before. With a quick step to the side, I countered, aiming a slash at his side. Reed parried the blow with precision, his movements fluid and practiced. He retaliated immediately with a swift lunge that narrowly missed my ribcage, his eyes gleaming with determination.

"Did I forget to mention? I was top of my class in sword fighting," he sneered. "One of the many reasons people like

Riaz hated me."

Reed lunged once more, his fury driving every blow. He brought his blade down with brutal force, pushing me to my knees as I barely managed to raise my sword in defense. With a roar, he drove his knee into my chest, breaking through my guard and sending me staggering backwards.

"I could have left with the *Angel's Wings* weeks ago, but I stayed behind to make sure you get what you deserve," he spat, his words biting with resentment. "First, I took away everyone you hold dear. And now I'm going to take away your life."

I stumbled, another blow catching me off guard. Reed seized the opportunity, grabbing me by the collar and slamming my head into his knee. A sickening crack echoed as pain shot through my nose, warm blood spilling down my face.

"I don't know how you survived the mermaids, but I won't make that mistake again," he growled, looming over me. With a cruel sneer, he picked up my rapier and hurled it over the side. "I'm going to finish the job I started. That money will be mine. Vengeance will be mine."

Sprawled on the ground, I struggled to focus through the haze of pain. Below, the chaos of battle raged on between my former crewmates and the crows. Fletcher and the crew worked tirelessly to press as many crows over the edge as they could, but they were still severely outnumbered. To my dismay, I could now see that a few more bodies now lay lifeless on the deck beside Travis.

"So much meaningless death," I heard Reed say. "And for what?"

I rolled over and found him standing above me, his cutlass now in hand.

CHAPTER 29

"This is all your fault. Only you had to die," he scowled, delivering yet another kick. Pain riveted through my ribs, and I grimaced, which only sent more blood into my mouth. "I was planning to kill you once we'd set off from this wretched place, but this will have to do. It's over now, Barnaby. I'm sorry it had to end this way."

Despite his hollow apology, his eyes betrayed no remorse, only a chilling determination.

I met his eyes, summoning the last bit of my strength, and spat a mouthful of blood into his face. His reaction was swift, wiping the blood away with a snarl before raising the cutlass high above my head.

"I'm going to kill you now."

It truly seemed to be the case. I closed my eyes, bracing for the final blow. In the darkness, memories of my journey to this place—to Lost Boys High—flooded my mind, as well as the people I had met, and the bond that had begun to sprout between Morgan and me.

I failed her. She'll stay underwater forever.

I felt the cold steel of Reed's blade lightly tap my neck as he aimed. A second later, it was lifted, poised to strike, and I knew I only had seconds to live. This was the end of the road.

God, please make it quick.

"GHAAAH!"

My eyes flew open, and Reed was no longer atop me. With an arduous grunt, I rolled over and saw him two feet away, reeling—a shiny red blade now poking out of his thigh. My shocked gaze went upward, and there was Miles, a thin stream of blood trickling from the corner of his mouth.

As Reed grimaced, panting with pain, Miles stepped over and helped me up. I opened my mouth to thank him, but before I could, he went tumbling onto the deck. Reed had grabbed his leg and tripped him—somehow doing this with a freaking sword sticking out of his leg.

"You think that will stop me?" He screamed through the pain as he stood up, raising his sword toward Miles. "I control the power of Davy Jones! I have the strength and energy of fifty souls inside of me! You can't defeat me!"

"Oh, yeah?"

Reed's raging, bloodshot eyes swiveled to me and widened when they saw my foot hovering over Melody's seashell. Before he could say anything else, I dropped my boot onto the deck, crushing the shell into dust.

One second passed, then another. Nothing happened.

Reed looked down at my boot, then back up to my face, and burst into laughter.

"Oh, you really had me going there, Barnaby," he chuckled.

The substantially large splash that came next wiped the grin off of his face.

Like a crescendo, several more followed, all around the ship. Miles, Reed, and I watched as a colossal, swampy mass suddenly shot out of the water and latched itself onto the ship. It was followed by another, then another, until the entire bow of the ship was swarmed with vines of kelp, seaweed, and just about anything else you'd find on the bottom of the ocean—even what appeared to be a tentacle of some sort.

What had initially been fright turned into relief as the vines slithered right past me and over to their target.

The first vine latched onto Reed's leg, dragging him toward the side. Terrified, he tried cutting the vine away with his sword, but every time he chopped some off, a new, thicker length would come and snatch him. Eventually, the mass had Reed by the chest, pinning him against the railing with a terrifying slam.

Reed looked at me with fear-filled eyes.

"What is this!" he cried to me. "What did you do to me?"

I was so stunned I didn't know how to reply.

More vines snatched onto Reed, quickly consuming him from the neck down, leaving only his horrified face visible. Bits and pieces of green, mucus-like tissue flew off as he continued to slice at it from the inside. He might've even cut into himself in the process, because one particular vine around his arm had a vague, red tinge to it.

"Help me, Barnaby!" he begged, full-on crying now. "Help, please. I'm so sorry. I was never really going to kill you. I only needed you to get to this place. Please, Barnaby—make it stop!"

But I didn't. I simply stared ahead and watched.

"Help me, Barnaby, pl—"

The vines now covered his mouth, silencing his pleas.

I then watched as the mass—forming what now looked like a cocoon—lifted Reed into the sky. It writhed violently, indicating he was still fighting to break free, but no part of him reappeared. The green mass disappeared over the side of the ship and into the water with an almost too-simple splash.

At that exact moment, the fighting on the deck abruptly ceased. Below, I heard dozens of voices murmuring in confusion, questioning what in the Seven Seas was happening, and why they were all covered in scars and bruises.

The crows had broken free.

Taking a deep breath, I stepped toward Miles to offer up a hand.

"Thanks for saving my life," I expressed.

Frowning, Miles swatted my hand away.
"Forget about it," was his curt reply.
And I had a feeling that he really meant it.

CHAPTER 30

Entering the Sword Hall and finding it empty, I let out a deep, satisfying sigh.

I almost felt like congratulating myself. Today officially marked a full month since I first set foot on the hidden island of Lost Boys High, a day that forever altered my life. I was still labeled as a freshie by most—even after basically saving everyone by thwarting Reed's dark plot—but nonetheless, I was beginning to grasp how things operated here. For instance, I'd discovered that the Sword Hall was always empty during the first two periods on Tuesdays.

In other words, the perfect place to find some morning peace and quiet.

Peace and quiet were hard to come by lately. The past forty-eight hours had been a complete whirlwind: from being interrogated by Blackbeard for hours after the battle; to the heart-wrenching memorial for the students who had lost their lives thwarting Reed's plans. Even at meals, I couldn't catch a break—what with being constantly bombarded with apologies from kids who, y'know, once accused me of being a murderer.

Desperate for a break, when Tuesday arrived, I chose to skip class altogether and head for the Sword Hall. The silence was indescribably welcoming. Settling in, I couldn't help but release a critical sigh of relief as I took a seat and began to relax. I'd brought with me my copy of *Treasure Island*—well, the library's first edition copy—and instantly lost myself in its pages. It felt amazing to just read, to find peace without a care in the world for a change.

Pity it only lasted seven minutes.

"Ahem."

My head jerked up to find Roberts, standing there.

"Enjoying some peace and quiet for a change, I see," he remarked. A pause followed. "I can come back another time..."

"No, it's all right, sir," I answered with a smile. Closing the green hardcover, I motioned for the Sword Master to join me on the bench.

Donning an awkward smile, Roberts took a seat and cleared his throat. He looked rather different than usual—more serious and unsure, unlike the confident Sword Master I sparred with. Something was bothering him.

"I see you've found yourself some reading material," he noted while gesturing to the book in my hand. "To be honest, after everything that's happened, I would've guessed that you'd had enough of Robert Louis Stevenson for a lifetime."

My grin widened. "You're not wrong. I just thought that, as so much of my life here has revolved around what's written within these pages, I thought it might be a good idea to get through it once and for all. For future context, y'know?"

Not to mention that the book is actually RIDICULOUSLY good, I thought. It was clear to me now why the novel was considered a classic. I found myself captivated by its characters, especially the charismatic cook, Long John Silver. A true antihero, Silver is the one who leads the mutiny described in the novel. Yet, by the end of the story, he switches sides, betraying his wicked crewmates—but only for his own gain. I couldn't help but wonder who Robert Louis Stevenson based him on.

Still not himself, Roberts remained visibly uneasy, fidgeting in his seat before finally responding.

"Not a bad plan, not bad at all," he murmured almost to himself.

Okay. I had to ask.

"Sir, is everything all right? You seem...troubled."

Running his hand through his long brown hair, Roberts eventually responded with a nod.

"Yes, yes, Barnaby. It's actually what *I* can do for you. You see, I came looking for you—looking to apologize."

I was taken aback. "But, sir, apologize for what?"

Roberts threw his hands up, a look of self-reproach on his face. "For the way I treated you—keeping my distance, shutting you out. I convinced myself I was doing the right thing by siding with and protecting the other students, but I was wrong. I should have trusted you. Instead, I acted impulsively and foolishly, never once pausing to consider your innocence. As your teacher, I let you down."

When Roberts had finished, his chest heavy with regret, I raised my hand.

"Sir, if I may," I began.

The Sword Master nodded for me to continue.

"Over the last two days, I've received countless apologies, mostly from people who never spoke to me before, let alone supported me. You, sir, have done more for me than I could have imagined. Your apology is one I cannot accept."

Lost for words, Roberts looked thunderstruck.

"You did what you thought was right," I continued, "standing by another student of yours, one whose older brother had just been revealed to be dead. Honestly, probably would've done the same. But even then, when I lost Miles as my sparring partner, you stepped in to make sure I continued my training. Perhaps that extra sparring session after Jefferson's attack had something to do with that?"

"I thought it might help," Roberts offered softly, tears forming in his bright green eyes. "Barnaby, I don't know what to say—"

"Say that you'll continue to train me," I finished for him. "If it wasn't for Miles, Reed would've had his revenge and killed me. I need to be better if I'm going to fight any more foes coming after me."

Roberts looked at me, visibly moved.

"I swear, on my title of Sword Master, I will keep training you," he affirmed. "I will do everything in my power to make you the greatest swordsman this island has ever seen."

"Thank you, sir," I replied, matching his smile with one of my own. But it faded quickly. "Oh, and I could do with a new sword if possible."

Ah, yes. One of the few bitter outcomes of this whole ordeal: my rapier was most definitely sitting on the bottom of the lake after Reed tossed it over.

My words seemed to strike a chord with Roberts. When he looked at me again, his wide, familiar smile had finally returned.

"Well, as Sword Master, I think I can help with that," he boasted. "Let me know if you want a different blade this time around. Perhaps something exotic, like a scimitar? Or would you like to try a cutlass? You name it, Barnaby, and I'll make it happen."

"Thank you, sir," I replied.

CHAPTER 30

"No, Barnaby," Roberts shook his head. "Once again—thank *you*."

Three hours later, after finishing *Treasure Island*, I made my way down to the mess for something to eat. As I walked, I noticed the corridor next to the hall was uncharacteristically empty. Normally bustling with people at this time—their chatter echoing all the way to the library—I was surprised to count fewer than a dozen students before reaching the large doorway.

The unusual silence continued inside the mess, although there were significantly more people there. In fact, the room was nearly full, but for some reason, no one was speaking.

Scanning the tables, my eyes landed on a hand raised high in the air, grabbing my attention. I looked over and saw, with certainty, the cause of everyone's unusual behavior.

"Ah, Barnaby," Blackbeard greeted me from the very table I used to share with Miles and Jefferson. "Shall we go for a walk?"

Ignoring the flabbergasted eyes fixed on him, the head of Lost Boys High stood up and approached me at the doorway. I hadn't actually responded to his proposal, but from the way he was already heading out, it was clear he wasn't really expecting an answer.

Reluctantly abandoning my thoughts of grabbing lunch, I followed Blackbeard back out into the corridor. Sure enough, within seconds of his departure, the noise inside the mess began to revive.

"My first time in the mess in quite a while," Blackbeard remarked as we walked. "I usually take my meals elsewhere, primarily during meetings. But the staff still seem to be serving you all rather nicely. Generous portions. That's good."

Unsure exactly how to respond, I kept quiet as I followed Blackbeard up the stairs to the deck. We passed several students along the way, all of whom froze in their tracks, as though they had just seen a ghost.

On the deck, Blackbeard proceeded over to the starboard-side railing, gazing out at the array of ships below in contemplative silence.

"Ye would think," he began after a moment, "that after centuries of looking at the same view every day, it would eventually get old, yes? But not this one. Never. This island is as close to heaven on earth as it gets."

Blackbeard now turned to face me, his expression serious.

"You saved it, Barnaby. If it weren't for your actions, Lost Boys High would've fallen into chaos. There would no longer be such a haven for all these young adults. I brought you here to offer my personal thanks for that."

My solemn expression must've surprised him, because his next words were measured.

"Why the long face, boy?"

I blushed and shook my head. "I'm sorry, sir, it's just... Morgan helped me solve the puzzle and find Reed's lair. Frankly, we probably would've never caught him if it wasn't for her. I wish she was here to take the credit with me."

Sadly, there was still no word from the mermaids. The uncertainty over Morgan's wellbeing gnawed at me. And aside from the scale tattoo on my forearm—which seemed to grow more permanent by the day—I had no real assurance that Melody and Harmony would keep their promise.

Another reason why I so desperately needed that morning

CHAPTER 30

off.

When we'd last spoken, Blackbeard was unable to offer me any update. Now, to my dismay, he once again—begrudgingly—shook his head.

"As much as I would like to give you some positive news, I've yet to hear anything from our neighbors in the lake. Rest assured, Barnaby, you will be the first to know as soon as I do. In the meantime, if there's anything else I can do to lift your spirits, just say the word."

"There is one thing, sir," I said after a moment's hesitation. "When Reed was leading us out of the lake, he referred to the person who hired him to steal the *Angel's Wings* as his master. The mermaids also used that term to describe Davy Jones."

"What's your point?" Blackbeard snapped, his tone almost defensive.

I swallowed. "Sir, Reed also claimed you knew exactly what was happening to your students. If that's the case, it means you lied to me that night in your cabin. So, is it true?"

I half-expected Blackbeard to shout at me to drop the question, but he sighed, as if he had anticipated such a query. To my surprise, he even nodded slowly in acknowledgement.

"Yes. I wasn't entirely truthful the last time we spoke of the matter."

No kidding, I thought, as Blackbeard continued.

"The truth dates back to the peak of the Golden Age. Back when The Offer was introduced. Just as we were about to accept, the meddlesome kings and queens of Europe revealed one final demand: to rid the Seven Seas of a *ghoulish pest* causing their trading companies serious damage."

It didn't take much to guess who he was referring to.

"Davy Jones?"

Blackbeard nodded. "Aye. Like I've already told you, Jones grew corrupt over the years. He'd begun using his powers for self-gain, not for the sake of those who'd fallen at sea. Slaughtering innocent sailors and enslaving their souls instead of guiding those lost at sea to the afterlife."

"So, what happened?" I asked. "What did you do?"

"We agreed to their terms. And we went to war."

I stepped back in disbelief. "So, you…actually *fought* Davy Jones?"

Blackbeard's eyes darkened as he stared into the distance, his voice lowering to a grave whisper. "We gathered our best men, prepared our ships, and set sail," he said. His grip tightened on the railing, his knuckles turning white. "The sea was a battlefield, cannon fire and screams filling the air. The battle was fierce, the waters red with blood. We went to war, and it was a fight unlike any other."

I took a step back, heart pounding in my chest. "But you won though, right?"

"Aye, we did," Blackbeard replied, his voice rough with the weight of memory. "But I lost many good men that day, my own first mate, Caesar, among them."

The great pirate hung his head mournfully, like the loss of his first mate was still fresh.

"And Jones? What happened to him?"

Blackbeard took his time in choosing his words before responding.

"I made certain he would never terrorize another soul. I spared his life but left him in a state of pain and weakness that he could never come back from."

"He's gaining strength," I said. "He had enough to manipulate Reed into stealing the *Angel's Wings* for him. He's coming

CHAPTER 30

back."

Blackbeard was silent for a long time, his eyes hard and unyielding.

"Even if he were to return, I've made arrangements to prevent him from rising back to full power. And that is all I will discuss on the matter. Besides, it should not concern you. You've already done a great service for me; you shouldn't worry about this."

"But—" I stopped myself. Arguing the matter with Blackbeard would be a waste of time. If he wanted to elaborate on what he said, he would've done so already.

"I will, however, acknowledge my mistakes," Blackbeard said suddenly, his tone softer. "When I took this island from Jones, I chose to hide his instruments of destruction. I believed I was the only person alive with the ability to reach them. Something I've now come to realize I'd been mistaken about. For once Reed found them, I was helpless. Only he who controls the gloves can find the cave."

"So, then, sir," I asked. "How did Morgan and I find it?"

Blackbeard offered me a faint smile. "*That*, Barnaby, is a mystery for another day. But we are short on time. I have several other responsibilities to tend to today, and there's another topic of discussion I need to have with you. You see, Barnaby, apart from simply thanking you, I'd like to offer you a reward. Not just information—a real reward."

I couldn't believe what I was hearing. Blackbeard rarely interacted with students, and here he was, offering me a favor. I wished I could ask for Morgan to be back, but I knew that was beyond Blackbeard's control. Still, I had a few other ideas that came to mind.

First, I thought about asking him to reinstate me on a crew, maybe even as an officer this time. But that felt like a waste given how everyone was now begging for my forgiveness. Besides, I liked my chances of my former crew taking me back, especially with my name being cleared and Amelia and Jefferson coming back as well. Apparently, they were scheduled to be cleared from the brig this evening. Hopefully, Miles wouldn't cause too many issues with me back.

A few more ideas fluttered through my head—exam exemptions, my own personal skeleton servant—but at the last moment, something else popped into my head. Something that felt more appropriate than everything else combined.

"We lost some friends in the battle on the *Angel's Wings*," I began. "I know the school treasures its secrecy with the mainland, but I think their families deserve to know about their sacrifice, if not be offered some sort of compensation for it. If not for their bravery, I don't know if we would've prevailed. They're the ones who really deserve the reward."

There was more to it than just that. Reed's prior comment about their deaths being my fault had left quite the gash in my heart—and my psyche. I already had one person's blood on my hands; hopefully, this would do more than just mend the hearts of the families of the fallen.

Blackbeard nodded. "Very well. If *that's* what you would like—consider it done."

I frowned. There was something off with how he said that last bit. Call me crazy, but it sounded like the head of Lost Boys High was surprised by my decision.

"Something wrong with my choice, sir?"

"Of course," he answered. "I'm just surprised that you didn't think about asking for a way home. After everything, I would think it would be the first thing on your mind."

CHAPTER 30

Um...where was he going with this?

"Sir. The last time we spoke about that, you laughed in my face and proclaimed it impossible. You called the idea 'inconceivable.'"

Blackbeard nodded. "All of that is true. But that was before," he explained. "Before ye proved your innocence." He then reached over and tossed me a pamphlet he'd been keeping in his large jacket. "I believe you may know a certain Sergeant Gallman? That is his testimony. He claims that you were kidnapped by Reed from a certain highway, one not so far from your former neighborhood. Ring any bells?"

Frozen by what I was hearing, I barely managed to nod.

"So...I can go home?"

Blackbeard nodded, and in that moment, a rush of emotions overwhelmed me. It felt as if fireworks were going off in my chest.

"Yes, although I should probably explain to you what that would entail. You'd be immediately placed into police custody until your case is heard. Now, Gallman will make sure that his testimony, along with other evidence I've gathered, is passed into the right hands. I also have a few more tricks up my sleeve I plan to use in speeding up the whole process. So, in other words, if you can hang on for a week or two, you should be able to return to your previous life. That's the best I can offer."

Everything from relief to disbelief flooded through me. I struggled to find my next words.

"I-I don't know what to say."

Blackbeard pointed at the watch on my wrist.

"Well, if it's a yes, it's got to be now. I've set a time for you to meet the local authorities. So, Barnaby, what do ye want to do?"

What do I want to do?

The joy of seeing Grandma again encompassed my thoughts, but the decision weighed heavily on me. Could I really leave, just like that? Unfinished business tugged at my conscience—Miles, Amelia, Jefferson—heck, Morgan hadn't even returned from the lake yet. Could I really leave them all without a proper goodbye?

As I stood there, grappling with the enormity of the offer, my mind drifted back to my first night at Lost Boys High. I recalled the solemn oath I had made just steps away from where I now stood.

"I'll come back to you. I don't know how yet, or how long it'll take, but I will find my way back to you. I swear on Grandpa's grave that I'll do it."

With a sigh, I acknowledged the difficult choice I ultimately needed to make.

CHAPTER 31

Making my way to the *Angel's Wings*, my heart did a somersault when I spotted two familiar faces peering down at me from aboard the large, white ship.

"What are you guys doing here?" I asked, stepping aboard as Jefferson and Fletcher welcomed me. My hug with Jefferson lingered a bit longer than with Fletcher—it had been almost a month since I last saw him, after all.

Fletcher smirked. "We heard you might be going. Couldn't let you go without a proper goodbye."

Just as I'd been with Blackbeard, I didn't know what to say.

"I...I'm sorry I didn't come tell you first," I said to Jefferson. "I did try visiting you and Amelia when I heard you were getting out, but they still wouldn't let me see you guys. Said the medical team was still running tests."

"Yeah, well, Blackbeard showed up about an hour ago and told them to quit with the tests. He also mentioned something about you going home, so I grabbed Fletcher, and we've been waiting here ever since." Jefferson stepped back, placing his hands on my shoulders. "Barnaby, it's really good to see you again—although I heard you kinda took over my place on the *Adventure Galley*."

I raised my hands with a smile. "It's all yours now, buddy."

Jefferson laughed. "In all seriousness, I hope that's not why you're heading out. I'm sure the crew could always make room."

The small, spectacled boy glanced over at Fletcher, who responded with a curt nod.

Despite the gesture, I shook my head. "Thanks, guys. That means a lot—but I need to go home. My grandma needs me right now, and I made a promise to her. I've got to keep it."

Jefferson's smile faded slightly, but he nodded, understanding. "I get it, Barnaby. At least they let me out in time to come say goodbye—and offer my thanks. I mean, if it wasn't for you...I'd probably still be in the brig."

I shrugged, trying to downplay the blush creeping up my cheeks. "I just did what anyone else would have done."

"Like kissing a mermaid?" Jefferson chuckled and winked at me. "The crew told me about that. Did you really...?"

I lifted my sleeve and revealed the mark, a small smile playing on my lips.

"Sick!" Jefferson exclaimed, his eyes wide.

"What was it like?" Fletcher asked, his curiosity evident.

"Like a full summer vacation, all in one kiss," I replied, grinning at the memory.

Fletcher nodded, clearly impressed. "Damn."

We all laughed, the tension easing for a moment. But then my gaze drifted across the deck, searching for someone. Jefferson noticed and shook his head.

"Miles isn't here, Barnaby. I'm sorry. He wanted me to tell you that he wishes you the best. It's just...he needs more time to process everything."

I nodded, feeling a pang of understanding. If anyone had

been through more than me recently, it was Miles. I couldn't imagine the turmoil he was in. But hearing that he cared enough to send a message brought me a small measure of closure. It would have to do.

"It just stinks, is all," Jefferson lamented, gesturing toward Fletcher. "They all got to know you for a whole month. I only had a week! Not even one single raid!"

"To be fair, I did try speaking to you when I visited the brig," I pointed out. "I don't know if you knew that or—"

"No, I heard you then. I chose not to answer," Jefferson replied sternly, as if he was mad at himself. "I'll live with the guilt of that forever."

There was an awkward moment of silence. Jefferson sheepishly crammed his hands into his pockets.

"Barnaby, I—"

I stopped him. "Don't, Jay. I get it now. Loyalty is everything in this place, and you needed to have Miles's back. I understand."

Jefferson opened and closed his mouth several times before finally nodding. "Thanks. Will you at least be able to write?"

"Not sure," I said with a shrug. "Guess I'll have to find a new crow to pass on my messages. Without committing another crime, of course."

"Oh, I'm sure we can arrange something," a voice rang out from the stairwell. A moment later, Amelia and Brent emerged. *Holding hands.*

My heart drummed as I scrambled over and threw myself into a hug with my captain. Crew or no crew, she will *always* be my captain.

"How are you feeling?" I asked.

"Like a pirate sitting on a mountain of gold," my captain said with a grin. "Being back with Brent here definitely lifts the mood."

I smiled, understanding now why Brent had been so adamant about seeing through my claim on Reed. If not for his help, I doubted we would have stopped him.

I watched as Amelia whispered something in the bosun's ear, who then nodded and proceeded to head off—but not before giving me a hug of his own and wishing me farewell.

After he left, it was just Amelia and me standing there.

"So," she began. "I see that you've come to a decision."

I nodded. "I made a promise when I got here, and I've got to stand by it. I have to."

"I get that. Honestly, I respect it. Just a shame—I'm gonna miss having you on my crew."

I smiled. "Believe me, Amelia. I'm gonna miss it as well."

Amelia smiled back, her eyes staring out at the lake while she spoke to me.

"Do you remember the first time I saw you? It was at the tryouts, remember those?"

"I remember them very well," I replied, not knowing where she was going with this.

"Do you know what I thought when I first saw you? I thought, *Jeez, they're gonna make a legend out of him*. And look at you now. You've grown so much. A lot of people would've quit after what you went through—but not you. You remained resilient and strong. No matter how fierce the storm, you stood tall through it all."

I was lost for words. Amelia's praise was higher than almost anything anyone's ever said to me. Her words struck a deep chord, sending a swell of pride and gratitude through me, but also a pang of doubt.

CHAPTER 31

Was there more for me to gain from being here? Was I making the right decision to leave?

A month ago, I wouldn't have hesitated. Now…

Amelia must have noticed my sudden uncertainty because she gently added, "If you're considering a last-minute change of plans, Barnaby, don't stay because of me. I may not be around for much longer."

My eyes widened. "What! Where are *you* heading?"

"To become a crow!" Amelia beamed. "Thanks to you, Blackbeard plans to offer a salary and benefits to all the crows. He's planning on making huge changes after everything with Reed. Probably wants to make sure that something like that never happens again."

"Not a bad plan," I replied, thinking back. Reed would appreciate that. "But I thought you still have a year of studies left!"

Amelia smiled warmly. "Prospective crows can give it a try in the final year. So, if the gig ever takes me down to Florida—which I intend to make sure it will—we can catch up. Oh, and before I forget…"

Only now did I notice the long, thin bag she'd been lugging around. As I looked closer, I realized it wasn't a bag, but a case—strikingly similar to the one Roberts had placed my sword in after fixing it.

Wait a minute…

I nearly squealed from delight when Amelia opened the tube and withdrew none other than my sword. Sharpened and sparkling like new.

"The mermaids found it below when they…*took* Reed. They gave it to Blackbeard when they returned Morgan to us."

I took the sword from her, then felt it slip through my fingers it as the second half of her message sank in.

"Wait. MORGAN'S BACK?"

Picking up my rapier, Amelia gave me a look. "Surely you knew? Blackbeard personally carried her down to the med bay an hour ago. She's still unconscious, but should wake up in a day or two, according to the mermaids."

A blend of relief and frustration flooded through me. I couldn't believe how much Blackbeard had outright lied to me. A pirate through and through, that man truly could not be trusted.

"Nope, guess he forgot to mention that," I murmured bitterly.

"Not that it really matters," Amelia noted. "Your grandma needs you more than Morgan does. Hopefully she'll understand."

Amelia's logic was sound, but this bombshell piece of news had me reconsidering my decision *again*.

"I'll do my best to explain to her." Amelia offered, seeing the conflict in my eyes. "You know what's the right thing to do here, Barnaby."

I nodded, still just processing everything. Amelia patted my shoulder, her touch grounding me. After handing me my sword, she turned to join Jefferson—who was now down on the docks—leaving me with my thoughts.

With a heavy sigh, I started walking to the helm. The weight of my rapier reminded me of the journey I'd been on. As I gripped the wheel, memories of my time here flooded my mind. The trials, the friendships, the battles—all of it had shaped me in ways I couldn't have imagined.

"Take care, Barnaby!" Jefferson called out.

Waving at my friends for the final time, I turned my focus

CHAPTER 31

on the horizon. The sun shone with promise and possibility.

I knew where I needed to go. I'd made a promise, and I needed to keep it.

"Home," I whispered, closing my eyes.

EPILOGUE

Havana, Cuba

The blistering Caribbean sun shone down on Havana's historic Plaza Vieja as a middle-aged American man settled at a table on the terrace of Café El Escorial. As the waitress arrived to take his order, he nearly asked for a Coke but stopped himself, remembering that they don't serve those in Cuba. He smiled at his mistake, appreciating the country's bold stance against the modern monarchies of the world. He knew quite a few people who would appreciate that as well.

In fact, one of those people was the very reason this man had traveled all the way to Cuba. Not that he'd been given much of a choice. This particular individual had forced his hand, and now Logan Stump was here to settle an old score. More specifically, he was going to kill him.

Watching the waitress retreat into the café with his revised order—just a bottle of sparkling water in the end—Logan Stump contemplated what he was about to do. Truthfully, if fate had swung his way back in Florida, he would've left the past buried. But here he was, about to confront it head-on, as he should have all those years ago.

EPILOGUE

It was this man's fault, after all, that had caused his separation from his son. And now, after years of agonizing absence, when moment finally seemed right to reenter Barnaby's life, he had to come along and ruin it. Logan had been at the tournament that day, planning to approach Barnaby after his final match. But before he could, the scoundrel dealt him another cruel blow by trying to have his son killed.

Thank heavens Barnaby inherited my talents with the sword, Logan mused to himself. It was a small comfort amidst the chaos that followed. Like the rest of the crowd, Logan had been immobilized, powerless to do anything but watch as one of Barnaby's opponents tried to take his son's life. By the time he regained control, it was too late—his son was being escorted away by the authorities. And to make matters worse, one of those damn crows ended up getting hold of Barnaby, taking him to the last place on earth Logan wanted him to go.

But Logan recognized the familiar grip of frozen helplessness that had seized him. He'd felt it before, years ago. It had taken time, and far more money than he ever intended to part with, but he finally tracked down the devil responsible. The trail had led him here, to this very café in Cuba, where the man came for breakfast every Tuesday morning—aside from the occasional trip to Florida

"I should've put a bullet in his head all those years ago," he muttered under his breath, clenching his fists with resolve.

A loud, clunking sound came from the porch steps, and he knew his target had arrived. Turning around, he glanced up from his table and found himself face-to-face with the monstrosity he thought to be long dead.

The thing is, he actually looked *worse* than dead—his bone-thin skin a sickly, pale green—as he limped onto the porch with his fake leg. From where he sat, Logan could smell the stench of his clothes, and they reeked. He wasn't the only one who caught the stench, as several of the café's other customers looked up from their food at the disheveled figure with disgust.

Not dead, but not quite living either, he thought with significant satisfaction. Well, at least there was that.

As the cripple's gaze landed on Logan, his face split into a wide smile. He began limping toward him, then slumped into the empty chair across from Logan, who braced himself. He knew this meeting would push his wits to the limit. While this man's reputation for chaos and mass destruction had terrified seafarers, sailors, and pirates alike, it was his mind games that were truly lethal.

Logan knew this better than anybody and faced his former... *acquaintance* with considerable caution.

"Well, well," Davy Jones said, his voice still as silky smooth as the last time they faced off, "the great Logan Stump honors me with his presence for breakfast. To what do I deserve the honor?"

The young waitress returned with Logan's drink and left just as fast with an order of white rum from the café's newest customer. When she left, Jones turned back to Logan with a grin.

"I really do appreciate the free breakfast, Logan. I'm actually a little short on cash these days, would you believe it? Not like yourself, I hear. Made quite the fortune over, what did the newspaper call it? *Deep sea treasure hunting*? Now...how would you know where to find all that booty?"

Saying nothing, Logan lowered his sparkling water and reached down to his waist. The one-legged man barely flinched as he felt the barrel of Logan's pistol being shoved

EPILOGUE

into his lone working leg.

"Now, now, Logan. Can we at least have a drink before talking business?"

The waiter returned with the rum, and Jones thanked the lady and put the straw to his mouth, taking a generous swallow of rum.

"Ah. Do you remember the slosh we used to drink at sea? Nothing like the filtered spirits they produce these days. Did a better job at turning boys into men than war or women, it did." He let out a hearty chuckle.

"Shut up," Logan told him. His eyes glowered with rage. "You tried to have my boy killed."

Jones pouted his lips. "Aw, jeez. Sorry, Logan, I won't do it again."

Boy, did Logan want to put a bullet in him right there, but he was smarter than that. Cuba was a nice place to vacation, but if there was one thing you didn't want to do during your stay, it was mess around with the country's police.

Still, he needed to maintain control of this confrontation, and so he kept the gun trained on Jones while he asked his first question.

"I thought you needed the gloves to pull off what you did at that fencing tournament."

The former ferryman of souls shook his head.

"Not quite. Think of the gloves like a battery, emanating a charge from the true source. At first, I could only conjure through them, but eventually, I learned how to control the power of the island on my own. Manipulating those boys' compasses to bring them to me and then controlling them was a piece of cake. Freezing everybody else, well, I'll admit—that took quite a bit."

Logan frowned. "But if you could still wield the power, why would you send them to the island? Unless…" Logan paused, his frown transforming into a smile. "You're finally out of juice, aren't you?"

For the first time since arriving, Jones seemed to shift uncomfortably from this revelation—much to Logan's satisfaction.

"I've been out for centuries," he hissed bitterly. "Do you really think you'd be buying *me* drinks, let alone have the ability to uncover my location with so much ease, if I still had an ounce of my power remaining? It took me *centuries* to summon enough strength to just get inside those boys' heads. Half a million," he snorted, "I haven't seen that much money since the Golden Age."

Not feeling the smallest ounce of sympathy, Logan shrugged and nonchalantly drank from his soda water.

"Well, it looks like they failed. Otherwise, you'd be back on the island instead of here, correct?"

Jones outstretched his arms as if to say, *You've got me.*

Enjoying his minor victory, Logan rapped his drink with his gold wedding band.

"Okay, but there's one thing that I still don't get. You could have sent any kid to the school. Why'd it have to be mine?"

Davy Jones's sour expression evaporated, and his mischievous smile returned, the same mischievous smile Logan had been given all those years ago when—

No, Logan. Shake those memories away. You are not letting Jones get to you. Never again.

"Consider it a contingency plan. It brought you here to me, after all."

"Ha! Like you knew that I would come after you. Even

more so, you still haven't given me a single reason as per why I shouldn't just put a bullet in you where you sit. So, I guess your plan backfired."

Jones shook his head. "Oh, why the rush, Logan? You haven't even heard my *real plan* yet."

"And why should I?"

"Because I could offer you everything you've wanted since that day on the island. Not only can I give you a beloved reunion with your boy, but I can also help you show him why you've been out of the picture for so long. I can get him to understand. But most importantly, Logan," Jones leaned over the table as he spoke, knocking the soda water off the table and onto Logan's lap. "I can help you kill Blackbeard."

A moment ago, Logan would've put a bullet into this peg-legged demon for spilling his drink on him. But now, his anger, though still simmering, found a new focus amidst the chaos of emotions. He leaned back slightly, eyes narrowing with intrigue as he studied the smelly, disheveled figure before him.

"Okay. I'm listening."

ACKNOWLEDGMENTS

This book has been a project over a decade in the making, and there are more than a handful of people who have been instrumental in getting it to this point.

Thank you to my editors, Taylor Morris and Marissa Graff, for helping me transform my story into the fully fledged novel you are reading today. Thank you, Pamela Moritz, for years of mentorship and guidance, not only in shaping this story but also in helping me sharpen my writing skills altogether.

Thank you to all my beta readers: Ilan Simmonds, Yechiel Sultzbacher, Avi Ostroff, Diana Breza, Yora Canter Visscher, Shania Bano, and Alana Manchien. Your invaluable feedback helped push this book to its fullest potential.

Thank you to my parents and grandparents, who nurtured my love for reading and storytelling from the very beginning. Mom, your beautiful poems and articles, as well as your insistence that I read every *Harry Potter* book before watching the movies, taught me the true power of the written word. Dad, your words about perseverance and the importance of seeing things through have stuck with me throughout this journey. You both reminded me, time and again, that the only way to finish a project is to keep pushing forward, no matter how difficult the road.

And finally, to my incredible wife, Rachel: You are my beginning and my end. Your unwavering love and support kept me going, especially on the days when I couldn't bear to look at my manuscript. You're the only critic whose opinion truly matters to me, and I know that I'd still be working on this book without you by my side. Thank you for everything.

About the Author

Ezra Snukal has been a lifelong lover of stories ever since his grandmother introduced him to the magic of *Harry Potter* as a child. Inspired by the works of J.K. Rowling, Rick Riordan, and other fantasy greats, Ezra seeks to channel his love for adventurous tales into crafting imaginative worlds and memorable characters for young and old readers. Ezra lives in Tel Aviv with his wife, Rachel, where he continues to dream up new adventures. *Barnaby Stump and the Soul Thief* marks his debut as an author.

www.ingramcontent.com/pod-product-compliance
Lightning Source LLC
LaVergne TN
LVHW041224080526
838199LV00083B/2426